AERIAL CATASTROPHE

On the morning of April 18, church bells echoed across the desert in the village of Navarin. It was Palm Sunday. The screaming pitch of engines on the American airfield intermittently drowned out the sound of church bells. By mid-afternoon, Gen. Carl Spaatz called off further aerial patrols. "It's obvious the Germans don't intend to do anything today," Spaatz said. "Anyway, it's a holiday, so we may as well give our airmen the rest of the afternoon off."

But NATAF had already ordered the next patrol. Spaatz shrugged and told his side to allow the 57th Group pilots to make the final patrol of the day.

The P-40s flew north, following the winding road that led to Soussa. The formations of planes, four abreast, soon turned northward and out to sea.

"Okay, left turn," the colonel ordered. "One more westward swing and we return to base."

"That's what I like to hear, Colonel," Major Knight answered.

The quartet of P-40s swung into the setting sun. In a few moment, the 57th Patrol would fly right into the most astonishing aerial target they had ever seen.

Within the next hour, the Germans would suffer the worst aerial disaster of the war.

OTHER BOOKS ON THE WORLD AT WAR
by Lawrence Cortesi

ROMMEL'S LAST STAND

BY LAWRENCE CORTESI

ZEBRA BOOKS
KENSINGTON PUBLISHING CORP.

ZEBRA BOOKS

are published by

Kensington Publishing Corp.
475 Park Avenue South
New York, N.Y. 10016

First printing: July, 1984

Printed in the United States of America

ROMMEL'S LAST STAND

CHAPTER ONE

By March of 1943, the war in North Africa had reached a desperate point for Germany. Less than a month after America's devastating defeat at Kassarine Pass in Tunisia, U.S. forces had rebounded and pushed Field Marshal Rommel's Afrika Korps deep into northern Tunisia. The field marshal had then asked to evacuate his 300,000 seasoned German and Italian troops from North Africa in what Rommel considered a hopeless cause, and thus avoid another Stalingrad. However Nazi dictator Adolph Hitler insisted that Rommel defend his North Africa positions to the end.

Field Marshal Erwin Rommel thus worked hard to get a steady infusion of reinforcements and supplies in order to hold Tunisia. However, the superior Allied navies in the Mediterranean Sea had sunk hordes of German supply ships that sailed from Italy or Sicily to Tunisia across the Strait of Sicily. So, the Germans began moving men and supplies by air, a new innovation that disturbed the Allies.

While German ground forces and Allied ground forces jockeyed for positions to hold or to capture Tunisia, the final outcome in North Africa would depend on air activities and not on ground battles. The adversaries would clash in a vital series of air battles during April of 1943, and, ironically, these aerial confrontations in the Mediterranean would reach their climactic conclusion on Palm Sunday.

By March, the Allies had made considerable gains in southern Tunisia following the Kassarine Pass debacle. The British 8th Army was now pushing hard against the German's Mareth Line that commanded the rail line between Sfax and Tunis. In the northeast, units of the same 8th Army had laid siege to Sedjenne, whose capture would open for the British the Sedjenne-Mageur Highway for a quick thrust to Tunis. The American II Corps was now threatening the Afrika Korps at El Guettar and Gabes on the Gulf of Gabes in eastern Tunisia, while in the central sector of southern Tunisia the U.S. IV Corps was threatening to breach the German defenses at Shietla and Fondouk to break into the open Tunisian plains and race toward Bizerte.

If the Allied ground forces reached Tunis on the Gulf of Bon and Bizerte on the Mediterranean coast, they could entrap some 300,000 Axis troops of the Afrika Korps. Thus, the Germans needed to devise a strategy that would assure a flow of supplies to Rommel in Tunisia. The answer was seemingly a series of aerial convoys and the first small flights in March had reached Tunisia safely.

Gen. Dwight Eisenhower, CinC of Allied forces in North Africa, had been quite upset by these aerial supply convoys. Eisenhower believed that the mish mash in air commands had kept the Americans and the British from carrying out effective air attacks against the Germans. There had been no specific responsibilities for the U.S. Air Force and the British RAF. And worse, the American commands included the 9th Air Force, the 12th Air Force, and the Mediterranean Air Force, all of them often operating without coordination with one another. Eisenhower thus created the North African Air Force (NAAF), a unified command of all American and British air units under Gen. Carl Spaatz.

General Spaatz, in turn, had set up specific responsibilities for all Allied units in North Africa. He formed two commands, the North Africa Tactical Air Force (NATAF) under British Air Marshal Arthur Conningham, and the North Africa Strategic Air Force (NASAF) under U.S. Gen. James Doolittle. He then planned a strategy called Operation Flax to deal with both the German ground troops in Tunisia and the German resupply system from Italy or Sicily to Tunisia. NATAF would be responsible for supporting the ground troops in Tunisia against the Afrika Korps and for patrolling the seas off the North African coast to intercept any German aerial or surface ship convoys. NASAF would be responsible for attacking German airfields and harbors in Italy and Sicily and Tunisia, and hopefully destroying Axis ships and planes on the ground before they could be sent to Tunisia with men and supplies.

On March 17, 1943, Gen. Carl Spaatz held a briefing at his NAAF headquarters in Algiers to discuss the proposed Operation Flax and to explain the roles of NATAF and NASAF in these operations. Among those called to the conference were Britishers Air Marshal Arthur Conningham and Col. Kenneth Cross of the NATAF command and the RAF 211 Group. Also here were Americans Gen. James Doolittle of NASAF, Col. John Stone of the U.S. 62nd Fighter Wing, and Col. Joseph Atkinson of the U.S. 47th Bomb Wing.

When his commanders had comfortably seated themselves around an oval table, Spaatz gestured to an aide who pulled down a map of the central Mediterranean.

"Gentlemen," the NAAF commander began, "we are faced with a new problem. The Germans have begun sending reinforcements into Tunisia for the past couple of months in aerial convoys. Our naval ships and air units have done a pretty good job on their surface ship convoys that sail across the Strait of Sicily, so now the Germans are trying to send in their men and supplies by air.

This is what they did at Stalingrad, and quite successfully, until the cold weather did them in. But there is no winter climate in the Mediterranean to deter them. So we'll need to take the initiative."

"What did you have in mind?" Air Marshal Conningham asked.

"The NAAF staff has drawn up a plan called Operation Flax and its purpose is to stop this German air traffic into Tunisia before it really begins to steamroll. They've had some success thus far with these air transport convoys, but the flights have been small and irregular. But if they can do this, they'll surely intensify the effort."

"How will we stop them, sir?" Colonel Cross asked.

"I see four major facets to this Operation Flax," Spaatz said. "First, we must continue to keep heavy pressure on the German ground forces in Tunisia. We must continue heavy and sustained tactical missions on all four Tunisian fronts: The Mereth Line, Gabes, Edl Guettar and Sedjenne. The second need will be to maintain continuous combat air patrols over the Strait of Sicily and along the North African coast to intercept both aerial convoys and surface ship convoys." Spaatz looked at Air Marshal Conningham. "These two operations will become the sole responsibility for the new NATAF command."

"Do you mean we will no longer be attacking airfields and harbors on the continent?" Conningham asked.

"Only if you can spare some units from your

primary task of supporting our ground troops and for maintaining the CAPs in the Mediterranean."

"I see," Conningham answered. There was a tinge of coolness in his response. The air marshal, like many other British commanders, had resented the establishment of the united NAAF command that had put an American in charge of all air operations in the North African campaign. Conningham was piqued because he felt the British had been undermined after they had spent more than three years fighting in North Africa and in the Mediterranean. Now the Johnny-come-lately Americans were assuming a dominant leadership role in the campaign. U.S. General Eisenhower had taken over the supreme command of all North African Allied Forces since the landings in North Africa in November of 1942, and now another Americans had taken command of all air operations. Conningham wondered if American commanders would not soon take over all naval operations in the Mediterranean.

Group commander Col. Ken Cross was also disturbed. His bombers from the RAF 211 Group had enjoyed considerable success against German targets in Sardinia, Sicily, and Italy. Now this upstart American air general had relegated him to ground support and CAP missions. Cross's airmen would surely be disappointed with this new assignment; and they would no doubt curse the Yank intrusion into their North African war.

However, the British had needed three years to reach Tunisia's eastern frontier, while the American had reached Tunisia's western frontier in three months from their landing sites at Casablanca and Algiers in November of 1942. Further, American airmen had caused more damage to the Germans during this three month period than the British had done in the previous three years. Perhaps the Americans had won the right to dominate the strategy of the North African campaign.

General Spaatz looked again at his map before he addressed his commanders once more. "While NATAF deals with the German ground forces in Tunisia itself and maintains CAPs in the Mediterranean, NASAF will carry out the other two objectives of Operation Flax. There are two factors," he gestured, "the points of embarkation and the points of debarkation. We know that enemy transport planes load up at Naples in Italy and fly south to stage at the Sicilian airfields of Gerbini and Comiso. The transports then dart across the Strait of Sicily to the German airfields of Sidi Ahmed or El Aouina in northern Tunisia. Their fighter escorts from Sicily operate from airfields at Trapani, Bocco de Falco, Borrizio, or Messina. NASAF aircraft will need to keep all of these enemy bases neutralized, and to knock out as many planes on the ground and ships in harbors as is possible."

"But sir," Colonel Stone asked, "even a Piper cub can make it from Naples to Tunisia. Why are they stopping in Sicily?"

Spaatz grinned. "So they can carry more men and supplies inside the planes. By refueling in Sicily, they reduce their gasoline load and thus they can increase the tonnage capacity of their transport planes."

Colonel Stone nodded.

"In any event the job of NASAF will be to hammer the airfields at both the points of embarkation and the points of debarkation. NASAF air units will also pound Sicilian and Italian harbors where the Nazis sortie their surface ship convoys. We'd especially like to hit air transport planes and surface ships while they've bunched up on airfields or in the harbors."

"That's a big order, sir," Colonel Atkinson of the U.S. 47th Bomb Wing said.

"We recently got new air units from the States and some of them will be joining NASAF," Spaatz said. "You'll have eight bomb groups to use against the Italian and Sicilian targets and against the Tunisian airfields. General Doolittle has been assigned the 97th, 99th, and 301st B-17 heavy bomb groups, the 17th and 320th B-26 medium bomb groups, and the 321st and 310th B-25 medium Bomb Groups. NASAF will also be getting the RAF 142 Wellington Bomber wing. I've also asked for two B-24 heavy groups from NACAF and if we get them, I'll assign these to NASAF."

"Yes sir," Akinson said.

Spaatz now looked at Col. John Stone. "It's imperative that your fighter units do a good job of escorting bombers to Sicily and Italy. They can expect considerable Luftwaffe interception around the ports and airfields."

"We've only got the 82nd, 1st, and 14th Groups," Stone said.

"You'll also have the 350th Fighter Group with their P-47s and the 3rd Recon Composite Group of mixed P-38s and B-17s. That should give you enough fighters for escort missions." Spaatz now looked at Conningham. "On the aerial resupply missions, the Germans are likely to have plenty of fighter escorts. So I'd suggest that each CAP fighter group have at least one additional squadron of fighters as escorts in the event they run into an aerial convoy. If our own fighters deal effectively with any ME 109s or FW 190s, the interdiction squadrons will have a much easier time of destroying enemy transport plane formations."

"Yes sir," Conningham answered. "But I have one question. How do we know when or if these German transport planes are flying toward Tunisia?"

"We'll have destroyers with the latest radar on twenty-four hour patrol about the Strait of Sicily. They'll notify your headquarters in Libya as soon as they get positive bogies. You must also maintain round the clock flights with your own radar equipped recon planes."

"Yes sir," the Britisher said again.

"Meanwhile," Spaatz continued, "you should keep your fighter units on continual alert, so they can take off at once from their Tunisian and Libyan airfields. Remember, flights from Sicily to Tunisia only take about a half hour, so you'll

15

need to be over the Mediterranean within fifteen or twenty minutes after you get a report. You'll need to intercept before the enemy transport planes can land on their Tunisian airfields."

"I understand," Conningham said.

Spaatz now looked at Doolittle. "Jim, we can assume the Germans will continue to send supply and transport ships across the strait as well as aerial resupply convoys. So I would ask that NASAF aircraft hit their embarkation ports quite hard." He tapped the map with a pointer. "Here, at Naples, and down here, at Messina and Trapani in Sicily: these are the German embarkation ports for supply ships. They all head for Bizerte or Tunis in Tunisia, so you'll also need to hit these harbors quite hard."

Doolittle nodded.

Spaatz shuffled through some papers in front of him, looked up and then spoke again. "I believe your NASAF command is strong enough to carry out your responsibilites against airfields and harbors. You have two B-25 groups, two B-26 groups, three B-17 groups, and a composite group. As I said, we'll try to get a couple of B-24 heavy groups transferred to your command for this operation."

"That would help," Doolittle said.

Spaatz looked at Air Marshal Conningham. "How about the NATAF complement?"

The air marshal looked at some papers in front of him and then spoke. "We have the American 12th Bomb Group with their Mitchells and five fighter groups from the American Western Desert Air Force: 57, 79, 324, 31, and 52 Groups. And of course, we have our own 211 Group RAF wings: number 239, 244, 285, and the South African 7 Wing. I believe we have enough aircraft to carry out our responsibilities for this Operation Flax."

Spaatz nodded and again addressed the assembly. "It's obvious to you that the purpose of this operation is to destroy in the air, on the ground, and on the sea any concentration of enemy air transport planes or surface ships that attempt to bring in supplies or personnel to the Afrika Korps. While I have the utmost faith in Air Marshal Conningham and the airmen in his NATAF command, there are too many possibilities of aerial convoys eluding a CAP. So I would prefer to strike such convoys, aircraft or ships, at their source. When there is a sufficient buildup of planes or vessels on an airfield or in a harbor, that will be the time for NASAF bombers to strike."

"But how will we know when the Germans have such a buildup?" General Doolittle asked.

"Intelligence, Jim," Spaatz grinned. "Bill Donovan of the OSS has agents everywhere and they've been keeping tabs on each of the transport areas: Naples, Messina, Borizzio, Bari, Trapani, Tunis, Bizerte, Sidi Ahmed, and El Aouina. These agents will inform Donovan when they believe the buildups are large enough to warrant air attacks on our part. These same agents will also keep us informed of departures, estimated arrival times, and routes followed. The agents will also give us information on the extent of anti-aircraft defenses and what kind of anti-aircraft defenses the Germans have at departure and terminal points."

"Good Lord, sir," Colonel Stone gaped, "how can they tell us all that? We'd need a lot of agents to keep us informed on all these operations."

"Donovan has assigned over two hundred people to Operation Flax," Spaatz said. "I can tell you—there's a lot of Italians, French, and Tunisians who hate the Nazis, and they're more than willing to carry out espionage activities for us. And as some of you know, we first proposed this Flax operation in February, but with the unfortunate set back at Kassarine Pass, we've had to postpone the plan until the crisis was over and we had reestablished our ground positions in southern and eastern Tunisia. Donovan has had plenty of time to line up agents in Italy, Sicily, and Tunisia. His people are ready and the OSS network will move as soon as we give the word."

"When will that be?" General Doolittle asked.

"In a couple of days," Spaatz answered. "We hope to begin these aerial operations about the first of April. Both NASAF and NATAF air units should be ready by then." He looked at General Doolittle. "I'd suggest, Jim, that you begin at once to assign your air units for attacks on the enemy airbases and port facilities, and possibly on surface ship convoys."

General Doolittle nodded.

Spaatz then looked at Arthur Conningham. "Air Marshal, you should ready immediately your fighter groups for sweeps, CAPs, and interceptions against any German air transport formations."

"Yes sir," Conningham said.

"You should also alert air groups in your command to conduct support missions in the vital Tunisia ground areas as I mentioned earlier: Mareth, Gabes, El Guettar, and Sadjenne. You should use fighters, fighter-bombers, and light bombers in these support missions."

The British air marshal nodded.

"Okay," Spaatz sighed, "I guess that's it. I suggest you get back to your headquarters and get to your group and wing commanders to ready their air units. They must be constantly on the ready to attack airfields, harbors, ship convoys, and most of all, any aerial convoy formations. Both NASAF and NATAF headquarters will be in liaison with the OSS headquarters in Algiers, and you'll take your cues from them. I needn't remind you that any messages or reports from the OSS must be kept top secret, and I suggest that only U.S. wing and RAF group commanders and their executive officers be allowed to accept OSS messages, which will be identified by the code name Roman. If you get such a call, only the authorized officers will respond. The wing or group commander will then make out an FO for an air mission. Any questions?"

None.

Spaatz nodded and looked at his watch. "Time for lunch, gentlemen. Let's enjoy our meal. Then you can head back to your own headquarters to get this show on the road."

The next day, Gen. James Doolittle of NASAF met with his 47th Bomb Wing and 62nd Fighter Wing commanders, along with bomber and fighter group commanders, at his headquarters in Algiers to outline the Flax operation. He would use his B-17 heavy bomb groups and the two B-26 medium bomb groups to hit the airfields and the port at Naples, and to hit the ports and transport airfields in Sicily. He would use his two B-25 groups to hit the German fighter bases in Sicily. His 3rd Composite Recon Group would use its P-38s and B-17s for reconnaissance as well as on escort and bombing missions.

The heavies and B-26s would be especially alert to bomb the German transport plane staging bases at Gerbini and Comiso in Sicily in the hope of knocking out such aircraft before they could make the run over the Strait of Sicily into Tunisia. The NSAF commander warned his B-25 group commanders, Col. Ed Olmstead of the 321st Group and Col. Anthony Hunt of the 310th Group, to prepare a series of missions to knock out the German fighter bases at Trapani, Borrizio, Bocco de Falco, and Messina in Sicily. Such successful attacks could cut down the number of fighter escort planes the Germans could mount to accompany aerial transport formations to Tunisia.

Doolittle was also concerned about surface ship convoys and he looked at Colonel Upthegrove of the 99th Bomb Group. "Fay, we can expect the Germans to still use ships, when they can. Your group and Col. Stan Donovan's 97th Group should gear your airmen for harbor attacks on shipping."

"We'll be ready," Col. Fay Upthegrove said.

"I understand," Colonel Donovan said.

Doolittle explained that on all strategic missions, one full fighter group would be assigned to escort two bomb groups. Some of the group commanders did not believe that one fighter unit was enough for two bomber units, but Doolittle said he could not afford to use any more. He explained that their air complements were spread quite thin, and they needed to attack a considerable number of targets. He was doing the best he could.

"After you return to your group campsites, make sure you put your aircraft in on-the-ready condition. We'll never know when a Roman message will come in from OSS to the wing commanders. You may need to take off on a mission within an hour or even a half hour."

"Yes sir," Col. Fay Upthegrove said.

Far to the west, in Tripoli, Air Marshal Arthur Conningham met with 211 Group commander Col. Kenneth Cross and with his American and RAF bomber and fighter unit commanders. In attendance here were the U.S. commanders of the 57th, 324th, 79th, 31st, and 52nd Fighter Groups, along with Col. Ed Backus of the 12th Bomb Group. Also here were the RAF commanders of the 7 SAAF, 239 and 244 Fighter Wings, along with the commander of the 285 Bomber Wing. Conningham pawed through

21

some papers in front of him before he spoke.

"Gentlemen, there has been a change in our plan of operation. We will no longer attack strategic targets on the continent. The North Africa Air Force commander has drawn up a plan called Operation Flax. The strategy is to stop the Jerry transport plane convoys that are coming into Tunisia. The North Africa Strategic Air Force will bomb port and airfield targets in Sicily and Italy in the hope of stopping such convoys at their source. The duty of the North Africa Tactical Air Force, aside from our usual ground support missions, will be to maintain combat air patrols continually over the Strait of Sicily and along the North Africa coast. We are to intercept and destroy any German transport planes that attempt to reach Tunisia. Since we know that such aircraft can dash across the strait within a half hour, we will need to maintain patrols off the coast at all times."

"All times, sir?" Lt. Col. Dan Loftus of the 7 SAAF Wing asked.

"All times," Conningham answered. "Each patrol will include a full American air group or British air wing and the stint will be for two hours before relief. I've decided that 211 Group will maintain these patrols and Colonel Cross will decide which units will conduct these patrols and when they will conduct such patrols."

"This might be quite monotonous, sir?" Lieutenant Colonel Loftus said.

"It is not for us to ask questions," Cross answered. "When you get the word, you'll scramble. Just make certain that by this time tomorrow your aircraft and pilots are ready, with planes fully loaded with machine gun belts and 20mm cannon shells. You may need to get off the ground within five minutes' notice and you may only have fifteen or twenty minutes to reach target."

"Yes sir," Col. Art Salisbury of the 57th U.S. Fighter Group said.

Conningham scanned the unit commanders. "Any questions?"

"I guess not," Salisbury answered.

"Get back to your units," the NATAF CinC gestured. "We'll be sending you a full FO sheet in the morning, although time, dates and places of attack will not be shown on the FO. You'll get these from group headquarters."

When the meeting ended, the British and American commanders of NATAF returned to their campsites in disappointment. They expected the NASAF air units to get all the glory in this new Operation Flax. Still, they understood the need to fly protective air patrols as well as to bomb enemy installations. Each duty was important to cut the German lifeline between Sicily and Tunisia.

But the Germans suspected that the Allies would sooner or later begin to frown on their aerial transport convoys that carried men and supplies to Tunisia. So they took steps to thwart the Operation Flax strategy.

CHAPTER TWO

Without doubt, in March of 1943, the busiest German base in Europe was Naples, that quaint Italian city with its perfect semicircle bay and a view of Mount Vesuvius. The city of more than a million offered a wide gap between the rich and the poor, the handsome villas and the seedy slums, or the wealthy business manipulators and the begging waifs. Wide boulevards interspersed with dark, narrow streets that were little more than alleyways, while handsome cars shared these same streets with donkeys and carts.

Among the citizens, a few cooperated fully with the Germans and thus enjoyed freedom and luxuries. A few others were diehard anti-Nazi partisans who tried to hurt the Germans, but who more often got themselves executed. However, the bulk of the population showed indifference. They viewed the German soldiers about their city as no different from Italian soldiers, or the conquering Etruscans of ancient times. For centuries, Neapolitans had seen one conquering army or another occupy their city, going back to the Romans, so they accepted the German presence as routine.

The Bay of Naples sheltered every conceivable type of vessel: from battleships down to harbor craft, large cargo and transport ships down to barges, from an array of auxiliary vessels to tugboats, from luxury yachts to leaky dinghies that were used by poor fishermen. The rich and the poor, the German military and Italian civilians, the less than enthusiastic Italian military, and the nonchalant Italian commercial sailors had all learned to live with each other.

The Bay of Naples had become the frequent target of American and British bombers in recent months and errant bombs had too often blown up commercial ships or pleasure boats along with an occasional Italian or German warship. After such Allied bombing attacks, the Neapolitans cursed the Allied airmen and wished they would simply go away and leave them alone.

If activities thrived in the Bay of Naples, activities at the four airfields outside of the city boomed even more. The Luftwaffe based its transport planes of Lufttransport Mittelmeer at the huge airbase of Capodichino, its KG 26 DO 17 and KG 100 HE 111 bombers at the Pomigliano bomber base, its German ME 109 and

Italian MC 200 fighter planes at Aquino Field, and most of its repair and service facilities at Montecervino Airdrome. More than 10,000 German and Italian air crews and ground crews, along with 20,000 employed Italian civilians, operated from these fields.

The civilians worked for the German military at these airdromes because the Germans paid them well, treated them tolerably, and provided them transportation. However, when the Allies began hitting these fields with long range B-17 and Lancaster bombers, the Italians not only cursed the American and British airmen but also the Germans who had subjected these emotional Neapolitans to bombing attacks. They began deserting their jobs by the score. After the first air raid, according to a German commander, "More than one thousand of these civilians at the airfields never returned."

Subsequent air attacks had prompted more desertions until by March of 1943 the Germans were forcing civilians to work at a point of a gun.

"We had the most elaborate kinds of shelters," said Gen. Ulrich Buchholtz, commander of Lufttransport Mittelmeer, "and few people were ever injured in these Allied air attacks. But the cowardly Italians ran like frightened rabbits at the first sound of an air raid siren. These people were next to useless for us, but we could not get help from Germany, so we had to employ them."

Without doubt, the Germans in Naples were quite contemptuous of both the Italian military and Italian civilians. They considered them lazy and unreliable as workers, lacking in patriotism, quick to pilfer anything from a can of sauerkraut to a motor vehicle, and unresponsive to needed training so they could work capably on aircraft and equipment.

However, the indifference of these Neapolitans at least left the German in command of Naples and free of the widespread sabotage and destruction that had plagued German commanders in other areas of occupied Europe.

Field Marshal Albert Kesselring was the CinC of OB South (Oberbefihlishaber Sud), commanding all Forces in Italy and Sicily, and also the Luftflotte 2 aerial arm of OB South. He said of Naples: "Our only problem was the occasional enemy air attacks and the unreliable Italian workers. Fortunately, the weather over Naples was usually as fickle as the populace, so the Allies did not bomb us with any kind of regularity to cause more effective damage."

Kesselring's main occupation during the early part of 1943 was the movement of men and supplies to the hardpressed Afrika Korps under Field Marshal Erwin Rommel in Tunisia. The OB South commander had been using Naples as a marshalling center to categorize and assign the hordes of troops and provisions coming down the boot of Italy before transshipping these resources to North Africa. Thus, transport and cargo ships continually came in and out of the Bay of Naples to reload before making new runs to Tunisia.

In January of 1943, 105 ships had arrived in

Italy from France to carry the estimated 3,000 tons of supplies the Afrika Korps needed daily to continue its defense of Tunisia. Supply vessels had been escorted by Italian destroyers, the German Air Force, and the Italian Air Force. The Germans had been bringing Rommel all the supplies he needed until the end of January of 1943, when the U.S 3rd Recon Group's B-17 snoopers began to pinpoint the locations and routes of German convoys with amazing accuracy.

Allied warships, British carrier planes, American submarines, and U.S. land based aircraft took a heavy toll against the German cargo and transport ships that skirted the southwest coast of Italy, steamed around western Sicily, and then raced across the Strait of Sicily to Tunisia. By mid-March the Germans could no longer send convoys safely to North Africa.

Kesselring, shattered by the blows to his surface ship convoys, began to use transport planes to supply the Afrika Korps. During the first ten days of March, JU 52 transport planes, with ME 109s, FW 190s, or MC 200s as fighter escorts, made regular shuttle flights to North Africa from Italy, bringing about 10,000 tons of needed supplies to Field Marshal Rommel. The airlift had hardly filled the needs of the Afrika Korps but the air shuttles had not suffered the severe losses of the German surface ship convoys, whose few vessels that reached Tunisia brought in only a trickle of supplies.

The JU 52s from Naples usually stopped at the German bases in Borrizo or Comiso in Sicily to refuel and then to make the half to three-quarter hour dash across the Strait of Sicily — before the Allies could mount adequate interceptors to attack the transport planes.

The early success of these air transport shuttles prompted Field Marshal Kesselring to use aerial convoys more and more along with the dangerous surface ship convoys. As head of Luftflotte 2 as well as OB South, Kesselring called on Gen. Ulrich Buchholtz of the transport command in Italy to devise a definite plan for a massive and steady transport supply effort to Tunisia.

Buchholtz, who had about 100 JU transport planes in his Lufttransport Mittelmeer's KVT 16 Geschwader, then scrounged the European continent to bring into Naples as many cargo planes as he could beg, borrow, or steal. He managed to commandeer an additional 100 JU 52 transport planes, about 50 JU 87s, and the promise of the KVT 5 Geschwader that included 100 of the huge long range ME 323 rear loading transports. These giant six engine Gigantens could even carry the famous 88 artillery piece intact or a Mark IV tank intact.

By mid-March, Buchholtz had amassed over 300 transport planes of all types. Then he and Kesselring, along with the Luftflotte 2 staff, drew up a plan called Operation Oschenkopf (Bulls Head) to transport a daily minimum of 500 replacement troops and 2500 tons of supplies, arms, and equipment for Tunisia.

U.S. agents from Gen. "Wild Bill" William Donovan's OSS carefully maintained a close watch on the arrival of these transport planes into Naples. The agents, part of the American OSS worldwide spy network, reported these developments to Donovan's intelligence headquarters at Algiers and the information had prompted Gen. Carl Spaatz to initiate Operation Flax.

At about the same time that U.S. General Spaatz had called his Operation Flax conference in Algiers, Field Marshall Albert Kesselring called a conference of his own in Naples to complete plans for Operation Bulls Head. Besides Kesselring and Buchholtz, other ranking German officers were there: Gen. Hoffman von Waldau, commander of Fleigerkorps Tunisien; Gen. Jurgeon von Armin, representing Field Marshal Rommel; Gen. Hannes Trautloft of Luftflotte 2's Fleigerkorps II fighter corps; and Gen. Erich Hammhuber, commander of the Luftflotte 2's Fleigerkampf Sud bomber corps.

When the German officers were comfortably seated at the oblong table in Kesselring's operations room, the field marshal scanned some papers in front of him and then spoke.

"No one here must be reminded of the critical situation in North Africa. The enemy is now pressing the Afrika Korps on all sides in Tunisia. We are fortunate to have a man like Field Marshal Rommel directing our defenses in Africa. He has shown a remarkable ability to stop the enemy, despite the overwhelming odds against him. But he must have a regular flow of supplies, or even a courageous kommandant like Rommel will ultimately fail. I am sure that we would all agree that if Tunisia falls, the enemy will surely come next to Sicily and even Italy itself. I must therefore agree with the Fuhrer, who says that Tunisia must be held at all costs."

Kesselring paused and then continued. "If Herr Rommel is to continue his stalwart defense in Tunisia, he must have tons of supplies and a steady flow of replacement troops to fill the ranks of the gallant Afrika Korps soldiers who have been killed or wounded in battle. We know that strong Allied naval units and air units have severely curtailed our attempts to send supplies and men into Tunisia by sea. We have lost too many merchant ships which we cannot afford to lose. And worse, we have lost hundreds of tons of provisions and scores of gallant men who have gone to the bottom of the Mediterranean along with these ships. We have now considered a plan to supply Tunisia mostly by air." Kesselring gestured before he turned to Buchholtz. "Ulrich?"

The Lufttransport Mittelmeer CinC nodded and then spoke. "We will launch a plan called Operation Oschenkopf that will increase the flow of supplies into Tunisia on a regular basis through aerial convoys. So far, we have been quite successful with the few transport flights we have made thus far."

"You must excuse my skepticism, Herr Buchholtz," General von Armin suddenly spoke, "but I do not believe that transport aircraft can bring in all the provisions necessary to support the three hundred thousand men of the Afrika Korps."

"I believe the same thing would be true for Fleigerkorps Tunisien," General von Waldau said. "We have about three hundred operable aircraft, fighters and bombers, to support our ground troops, but too often they must remain grounded for lack of fuel and spare parts. We are simply not getting enough gasoline, and I cannot see how aircraft alone can bring in the fuel we need for our bombers and our fighters."

"All that will change," Buchholtz said with a grin. "Up to now, we have used only about one hundred transport planes, but soon, the Pomigliano as well as the Capodichino airdrome in Naples will be housing more than three hundred transport aircraft. Included will be up to a hundred of the large ME 323 cargo planes from KVT 5 that can carry vehicles up to Mark IV Panzer size. The Giganten can also carry cannon pieces as large as the 88mm gun."

"So many transports?" von Waldau asked in surprise.

"One ME 323 alone can carry enough gasoline to allow each fighter and bomber of your Fleigerkorps Tunisien to conduct five sorties. Or," Buchholtz gestured, "one of these giant transport planes can carry enough spare parts to keep your Fleigerkorps Tunisien supplied for a month."

"I did not realize that the new 323 transport plane had such a capacity," General von Waldau said.

"As I said, we may have up to a hundred of these," Buchholtz continued. "So it is not a question of our means to supply the Afrika Korps with three thousand tons of supplies daily, but if we can get these transport formations safely from Naples to Tunisia in a regular shuttle service."

Kesselring turned to Hannes Trautloft of the fighter command. "Well, General?"

Trautloft fumbled through some papers before he answered. "When General Buchholtz first told me of this proposed operation, I was sure the plan was not practical. But it is true that he has already succeeded in several small aerial convoys, and I am now convinced that we could be just as successful in large airborne convoys. We can easily fly these transport aircraft from Naples to staging bases in Sicily without fear of interception from enemy fighter planes, as General Buchholtz pointed out to me. We then need only slip across the strait to Tunisia, a less than one hour flight. In this short period, the enemy cannot likely mount massive squadrons of fighter aircraft from North Africa to intercept. The enemy could only have available for interception the few aircraft on combat air patrol over the Mediterranean, and our own fighter escorts can easily deal with such a small formation."

"We are improving our Comiso and Borrizo staging airdromes in Sicily," General Buchholtz, said. "Since we have fighter units based in Sicily, we can easily coordinate an escort gruppen with a transport gruppen."

"I have already designated certain fighter geschwaders that will participate in Operation

Oschenkopf," Trautloft spoke again. "We have the well experienced JG 77 at Trapani, Sicily, under the capable Lt. Col. Johannes Steinhoff. He has at least one hundred and twenty FW 190 fighters in his geschwader. We also have in Sicily at Catania the II Gruppen of JG 53 under Hauptman Wolfgang Tonne. He has forty ME 109s in his unit. At Boco de Falco, Sicily, the erstwhile Maj. Hartman Grasser has some forty Messerschmidt fighters in his II Gruppen of JG 51."

Trautloft looked at some papers and then continued. "I have also assigned the JG 27 to this operation. Colonel Neuman has about one hundred and twenty fighters. He is based at Reggio de Calabria in southern Italy, so his geschwader is within close proximity to escort transport aircraft across the Strait of Sicily."

"Very good," Field Marshal Kesselring said. He then looked at General von Waldau. "What of your fighters and bombers from Fleigerkorps Tunisien? Can you assign some units to aid in this plan?"

"I really need every available aircraft to support the Afrika Korps ground forces," von Waldau answered, "but perhaps I can release the III Gruppen of JG 51 and some of our attack bombers."

Kesselring nodded and then looked at some more papers in front of him before he continued. "It would surely be foolish to send only a few aircraft at once over the Strait of Sicily. We would be wiser to wait until we have a large number of transport aircraft fully loaded. We could then use a full gruppen of fighters, even two gruppen, to escort these transport planes."

"I might add," General Buchholtz spoke again, "that the ME 323s will carry gunners with .57 caliber machine guns to defend themselves against interceptors. Naturally, we expect our fighters to be the major protectors of the transports. Yet should some of the enemy fighters break through the escort screen to reach the transports, the gunners will at least be able to make some defense." He gestured to Kesselring who spoke again.

"We will send out at least a full gruppen of transport aircraft on one flight, no less than fifty aircraft," the OB South CinC said. "They will have at least fifty fighters to accompany their formation. Never will we send out less than a hundred aircraft in one aerial convoy. The firepower of such a large number of aircraft will be quite intense against British or American units who rarely keep more than a staffel of fighters on combat air patrol."

"But could they not mount two or three gruppens of fighters to intercept our formation?" General von Armin asked.

Kesselring and Buchholtz exchanged glances before the Luftflotte Mittelmeer CinC spoke. "We will not give the enemy an opportunity to mount such large numbers of fighters against our aircraft formations. First, as Herr Kesselring pointed out, we do not intend to send out these aerial convoys on a scheduled basis so that the enemy can take measures to meet our aircraft over the Strait of Sicily. No," he gestured emphatically, "we will first make certain we have at least fifty transports fully loaded before we make a flight from Naples to Tunisia. And, to deceive the Allies even further, we will sometimes make direct flights and sometimes we will stage from our airbases in Sicily at Comiso and Borrizo."

"Are these fields prepared to receive and deal with these transport aircraft?" von Waldau asked. "Especially the large ME 323s?"

"As I said, our engineers have been working diligently on the fields," Kesselring now spoke. "They will have expanded runways and many more revetments completed by the end of March."

"But will not the enemy become suspicious?" General von Armin asked.

"We will send a staffel of large DO 200 four engine bombers to Comiso," Gen. Erich Hammhuber said. "The arrival of these bombers at this base should deceive the enemy into thinking we are preparing these fields in Sicily for long ranger bomber operations. And in fact, these bombers will be used. Not only the DOs but also a gruppen of light bombers and a gruppen of anti-submarine bombers will move to Sicily so that they can be used to support the Afrika Korps in whatever way they can."

"Very clever, Herr Hammhuber," von Armin said.

"If the enemy's spies in Naples do report that a large formation of transports had left the city," Kesselring said, "the Allies will not find such a formation conveniently over the Strait of Sicily in two or three hours so the enemy can attack them. We may keep the transports at Comiso or Borrizo for several hours or even for a day or two. Then, at an unexpected moment, these loaded transports will suddenly leave the airfields and fly to Tunisia. Even if enemy spies in Sicily observe these transport aircraft planes taking off, the aircraft will arrive safely in Tunisia within an hour, before the Allies can react to intercept them."

"You have planned well," General von Waldau said.

"We have tried," Kesselring said, "but I must ask that the transport airfields at Sidi Ahmed and El Aouina in Tunisia be prepared for these formations."

"We have been laboring hard, Herr Field Marshal," von Waldau said. "But, these two fields have been frequent targets for Allied aircraft and the work has not been easy. However, we intend to maintain only gravel and hard clay runways so that they can be quickly filled if enemy bombs cause craters. This will mean, of course, that you cannot send in aircraft during heavy rain storms that will turn these runways into strips of mud. But then," he grinned, "we do not see much rain at Sidi Ahmed and El Aouina."

"Very good," Kesselring said. He looked at General Hammhuber. "Of course, we would like to cause some grief to the enemy's positions and airfields if we can. Have you made arrangements for such air attacks?"

"We intend to concentrate on the bases that

house the enemy's big bombers in Algeria," Hammhuber said. "If we can keep these airfields out of commission, we could surely avoid heavy B-17 bomber attacks on Naples, from whence these aerial convoys will begin."

"A wise suggestion," Kesselring said.

"We will, of course, also continue to attack enemy warships and submarines when the opportunity arises," Hammhuber continued, "and we will make attacks on the fighter bases in southern Tunisia whenever we can spare the aircraft. I can promise all of you, the bomber force of OB South will not remain idle while the fighters and transports are busily engaged in Operation Oschenkopf. We will do our part to assure the success of this operation."

"I have every confidence that you will, Herr Hammhuber," Kesselring said. He scanned the papers in front of him and then continued. "We must now turn to Fleigerkorps Tunisien, General," he looked at von Waldau. "I hope that you will indeed keep the full gruppen from JG 51 on constant alert. They must protect the fields at Sidi Ahmed and El Aouina during the arrival of aerial convoys and until every pound of supplies and every last man has been safely discharged from the aircraft. This III Gruppen of JG 51 must have no other duty than to participate in Operation Oschenkopf."

Von Waldau rubbed his face. "I do not like the idea of keeping fifty fighters on such alert, with no opportunity to perform other work except to maintain combat air patrols. The Afrika Korps is quite badly harassed in Tunisia by the pressing Allied group forces. While I am willing to release JG 51/III to protect these airfields, I would also like to use them to support our ground forces when necessary."

"I am afraid, General, that you must choose between protecting the airfields or supporting ground troops. I would believe that vitally needed supplies and soldier replacements would take first priority."

"Of course," von Waldau sighed. "Very well, I will inform Major Rudorffer of JG 51/III that his sole responsibility now will be to defend these airfields in Tunisia and to defend aerial convoys when necessary. I can tell you that the major who commands this unit is one of the finest air officers of Fleigerkorps Tunisia. Rudorffer has some of the best fighter pilots in the Luftwaffe, and these fliers are fully capable of dealing with any American or British pilots. This unit was largely responsible for our success in the Kassarine Pass against the Americans because the JG 51/III did an excellent job in supporting Wehrmacht troops during the battle. I am quite reluctant to use this unit solely for Operation Oschenkopf, Herr Field Marshal. But, as you say, we must have supplies and reinforcements in Tunisia and we must spare no effort."

"Good," Kesselring said. He then sighed before he spoke again. "It appears we have discussed all aspects of this operation." He looked at Trautloft. "Of course, the geschwaders you have assigned to escort the aerial convoys must be on constant alert. As I said, you may be called upon on a moment's notice to mount a gruppen of fighters or even a full geschwader for the short flight over the Strait of Sicily."

"I will notify at once the kommandants of these fighter geschwaders and gruppens that I have assigned for this operation," Trautloft said.

Kesselring scanned his officers again. "If there are no more questions I believe this conference is over. We will retire to the dining room for the noon meal. Then you must all return to your units and acquaint your subordinates with these plans which, of course, must remain top secret."

"Yes, Herr Field Marshal," General Hammhuber said.

Thus did the Germans complete plans for Operation Oschenkopf (Bulls Head).

While Allied and German ground forces battled to conquer or to hold Tunisia in this last battle of the North African campaign, the fight would be won or lost in the air and not on the ground.

CHAPTER THREE

On the morning of 28 March 1943 at Berteaux Field, outside of Bougie, Algeria, Col. Bill Covington called his squadron commanders of the U.S. 82nd Fighter Group into his office after breakfast. Among those present with the colonel of the Blue Gulls group were Capt. James Lynn of the 95th Squadron, Maj. Harley Vaughn of the 96th Squadron, and Capt. Richard McAuliffe of the 97th Squadron.

The 82nd Blue Gulls Group had been activated in May of 1942 with new personnel coming into Harding Field, Louisiana, to train as a fighting unit. The group had then moved to California for advanced training with the new P-38 fighter plane. Lieutenant Colonel Covington, who had been working with the Lockheed Company itself with the new forked tail Lightning, took over command of the group in the summer of 1942.

No man in the 82nd doubted for a moment that the group would not move to the Pacific to spring the new fighter plane against the Japanese Zero that thus far had dominated the Pacific war against Allied fighter planes. The bulk of the group personnel had finally boarded transport ships in September of 1942, but the convoy had taken a long sail through the Panama Canal, over the Caribbean Sea, and then across the Atlantic to the 8th Air Force base in northern Ireland. The group's officers and enlisted men now believed they would go into combat over Europe.

But only two months later, after more combat training, the Blue Gulls boarded transport ships again and sailed to Telergma, Algeria, to join the air war in North Africa. A month later, the group moved to a new airfield at Berteaux, also in Algeria, and began a series of both ground support and escort missions for heavy and medium bombers that attacked German targets in the Mediterranean area.

Covington, who had been apprised of Operation Flax at NASAF headquarters, now spoke to his own squadron commanders. "Well, gentlemen, we're being relieved of all missions except escort missions."

"No more ground support?" Capt. Jim Lynn of the 95th Squadron asked.

"NAAF will launch a special operation for the month of April," the 82nd Fighter Group commander said, "a strategy to destroy German air transport operations between Sicily and Tunisia. Our navy, the British Navy, and Allied air forces have done an awful job on German and Italian shipping, so the Germans are now moving more and more supplies and men to Tunisia by air. Our missions for the month of April will be to escort bombers that make a series of air attacks on German airbases and port areas, where these aerial or merchant ship convoys sortie for a flight or a sail to Tunisia. The Germans are pretty cagey. They seem to know just when to make an aerial convoy run across the strait to avoid our CAPs. They've landed and unloaded before we even know what happens. So we'd like to get them at their source."

"How do we know when we can catch them, Colonel?" Maj. Harvey Vaughn of the 96th Squadron asked.

"General Doolittle has our phase of the operation down pat," Covington said. "NASAF says we'll know when German air convoys are ready to leave Italy or Sicily because Allied agents will find out. They say we have a swarm of OSS spies covering every German airfield and shipping harbor in Sicily and Italy, and they'll inform OSS headquarters in Algiers as soon as a flight of transport planes or a fleet of supply ships is ready to leave for Tunisia."

"Do you believe that, sir?" Captain McAuliffe asked with a grin.

Covington shrugged. "That's what they tell me. Our orders are to keep our P-38's on the ready continually, fully alert, so we can be off within five or ten minutes on any call. That means pilots will need to scramble on a minute's notice, while line crews will need to have our plans fully loaded with fuel and ammo at all times. They'll also keep aircraft engines warmed up."

"Do they expect one fighter group to handle a swarm of 109s or 190s that might try to intercept a bomber formation?" Captain Lynn asked.

"That's the plan," the Blue Gulls commander said.

"Will our group be working with any particular bomb group all the time?" Capt. Dick McAuliffe of the 97th Squadron asked.

"I don't know," Covington answered. "They just told me to be ready."

"Yes sir," McAuliffe said.

"I'd like you to meet with your flight leaders and line chiefs to acquaint them with these instructions," Covington said. "Make sure they understand. As you know, it doesn't take long for a German air formation to get off the ground. So we need to be over a target area as quickly as possible when we get a call to scramble."

"Yes sir," McAuliffe said again.

Fifty miles to the east, at the U.S. Telegram airbase in Algeria, the 14th Fighter Group also prepared for Operation Flax. The 14th had been activated on 20 November 1941 at Hamilton Field, California, under a mere second lieutenant, Tony Keith. The new unit began preliminary training and then moved to March Field in June of 1941 where Lt. Col. Thayer Olds assumed command of the group. The fighter unit was ready for overseas duty by the spring of 1942 and they moved to Atchen, England, expecting to join the U.S. 8th Air Force. However, shortly after the Allied invasion of North Africa in November of 1942, the group sailed to Morocco to join the new U.S. 12th Air Force at Maison Blanche.

Tony Keith, now a lieutenant colonel and a ten year veteran of the U.S. Army Air Force, again assumed command of the 14th. The Avengers then moved to Algeria where they went into combat at once with their new P-38s to support Allied troops against the Afrika Korps, or to escort bombers on missions to Italy and Sicily. In March of 1943, the 14th Fighter Group moved to Telergma, Algeria, its present base.

The 14th Group airmen had found their new station abruptly different from Maison Blance where they had enjoyed barracks quarters, good food, and frequent visits to Oran with its restaurants, movie houses, bars, and friendly Algerian populace. Now in the remote desert of eastern Algeria, the Avengers lived in tents, plagued by heat and black flies during the day and a cold chill at night. They had also come under frequent air attacks by ME 110 fighter bombers and DO 17 light attack bombers from General von Waldau's Fleigerkorps Tunisien. However, the 14th Group airmen had learned to accept these inconveniences because they had the job of trying to chase the Germans out of Africa.

On the morning of 28 March, 1943, Lt. Col.

Tony Keith called into conference his squadron leaders: Maj. Bill Levelette of the 48th Squadron, Maj. Lou Benne of the 49th Squadron, and Capt. Jim Griffith of the 37th Squadron.

"The word has just come done from NASAF," Keith told the three officers. "We'll be launching Operation Flax during the first week of April. This group will be devoting its efforts to escorting bombers that hit German ports and airfields in Italy, Sicily, and Tunisia."

"What about ground support and fighter-bomber missions?" Captain Griffith asked.

"For the time being we won't be engaged in any tactical missions," the lieutenant colonel answered. "The ground support missions will be carried out by the American and RAF units from NATAF. Almost every American fighter unit from NASAF will be engaged in escort duty during this Flax operation."

Major Benne grinned at Keith. "The British won't like the idea of no strategic bombing targets."

"General Spaatz is in command and that's his plan."

"Colonel," Capt. Jim Griffith said, "haven't the Krauts been sending their transport planes into Tunisia for some time now? What makes them think we can stop them with bombing raids? B-17s and B-26s haven't hurt them too much up to now."

"True," Keith nodded, "but it looks like the VIPs have come up with a new strategy. They've brought in OSS intelligence and they claim that

Allied agents will keep us fully informed on the massing of German air transports at Naples or in Sicily. When the OSS gives the word, we make an air strike. That's why we need to be on full alert. It's not much of a hop across the Strait of Sicily from Sicily to Tunisia. So we'll have to be over an embarkation airfield as soon as possible to hit those planes on the ground, before they take off."

"Jesus, it's a long way to Naples, sir," Captain Griffith said.

"That's why your squadron personnel will need to be alert at all times," Keith answered. "Our P-38s will need to be fully fueled and loaded with strafing belts and cannon shells from now on. We could get called out in the middle of the night for a dawn attack. Ground crews will need to keep aircraft on constant combat ready and your pilots will need to get off within five minutes. I'd suggest that crew chiefs preflight our fighters at least three or four times a day, so the aircraft can take off immediately."

"Colonel," Major Benne said, "like Jim Griffith says, we've been on the lookout for massive German aircraft buildups for some time and we really haven't done much. Is NASAF sure we can do better this time?"

"As I said earlier," Keith answered, "we'll have agents in Sicily and Italy to keep us informed as to when such air fleets are ready to take off. Secondly, NATAF will have continual CAPs over the strait in case we miss and a German air fleet is on the way to Tunisia."

"Yes sir," Benne answered.

Keith sighed. "Get back to your squadrons and meet with your own flight leaders, pilots, line chiefs, and crew chiefs to relay my instructions."

At other NASAF fighter bases, fighter group commanders also briefed their squadron leaders on Operation Flax. At Rhumel, Algeria, Col. Ralph Gorman spoke to his officers of the 1st Fighter Group. At Maison Blanche, Col. Marv McNickle talked to his squadron commanders of the 350th Fighter Group. Finally at Soukel Khemis, Tunisia, Lt. Col. Gordon Austin briefed his P-47 squadron leaders of the Checkertail 325th Fighter Group on details of Operation Flax.

In southeast Tunisia, at Theleple, the RAF's 7 SAAF Wing maintained its Spitfire fighters. The South African wing (an RAF wing the equivalent of a U.S. group) had originally come to England in June of 1940 to join the RAF for the Battle of Britain. The 7 Wing had excelled quite well, shooting down more than a hundred German planes during this hard fought, precarious campaign in the skies over Britain and the English Channel.

By the end of 1940, after the Battle of Britain, 7 Wing moved to North Africa to join the 211 RAF Group (RAF Group equivalent to a U.S. wing). From bases in Egypt, and then in Libya, the 7 Wing hit German airfields, base installations, railroad yards, and troop concentrations. The South Africans had also conducted missions against German shipping in the Mediterranean

Sea or they conducted ground support missions for Tommy troops against the Afrika Korps.

Seven Wing had moved to Tripoli in late 1942 to fly ground support missions during the British drive into Tunisia or to hit vital German installations in Tunisia or their ships at sea. During these missions, the South African pilots had continually clashed with German 109 and 110 fighter pilots over the skies of North Africa or the Mediterranean. By March of 1943, 7 Wing had downed 173 German planes in the North African campaign, although they had lost 113 planes of their own.

"The Jerry pilots are good," Lt. Col. Dan Loftus, the 7 Wing commander told a correspondent, "and we're lucky to come out even most of the time."

Seven Wing, so accustomed to walloping German installations and Afrika Korps ground troop concentrations, or battling German pilots in vicious dogfights, had amassed a horde of good, experienced pilots. They would be in for a disappointing shock when they learned their assignment for the Operation Flax campaign.

Lieutenant Colonel Loftus called a meeting of his squadron leaders on the same morning of 28 March. "We will soon join NAAF in a campaign called Operation Flax. It's a complex strategy that includes simultaneous attacks on German shipping, airfields, and transport planes. Unfortunately, our role in this operation will not include any offensive missions."

"No offensive missions?" Maj. Ed Parsonson

of 5 Squadron asked.

"As of now, we will no longer conduct ground support missions or dive bombing missions," Loftus said. "Such missions are now the responsibility of other NATAF air units. Our role will simply be to patrol the Strait of Sicily and the North African coast to attack any Jerry aerial transport planes that attempt to fly into Tunisia."

"Patrols?" Capt. John Hauptfleisch of 2 Squadron gaped. "That's the kind of bloody duty for newcomers. Why are they doing this to us?"

"I don't make the assignments," Loftus shrugged. "All I know—as of 1 April we begin these combat air patrols. The German can send an aerial convoy across the strait in a hurry, less than an hour's time from their bases in Sicily. 211 Group will have full RAF wings or American groups on two hour patrols during a round the clock period."

"That's a bloody shame, Commander," Lt. John Green of 4 Squadron grumbled.

"We do as we're told," the 7 Wing commander said. "I'm giving you copies of the Operation Flax plan. Read them carefully and then discuss the plan with the airmen of your squadrons. Make sure that every pilot, line chief, and ordnance man knows we need to be ready twenty-four hours a day from now on."

"Yes sir," Lieutenant Green said.

At the same Theleple fighter base, the U.S. 57th Fighter Group based its P-40 fighters on the El Djem airstrip, a large airdrome that the 57th shared with the U.S. 79th and 31st Fighter

Groups. While the 57th flew P-40s, the other American groups at Theleple were still using Spitfires while they waited for the new P-38 American fighter planes that had not yet arrived in North Africa for them.

The 57th Black Scorpion Group had been activated in January of 1942 at Mitchell Field, Long Island, beginning their training with P-40s. The 57th had then moved to the Northeast, to Windsor Lock Airbase in Connecticut. Here, the group had continued training with P-40s until mid-summer of 1942 when the group moved overseas to the Middle East.

The ground echelon of the Black Scorpion group had sailed to Palestine aboard the transport ship *USS Pasteur,* while the group's 72 P-40s left Rhode Island aboard the carrier *USS Ranger.* When the carrier came within a hundred miles of the West African coast, the Warhawks had zoomed off the deck and flown to Palestine in a series of hops, finally arriving at Mugeibile in the Near East on 20 July 1942.

The 57th had become part of the British 211 Group and the Americans were soon supporting the British 8th Army during the ground war in North Africa. Thus, the Black Scorpions became the first U.S. air group to conduct combat missions in the Mediterranean area. The 57th had conducted its first mission in August of 1942, nearly three months before the invasion of North Africa. In fact, in September of 1942, the Scorpions moved to the RAF airbase in Cairo, Egypt, where they were closer to the North African war, and where they could now support British ground troops moving across Libya.

Not until November of 1942 did this American fighter group detach itself from the RAF to join the new American 12th Air Force. The group had then moved to Les Sers, Tunisia, to join other U.S. fighter groups of the North African Air Force. The group never got its promised P-38s, but continued to use its P-40s. Then, when Eisenhower ordered the reorganization of the various Allied air forces in North Africa, the 57th again came under the jurisdiction of the RAF 211 Group in the new NATAF command.

Col. Arthur Salisbury, who became the 57th Group commander in December of 1942, probably had more combat experience than any American fighter group commander in the Mediterranean theatre. He had been flying combat against the Luftwaffe for several months before leading this group in ground support missions in Tunisia. In fact, the Afrika Korps troops knew well this American air unit that flew with the RAF.

Salisbury had been among the many young Americans who had joined the Air Corps during the late 1930s and he had been a U.S. Army Air Force pilot for six years. His rise to colonel by December of 1942 had been phenomenal. He had always shown exceptional leadership, remarkable ability as a pilot, and an aggressive attitude in combat against the Luftwaffe. His men liked him because Salisbury was quite sympathetic to their problems, even while he maintained that stern discipline that was so necessary to run a combat air unit effectively.

In fact, under Salisbury's leadership, the 57th Fighter Group had earned a King's Victoria citation from the RAF, one of the few American air units so honored.

Salisbury, like other American air group commanders, had also been thoroughly briefed on Operation Flax, and he too called a meeting of his squadron leaders in late March. He shuffled through some papers before he spoke to these squadron commanders: Maj. Archibald Knight of the 64th Squadron, Capt. Ray Whittaker of the 65th Squadron, and Capt. Jim Curl of the 66th Squadron. All of these men and many of their pilots had seen considerable combat in North Africa.

"We've got a rather unique mission," Salisbury told his officers, "and maybe a lot of you won't like it. NAAF will be launching an operation throughout the month of April to destroy the German air transport system between Italy and North Africa. The brass is getting quite concerned because German supply planes have been coming into Tunisia with men and materiel for the past month or more. The Germans have apparently changed tactics because they've suffered so many losses in their surface ship convoys. The advantage of using air transports, of course, is the ability to make aerial runs across the Strait of Sicily within an hour."

"Some of the 211 air units have already run combat missions against these air transport formations," Maj. Archie Knight said.

"Yes," Salisbury answered, "but General Spaatz has now ordered a special effort against the Luftwaffe transport system, including heavy raids on the German airfields involved in this aerial shuttle system. Under the new NAAF organization, the NASAF units will engage in the bombing attacks and the NATAF units will conduct ground support missions and maintain heavy CAPs over the Strait of Sicily and along the North African coast. Some RAF units will handle the ground support, but the 211 Group units will get assigned strictly to CAP."

"CAP?" Capt. Ray Whittaker huffed. "My God, that's like taking us out of the war."

"I didn't cut the orders," the 57th Group commander shrugged. "I only follow them. Anyway," he referred to his papers again, "we've been told to keep our Warhawks on continual alert. All aircraft must be loaded with fuel, strafing guns, and cannon shells at all times, but no bombs. Our mission will be strictly interception against German transport planes and their 109 or 110 escorts, if or when we see any during our patrols."

"Who else is pulling this duty?" Capt. Jim Curl asked.

"The American 79th, 31st, and 52nd Fighter groups and the RAF 285 and the South African 7 Wing. NAAF has apparently devised an espionage plan to notify us as soon as any German air transport formations get ready to leave a base in Italy or Sicily. NASAF bombers and their escorts will try to catch these planes on the ground, but if they don't, we're expected to hit such transport plane formations while they're crossing the Strait of Sicily into Tunisia. This means we'll need to be on alert during our CAP stints."

"Hell, Colonel," Major Knight scowled, "the chances of hitting anything like that are practically nil."

"Nonetheless, that's how it is," the colonel said. "I want all of you to meet with your pilots and ground crews to make certain that pilots and planes are continually on the ready. Any questions?"

"No sir," Captain Curl said.

Salisbury nodded. "Let's get moving."

At the same Theleple, Tunisia, airbase was the U.S. 324th Fighter Group that had been activated in June of 1942, also at Mitchell Field, Long Island. The unit had also trained with P-40s before moving overseas in the fall of 1942. The Hawk airmen of the 324th had arrived at the RAF airbase in El Aneriya, Egypt, in December of 1942, but no P-40s had come with them. After a month of idleness, crated aircraft finally arrived, but the 324th airmen were astonished to open them and find British Spitfires instead of Warhawks. RAF personnel needed to help the Hawk ground crews to put the planes together.

"It really didn't make any difference to us," said then Maj. Bill McKnown of the 324th's 314th Squadron. "At least we had planes and we could get into action."

As soon as the 324th got their Spitfires, they

began combat against the German Afrika Korps. The group supported Tommies of the British 8th Army for more than two months before their release from the RAF command to join the 12th U.S. Air Force. At their new base in Kairouan, Tunisia, they traded in their Spitfires for P-40s.

The Hawks, however, did not remain with the 12th Air Force for very long. They soon moved to the expansive desert airbase in Theleple to join the British 211 Group under the new North African Tactical Air Force. Bill McKnown, now a lieutenant colonel, took command of the 324th Group.

As with other fighter group commanders, McKnown had also called his squadron leaders into conference to outline the plan for Operation Flax. The 324th would see its group split up for Operation Flax, with each of the three squadrons joining an American fighter group as a bolster unit during the combat air patrols.

"All I know," McKnown told his squadron leaders, "is that each squadron will be assigned to a different group during this Operation Flax campaign. Major Worley's 314th Squadron will remain here at Theleple, attached to the 57th Group. The 315th Squadron will join the 31st Fighter Group, also here at Theleple, and the 316th Squadron will join the 52nd Fighter Group at Le Sers. I'll maintain the group headquarters here in Theleple and fly out myself with the 314th or 315th Squadron."

"Sir," Lt. MacArthur Powers of the 314th Squadron asked, "do you mean that from now on we don't do anything except to pull CAP? No more ground support and other tactical missions against the Krauts? And no more attacks on shipping?"

"The first priority will be the CAP stints," McKnown said, "but that doesn't mean we will not also conduct tactical missions when the opportunity comes."

"Yes sir," Powers answered.

"I'd like the squadron leaders to check in at once with his assigned group, the 57th, 31st, or 52nd, to determine how they want to use you during these operations." He paused. "Any questions?"

"I guess not," Maj. Roscoe Wortley of the 314th Squadron said.

On 31 March, 1943, 92 Squadron of the RAF 285 Wing also arrived in Theleple to join the Americans. They too would be attached to one of the American U.S. fighter groups for the CAP duties. Maj. Neville Duke, the squadron commander, had led these British Spitfire pilots through more than two years of war in the North African campaign. The Britishers had engaged the Germans in countless aerial combat, having downed more than 200 Luftwaffe planes in combat, while they lost more than a 100 planes of their own. They had also run ground support missions for the 8th Army, attacked Afrika Korps installations, and hit shipping in fighter-bomber strikes. The 92 Squadron airmen expressed utter dismay at the new assignment — patrolling the sea and coastline. They felt degraded and demoted in these new duties and they cursed American Gen. Carl Spaatz who had relegated them to this role.

"We do as we're told," Major Duke told his angry pilots.

The 92 Squadron airmen agreed, however reluctantly.

Besides these NATAF units, other American and British air units of the 211 Group would also be assigned to these CAP missions. Squadron leaders also met with other commanders: Col. Earl Bates of the P-40 79th Group, Col. Fred Dean of the U.S. 31st Fighter Group at Theleple, and Col. Graham West of the 52nd Spitfire Fighter Group at Le Sers. Among the Britishers, squadron leaders of the 285 Spitfire Wing met with Air Commander Paul Hastings.

Most of the NASAF fighter pilots from the 82nd, 1st, 14th, 325th and 350th Fighter Groups looked forward to Operation Flax. They would be escorting bombers and the fighter pilots would get plenty of chances to mix it with German fighter pilots over the skies of Sicily or Italy.

However, the American and British fighter pilots of NATAFs 211 Group were disappointed in their role of maintaining a monotonous and perhaps docile time in combat air patrols. The pilots of the 57th Fighter Group, the 324th Fighter Group, the 7 SAAF Wing, and the 92 Squadron could not guess that they would play a major role in Operating Flax.

CHAPTER FOUR

While the U.S. and RAF fighter units of NAAF prepared for Operation Flax, the U.S. bomber groups of the 47th Bomb Wing had also received orders for their particular responsibilities in this operation.

At the bomber base in Berteaux, Algeria, the 310th Bomb Group based their medium B-25 bombers. The 310th had trained with B-25s at Davis-Monthan Field, Arizona, jelling crews and squadrons into an organized air unit. After further training at Jackson Air Force Base and Key Field in Mississippi, the 310th had moved to Mediouna, French Morocco, only six days after the Allied invasion of North Africa on 9 November 1942. Here, the 310th had joined the U.S. 12th Air Force to begin bombing missions against the

Afrika Korps.

"The airbase at Mediouna was a hell of a change from the states," said Lt. Col. Tony Hunter, the group commander. "I remember we walked toward some tents with a Frenchman carrying a lantern and leading the way. But all the tents were full and we had to sleep under the stars in our blankets. It was cold as hell at night and during the day we were plagued by flies, the most persistent and annoying insects imaginable."

The group did not even find tents to sleep in before they were off on close support bombing missions against Rommel's Panzer columns, German storage areas, motor transports, troop concentrations, and Luftwaffe airfields.

In March of 1943, the 310th along with the 321st Mitchell Bomb Group changed its tactics from medium height bombing to the level commerce destroyer technique. The two air groups installed the forward firing nose machine guns on their B-25s in place of the bombardier compartment to become heavy strafers. They also began using the delayed fuse skip bomb that enabled the B-25 to hit surface vessels at extremely close range. Thus the Mitchells then specialized in hitting shipping.

Late in March, the 310th moved to their base at Berteaux, and Lieutenant Colonel Hunter was invited to attend Doolittle's NASAF conference to get the full details of Operation Flax. The 310th Group would no longer direct its energies to ground support, but would now be responsible for attacking German surface ship convoys and airfields in Sicily during the Flax campaign.

Colonel Hunter, a ten year veteran of the U.S. Army Air Force, had been in bomber units since he graduated from flying school in Houston, Texas. He had been in both low level attack groups with light bombers and in medium bomb groups. Hunter had shown great leadership qualities and excellent flying ability. The Air Force had thus assigned him to command the 310th. Under his leadership, the B-25 unit had done well during its service with the 12th Air Force.

On 29 March, Hunter called into conference his squadron leaders: Maj. Pete Remington of the 39th Squadron, Maj. Bill Plant of the 381st Squadron, Maj. Ed Crane of the 380th Squadron, and Maj. Frank Wood of the 428th Squadron.

"NAAF is launching a special air operation for April," Hunter began. "All the groups of the 47th Bomb Wing will be involved. Our part in this operation will be to attack merchant ship convoys that sail from Italy or Sicily to Tunisia or to hit German fighter bases in Sicily."

"What's so special about that?" Major Remington grinned. "We've been hitting shipping ever since we came to North Africa."

"This time, we'll be concentrating only on these targets," Hunter said. "The fighter groups from NASAF will escort bombers that attack shipping, port facilities, and airfields."

"No more ground support for us?" Maj. Ed Crane asked.

"That's correct," Hunter nodded. He pulled

down a map of the central Mediterranean on the wall behind him. "We know that most of the German ship convoys to Tunisia come from Messina and Trapani in Sicily or from Naples in Italy. NASAF intends to have recon planes out continually to keep us appraised of such convoys. They'll track the convoys and then tell us where to hit them; or, they may also have us hit the German fighter plane airfields."

"The Germans haven't done too well lately with surface ship convoys," Major Remington said. "Between air strikes and navy warship attacks, we and the British have sunk an awful lot of German and Italian vessels. Do you think they'll still try to run convoys to Tunisia out of Sicily or Italy?"

"If our fighter and bomber units in this Operation Flax plan can hurt their aerial convoys, they'll send out more ships," Hunter said. "In any event, we've got orders to keep our B-25s fully loaded with GP and incendiary bombs and to keep our guns fully loaded with strafing belts. They may call on us at a moment's notice, so we'll need to be ready. I want you to keep your squadron air crews and line chiefs on full alert from now on. We can't waste time getting our planes airborne once we get a call to take off."

"Okay, Colonel," Major Plant said.

"Are we the only group assigned to shipping during this operation?" Maj. Frank Wood asked.

"No, the 321st Group will also be involved." Then Hunter sighed. "Okay, get back to your squadrons."

To the west, at the U.S. airbase in Bougie, Algeria, Col. Ed Olmstead of the 321st Bomb Group, another B-25 unit, had also met with his squadron commanders: Maj. Ellis Cook of the 446th Squadron, Maj. Dick Smith of the 445th, Cap. Frank Schwane of the 447th, and Maj. Ed Sampson of the 448th Squadron.

The 321st Group Ruinators had been activated in June of 1942 and had trained hard for the next eight months with their B-25s before moving to the DeRidder airbase in Louisiana and then to Bougie, Algeria, in early 1943. The Ruinator group had already been out on ship hunting missions in the Mediterranean, and in fact the 321st had sunk six German merchant ships and two Italian destroyers, while claiming damage to at least nine other Axis vessels.

Colonel Olmstead had worked in coastal defense units in the states for several years before assuming command of the Ruinators when the group moved overseas. Now he would lead the 321st in bombing missions on enemy shipping and airfields only during Operation Flax.

"Hitting ships will be nothing new to us," Olmstead told his squadron commanders, "but for the next month we will not conduct any tactical missions, only enemy surface ships and enemy fighter bases in Sicily."

"Hell, Colonel," Maj. Ellis Cook scowled, "I don't think the Krauts will even send any more ships to Tunisia. They've lost too many."

"They can't supply the Afrika Korps with enough men and materiel by aircraft alone,"

Olmstead answered. "At least I don't think they can. So we can expect them to continue sending troops and supplies across the strait by ship. We've got to keep air crews and ground crews on full alert. All aircraft must be ready to fly off at a moment's notice."

"Yes sir," Maj. Ellis Cook said.

"Please return to your units and meet with your own officers to relay these instructions. All the details for these operations are spelled out in the orders my aides have passed out to you."

At Navarin, Algeria, Col. Fay Upthegrove, CO of the 99th Heavy Bomb Group, also met with his squadron commanders to outline the strategy for Operation Flax. Among those here were Maj. Leon Lowry of the 346th Squadron, Maj. Warren Whitmore of the 348th Squadron, Maj. Harry Burrell of the 347th Squadron, and Maj. Al Orance of the 416th Squadron.

The 99th Group had trained with B-17s since January of 1942 and had remained in training at various airbases in the United States until December of 1942 when they left the Sioux City Air Force Base in Iowa and moved to the new U.S. heavy bomber base at Navarin, Algeria. From here, almost at once, the Ninety-Niners began long range bombing raids against German airfields, railheads, and port facilities in both Sicily and Italy. By March of 1943, the group had already conducted sixteen long range missions.

Col. Fay Upthegrove, the group commander and U.S. Army Air Force pilot for more than ten years, had already served a short tour of duty in the Pacific. On his return to the States, he had only had one month of rest before assuming command of the 99th Bomb Group in September of 1942, the month in which the 99th moved to North Africa. Upthegrove was thus an experienced combat commander and he had the full confidence and respect of his men.

"For this Operation Flax campaign, our targets will be German airfields or harbors in both Sicily and Italy," Upthegrove told his squadron leaders. "The Germans have been switching from surface ships to aerial convoys to reinforce their troops in Tunisia. Almost all of these transport air fleets initiate on the Naples airfields. They usually stage out of Sicily, where they pick up their fighter escorts. So our first missions are likely to be German transport or fighter airdromes in Sicily. We'll be hitting these airbases frequently, whenever weather permits."

"Will our strikes be confined to airbases?" Major Orance of the 416th Squadron asked.

"We may also be called upon to hit harbor shipping and facilities," Colonel Upthegrove answered. "NASAF has assigned us the 301st Group, the 2nd Group, and the 97th Group to these same types of targets. NASAF wants all the B-17 groups to specifically concentrate on the Trapani, Boco de Falco, and Catania fighter bases in Sicily, and the transport staging bases of Comiso and Borrizo, also in Sicily. Harbor targets will probably be at Messina, Trapani, and Naples. We may also hit airbases in Naples."

"What about escorts?" Major Burrell asked.

"They'll assign one fighter group for each two bomb groups."

"When would we start these missions?" Major Orance asked.

"Within the next couple of days," Upthegrove answered. "So I want you to alert all ground and air crews. They say that right now the Germans are massing hordes of fighter planes on their Sicily airbases and another horde of transport planes at Naples. As soon as recon reports say the time is ripe, we'll strike." Upthegrove then gestured. "Okay, get back to your units."

Other bomber group commanders also alerted their crews for Operation Flax missions: Col. John Fordyce of the B-26 320th Bomb Group at Montesquieu, Algeria; Col. Carl Baumeister of the B-26 17th Bomb Group at Telergma; Col. Stan Donovan of the B-27 97th Bomb Group; Col. Ford Lauer of the 2nd B-17 Group; and Col. Sam Gormley of the 301st B-17 Group.

Thus the Allies had prepared to knock out German reinforcements to Tunisia and thus expedite the end of the North Africa campaign.

The Germans, of course, fully realized that the Allies would make every effort to thwart their own Operation Bulls Head, and they took steps to assure the success of their resupply operations into Tunisia.

At the JG 27 fighter base at Reggio de Calabria on the heel of Italy's boot, Col. Edu Neumann met with his gruppen kommandants, including the renowned fighter ace, Maj. Gustav Rodel.

Neumann had already enjoyed a long record of success as a Luftwaffe pilot and a unit commander. The JG 27 kommodore had served with other top Luftwaffe pilots like Galland, Moelders, and Oseau in the Condor Legion during the Spanish Civil War in the mid-30s. Neumann had thus acquired considerable combat experience by the outbreak of World War II. He had then served on the western front during 1940 before transferring to North Africa when full scale war broke out there. By mid-1942, the air veteran had risen to gruppen kommandant and by early 1943, when JG 27 withdrew from Africa to Italy, the Luftwaffe high command assigned Edu Neumann as the new kommodore for JG 27. Neumann had molded a strong geschwader that had enjoyed almost even terms against the Allies, although conditions had worsened recently because of the growing Allied air strength.

Major Rodel had been a German fighter pilot since early 1939 and he had scored his first combat victories during the Blitzkrieg in Poland in 1939. During 1940, he had scored more victories on the western front against England and in 1941 he had increased his kill score dramatically against the Russians on the Eastern Front. By early 1942, Gustav Rodel had become a staffel leader in JG 27, downing 17 British planes in North Africa. By the time JG 27 had retired to Italy, Rodel had scored a total of 83 kills and he had won promotion to kommandant of II Gruppen in JG 27.

On this late March morning, Neumann spoke to his gruppen leaders. "All of you know, of course, that Luftflotte 2 will soon launch a determined campaign to bring supplies, arms, and men to our hard pressed troops in Tunisia. Lufttransport Mittelmeer will mass huge transport fleets for this purpose. We have drawn the responsibility of escorting such formations that stage out of Sicily airfields at Comiso and Borrizo. We can expect the first air transport fleet to leave within the next few days."

"Will the entire geschwader escort this air fleet?" Major Rodel asked.

"We have at the moment one hundred and twenty available fighters," Neuman said, looking at a sheet in his hand. "We may use one, two, or all three gruppens from JG 27, depending upon the size of the aerial convoy."

"Is it possible the Allies will learn of these movements and intercept?" Lt. Wolfgang Fisher asked.

"We hope not," the JG 27 kommodore said. "As you know, air transports can leave Sicily bases and land in Tunisia within an hour. If these flights are made swiftly and with enough secrecy, we may not meet enemy interceptors at all. The enemy's radar may pick up as we approach Tunisia, but by the time they can respond with interceptors, the transports will have already landed and discharged their cargos of men and supplies."

Neumann looked at a second sheet in front of him before he continued. "In any event, all gruppens must be on full alert from this day on. We may get a call for escort duty at any hour. Field Marshal Kesselring does not intend to send these transport fleets on any specific day or at any specific hour to give the enemy the slightest hint of our schedule. We will simply be notified and we will need to take off at once."

"Can the enemy intercept our messages?" Lt. Otto Stranglmeier asked.

"The message will be a simple word: Bull Market. A different code word will be used for each succeeding message. We will then get a code on where to rendezvous with transport formations. So, please return to your gruppens and staffels and inform your ground crews and pilots."

At Trapani, Sicily, Col. Johannes Steinhoff, Kommodore of JG 77, met with his gruppen and staffel leaders. This geschwader had been in service since 1939, flying combat missions in both France and Russia. In 1941, the geschwader supported the German assault on Crete before JG 77 transferred to North Africa along with JG 27 and JG 51 gruppens to support the Africa Korps. However, the improving RAF and the arrival of American air units had nearly exhausted the overworked JG 77. The geschwader had lost some of its foremost aces, men like Marseille and Mayer. Finally, in January of 1943, JG 77 retired to Sicily.

Steinhoff was probably the most respected man in the Luftwaffe. He had joined the German navy in 1934. But as an aviation enthusiast, he had wheedled his way out in 1936 and had then joined the rapidly expanding Luftwaffe. By 1941, he was a staffel leader who began his combat career on the Eastern Front, scoring 27 kills in three months. In mid-1942, the OKL transferred Steinhoff to the North African desert war against the RAF. In January of 1943 he assumed command of JG 77 and a month later, the geschwader retired to Sicily. By this time, Steinhoff had racked up more than a 100 kills.

Steinhoff's excellent leadership qualities and remarkable combat record had earned him the admiration of every man in his command. Now, the JG 77 kommodore spoke to his men.

"No one need remind you of the desperate situation in Tunisia. We ourselves are now in Sicily instead of North Africa because of the serious reverses. However, the move north has not ended our responsibilities to the Wehrmacht troops who are fighting so hard in Tunisia. Luftflotte 2 has devised Operation Oschenkopf, a plan to keep Field Marshal Rommel supplied with men and materiel so that he may continue the Tunisian campaign. The plan is to move such reinforcements by air, and our duty will be to escort these fleets to North Africa. We can expect the Allies to challenge us with interceptors, but if we are determined and aggressive, we can succeed in this endeavor."

"When will the operation begin, Herr Kommodore?" Maj. Henrich Ehrler of I Gruppen asked.

"Within a few days," Steinhoff answered.

Major Ehrler nodded. The Gruppen kommandant was himself already a German air ace who had won two Oak Leafs. Ehrler had begun his career in the Polar Wing, JG 5, flying out of northern Norway to attack the Allied convoys carrying supplies to Russia over the Arctic Murmansk route. He had downed 102 Russian planes during his tour with JG 5. The major had then been transferred from the extreme cold climate to the hot desert war where he had joined the renowned JG 77.

"Please return to your gruppens and staffels and hold conferences with your own pilots and ground crews. All of your airmen must be on full alert, with aircraft ready to take off at a moment's notice. We could be called upon at any time to escort an air formation of transport planes."

"Yes, Herr Colonel," Ehrler said.

Also in Sicily, at Boco de Falco airbase, Maj. Hartman Grasser met with his staffel leaders of II Gruppen, JG 51. Grasser had also received orders from Fleigerkorps 2 to prepare his gruppen for Operation Bulls Head.

Grasser had won his wings as a Luftwaffe pilot in 1938 before he flew an ME 110 fighter-bomber at the outbreak of war in 1939. He had survived early air battles in France and later air flights during the Battle of Britain, while he shot down 56 British, French, and Belgian planes. He had then joined JG 51 on the Eastern Front where he had shot down an additional 76 planes. In July of 1942, when II/JG 51 was detached from the wing and sent to North Africa, Grasser had taken command of the gruppen. He had then fought against the RAF in the vicious desert and Malta air battles before II Gruppen withdrew to Sicily.

II/JG 51 had seen little action for the past few weeks, but with the imminent onset of Operation Bulls Head, Grasser expected some heavy air fighting.

"This operation will be vital if Field Marshal Rommel hopes to hold Tunisia," Grasser told his staffel leaders. "We can expect the Allies to note the buildup of transport air fleets that will fly men and supplies to North Africa, and we can be sure that Allied air units will attempt to knock out the transport fleets that stage from Comiso and Borrizo. Our units, along with II/JG 53 have drawn the assignment of defending the transport airfields and the port areas at Messina and Trapani."

"We will have no other duties, Herr Grasser?" Lt. Herman Schneider of 3 staffel asked.

"I assume we could also be used to escort these aerial convoys," Grasser answered. "I suppose it depends on when and where the Allies respond to this new operation. Still, it is my belief that protecting the airfields will be our first priority as we can expect the enemy to attack our airfields. I ask that you keep all fighter planes fully loaded with ammunition, shells, and fuel to fly at a moment's notice. You should work closely with the airmen of your staffels so we can be airborne at once to stop any approaching enemy aircraft."

"Yes, Herr Grasser," Lieutenant Schneider answered.

At Catania, Sicily, Maj. Wolfgang Tonnes

called to a meeting his three staffel leaders of II/ JG 53. Tonnes, one of Germany's greatest air aces with 153 kills during his four year combat career, had been fighting in the Mediterranean for more than two years. He had seen the Luftwaffe's fortunes in the MTO go from complete dominance over the RAF to an inferior air force against the Allied air might of 1943. Still, he and his experienced II/JG 53 pilots had held their own against RAF and U.S. pilots. He scanned the Bulls Head operation sheet in his hand before he addressed his officers.

"Bulls Head is vital to the Afrika Korps if they are to hold Tunisia. Our gruppen will have the responsibility of protecting the fighter and transport airfields in Sicily, especially the transport staging fields at Comiso and Borrizo. JG 51 will aid us in this duty."

"Are we strong enough to stop a horde of enemy bombers with their mass of escort fighter planes?" Lt. Harti Schmeidel of 2 staffel asked.

"Let us hope so," Tonnes answered. "We at least know that our pilots are more experienced than the Americans and this should give us an advantage."

"Yes, Herr Major."

"You will make certain that our pilots are on full alert and that our aircraft are ready to take off on a minute's notice."

"We will be ready," Schmeidel promised.

Across the strait, at Dejedeida, Tunisia, Maj. Erich Rudorffer of III/JG 51 had also received orders on Operation Bulls Head. Of all the German units in the MTO, Rudorffer's unit had been the most harassed in the Mediterranean war. Almost daily, British or American planes attacked his airdrome and he was constantly forced to scramble his pilots against these interlopers. He, his pilots, and his ground crews were all but spent since they had not relaxed for a moment during the past couple of months.

Rudorffer, however, was accustomed to fighting against heavy odds by late March of 1943. He had often met twice his number in RAF Spitfires or Hurricanes during the Battle of Britain and he had often met two or three times his number of aircraft during air battles on the Eastern Front. He and his pilots had done well in these circumstances, with Rudorffer himself already scoring 102 kills.

Rudorffer had been among the German aces who had been transported from the Russian front to the Mediterranean. But unlike many other Luftwaffers, the major had been evacuated from North Africa as Allied ground troops squeezed the Afrika Korps into northern Tunisia. Now, only his gruppen and several other Fleigerkorps Tunisien units still fought out of North Africa. These gruppens rarely got replacements in pilots, crews, or aircraft to replenish their losses. Still, the Luftwaffe airmen in Tunisia did what they could.

"This new operation is extremely important," Rudorffer told his staffel leaders. "No matter how secret the plan might be, we cannot assume that the Allies will not learn of Operation Bulls

Head. They will easily guess that transport planes in this operation will land at Sidi Ahmed or El Aouina in Tunisia and they will make every effort to knock out these airfields."

"They have already made heavy attacks on these fields as they have on our own here at Dejedeida," Lt. Heinrich Perzina of 2 staffel said.

"True," Rudorffer nodded. "but when they learn of this new operation they will no doubt intensify their efforts. We must be more vigilant than ever. I must ask that you double your guard, keep aircraft camouflaged, and make certain that aircraft are ready to intercept quickly. Be sure that crews are ready to repair runways."

"We understand, Herr Major," Perzina said.

And finally, at Gerbini, Sicily, Lt. Col. Bruno Dinort of the KG 26 Dornier 17 bomber geschwader also met with gruppen leaders. Dinort had been a medium bomber pilot since the onset of hostilities and he had carried out extensive bombing raids on the Russian front, over England, over France, and in North Africa. His KG 26 had been the main bomber unit in North Africa during early 1943 and now he had the impossible task of knocking out Allied airfields, which now numbered in the dozens all along the North African territories.

True, the new version of the DO 17 twin engine bomber with Daimler-Benz engines had made the medium bomber more powerful and much speedier. The Flying Pencil could now fly more than 300 MPH. But the DO 17 only carried six guns and a mere 4,000 pounds in order to maintain this speed.

Dinort was hardly pleased with his assignment, but he would do his best.

"It is my understanding," Dinort told his men, "that we will leave on a bombing mission an hour before the transport planes leave Sicily. If we can attack the enemy's fighter bases before their interceptors take off, we can stop the enemy's fighters from attacking the transport planes. KG 100 will also be doing this with their Heinkel bombers."

"Will we be furnished escorts?" Maj. Gunther Unger of II Gruppen asked.

"Let us hope so," Dinort answered.

Neither Unger nor the other gruppen kommandants answered. On paper, the plan appeared sound. But with swarms of Allied fighter planes in North Africa, the KG 26 bomber crews might get shot out of the air before they reached any Allied bases in North Africa.

"Please return to your staffels," Dinort gestured to his gruppen leaders. "Make certain that all aircraft are fully loaded with bombs and ammunition. We could get a request for a bombing mission on an hour's notice."

"Yes, Herr Dinort," Major Unger said.

Thus did the Germans make arrangements to protect the transport air fleets for Operation Bulls Head. But could Luftflotte 2 carry out this ambitious plan in view of the powerful Allied air strength in North Africa?

CHAPTER FIVE

Gen. William "Wild Bill" Donovan of the OSS had made good on his promise. He had met with cell leaders who directed more than 200 agents throughout Italy and Sicily and who would keep the Allies informed of any German air transport of merchant fleet movements. At least a half dozen OSS agents had been assigned to every German airfield in Italy and Sicily, while other agents kept a clandestine eye on the major German ports of Trapani and Messina in Sicily and at Naples, Italy. Coded information from Franklin (Italy) and Pilgrim (Sicily) had been coming back to OSS headquarters in Algiers for two days, on 1 and 2 April 1943. The messages from Franklin were quite clear:

"German airfields: nearly 100 transport aircraft are loading up with men and supplies and assembling for movement out of Capodichino and Pomigliano airfields in Naples area. It is expected these transport aircraft will be ready to fly out of Naples on afternoon of 3 April."

A second series of messages had come from Pilgrim regarding the port areas: "German merchant ship convoy is completing loading operations at Messina and should be leaving the harbor within 24 hours."

Donovan wasted no time in notifying NAAF in Algiers of these developments. General Spaatz then met immediately with General Doolittle and his NASAF staff to consider the OSS reports and to decide on a course of action.

"It's obvious the transport planes and ships will be the first to carry out a massive reinforcement effort to Tunisia," Spaatz said. "I suggest you make arrangements at once to hit the harbor and the staging areas and fighter bases in Sicily to break up this movement before it starts."

"We'll act at once," Doolittle promised.

"I'll notify Air Marshal Conningham to begin his CAP patrols immediately, while you are carrying out bombing attacks," Spaatz said.

"We'll do our part," Doolittle said.

Doolittle quickly acted. The NASAF commander prepared all fighter and bomber units to hit the Germans at the source. He cut orders to attack both the airfields in Sicily and in Tunisia. The plans called for the 14th Fighter Group to make sweeps over Sicily and off the coast during the day to reconnoiter German activities. The

2nd and 99th Bomb Groups would prepare their B-17s for high altitude bombing raids on the Sicily fighter airfields. The 310th and 321st medium Bomb Groups would hit the transport staging bases at Comiso and Borrizo with their B-25s, while B-17s of the 301st and 97th Bomb Groups would hit the debarkation airfields of Sidi Ahmed and El Aouina in Tunisia. The 320th and 17th B-26 medium bomb groups would hit Messina Harbor in the hope of catching the Axis merchant ships before they could sail.

Long range P-47 fighters of the 350th and 325th Fighter Groups would escort the 2nd and 99th heavy Bomb Groups to the Boco de Falco and Trapani fighter bases, while the P-38s of the 82nd Fighter Group would escort the B-25 groups to the Borizo and Comiso staging airfields. The 1st Fighter Group would escort the B-17s to the Tunisian airfields and a borrowed RAF wing of Spitfires would escort the B-26s to hit Messina Harbor.

Doolittle had acted wisely for the Germans were indeed toiling hard to send off both an air transport fleet and a surface ship merchant fleet for a run to Tunisia. On the first air transport mission, Gen. Ulrich Buchholtz had decided to use only JU 52s, the tri-engine transports. Each Junker would carry a full platoon of men or 10,000 pounds of freight.

Wild Bill Donovan's spies had sent accurate information because for two days Lufttransport Mittelmeer service crews had been loading 70 transport planes at the Naples airfields of Capodichino and Pomigliano. Buchholtz had spared no effort to enlist as many men as possible in this effort. By the late afternoon of 2 April, the chore had been completed and the Mittelmeer CinC met with Field Marshal Kesselring, General Trautloft of Fleigerkorps II and General Hammhuber of Fleigerkampf Sud-Ost.

"We have completed our loading activities and the transports will depart tomorrow," Buchholtz said. "The JU 52s will land at Comiso and Borrizo in Sicily to refuel."

"Good," Kesselring nodded. "And of course, the transports will remain in Sicily only long enough to refuel and then continue on to Tunisia."

Buchholtz grinned. "No, Herr Field Marshal. I intend to keep the aircraft in Sicily, fully loaded with men and supplies, until the morning of 4 April or even the fifth."

"What?" Kesselring gasped.

Trautloft and Hammhuber also raised their eyebrows, but they did not speak.

"Surely, you do not intend to delay the movement of these reinforcements for two or three days?" Kesselring said. "Field Marshal Rommel will be furious."

"I do not understand, either," General Trautloft said.

"Do any among you doubt for a moment that Italy and Sicily are full of enemy spies?" General Buchholtz asked. "Do you doubt that the loading process at the Naples airfields have not been under constant surveillance by these spies?"

No one answered the Mittelmeeer CinC.

"No, of course not," Buchholtz continued. "And I will tell you something else," the general pointed. "Even though the loading will be fully completed by dusk today, I shall continue to send trucks masqueraded with crated provisions or combat soldiers to these JU 52s. The trucks will operate throughout the night and into the morning, carrying on these simulated loading activities until the transport planes are actually taking off."

Kesselring frowned.

"Please, Herr Field Marshal," Buchholtz said, "we know what we are doing. The enemy, on the basis of information sent him by these spies, will not expect us to take off until at least mid-day tomorrow. By then, the transport aircraft will have left Naples and if enemy bombers come over the transport airdromes, they drop their bombs on empty airfields. And even if the enemy suspects that we will stage from Comiso and Borrizo, we will be ready for them. The kommandants at these airfields have prepared dozens of dummy aircraft to scatter about the fields while we hide the transports at Comiso and Borrizo until the JU 52s are ready to make their dash into Tunisia."

"I can see that you have planned well, Herr Buchholtz," Kesselring grinned. "Very well, I will not interfere with you."

"I have a second suggestion, Herr Field Marshal," Buchholtz said. "The transport ships at Messina should leave the harbor by night. They would be far at sea by sun up. Do not be surprised if enemy bombers also visit this Sicily port tomorrow morning. Between the enemy's spies and his reconnaissance planes, he must be fully aware of the activities at Messina. Frankly, I am surprised that the enemy has not already carried out bombing raids on Messina Harbor."

"They are waiting for the proper moment," General Hammhuber gestured. "They would rather sink loaded vessels instead of empty ones. I know I would, and I'm sure the enemy bomber command thinks the same way." He leaned forward and grinned at Buchholtz. "I am inclined to agree with you; Messina can expect a visit by enemy bombers some time tomorrow, perhaps in the early morning."

Buchholtz did not answer.

"I have confidence in your opinion, General Buchholtz, and also in yours, Herr Hammhuber," Kesselring said. "I will issue orders to get the merchant ships at Messina out of the harbor by 0400 hours, so the ships can be far out to sea by daylight."

Buchholtz nodded.

"Meanwhile," Kesselring gestured, "what might we expect from those seventy transport aircraft?"

"We are transporting two thousand men of the 36th Grenadier Division's 5th Regiment, two reinforced battalions," the Mittelmeer CinC said. "These men can be used to strengthen the Gabes Line below Tunis. We have also loaded ten thousand tons of supplies that include fifty small vehicles, thirty-four armored personnel carriers, and seventeen 37mm artillery pieces. These supplies and armaments can provision the grenadiers for a week. The vehicles, of course, will make these combat forces quite mobile, so they can move swiftly into whatever positions they are needed by Herr Rommel."

"While I appreciate this report," Kesselring said, "two reinforced battalions cannot be considered a major contribution. It is obvious that we must still use surface ship transports."

"I cannot argue that point, Herr Field Marshal," Buchholtz said. "But still, these reinforcements are useful and we will send as many as we can by air. On our next mission, we will be using the huge Gigantens, the ME 323s of KVT 5 that can carry three times the number of troops or tons of supplies as can the JU 52s. I merely await the arrival of fifty of these giant transports, since I prefer to use a massive formation rather than a few at a time. In that way, even if they are intercepted by fighter planes, most of the transport aircraft will get through."

"Very well," Kesselring said. He now turned to General Trautloft. "Obviously, Hannes, we need considerable fighter support, not only to escort the transport planes, but also to protect the airbases so that the enemy cannot destroy the loaded JU 52s or our fighter planes on the ground. Should they miss the planes at Naples, they will quickly realize that the JU 52s have probably gone to Sicily. I would not be surprised to see enemy bombers tomorrow to catch the transports on the ground. While I appreciate General Buchholtz' ruse to use dummy aircraft, we must do what we can to protect the Comiso and Borrizo airfields."

"We are prepared," Trautloft said. He looked at some papers in front of him and then gestured to Kesselring. "We have assigned both JG 27 and JG 77 for escort duties to protect the transport planes and the merchant ship convoy. Major Rudorffer's III/JG 51 in Tunisia will protect the Sidi Ahmed and El Aouina airfields in Tunisia, and they will also help out in escorting the JU 52s into Tunisia. The II Gruppen of JG 52 at Catania and II Gruppen of JG 51 at Boco de Falco will protect the Sicily airfields. Colonel Neumann and Lieutenant Colonel Steinhoff of JG 27 are excellent geschwader kommodores, as are Major Tonnes of II/JG 52, Major Grasser of II/JG 51, and Major Rudorffer of III/JG 51 very good gruppen kommandants. Most of their pilots are reliable and experienced combat airmen."

"What will be the duty of Major Grasser's gruppen?" Kesselring asked.

"He will be on alert to also escort transport aircraft to Tunisia," the Fleigerkorps II fighter command CinC said. "I must tell you of course," Trautloft pointed, "that the assigned duties of these units are not hard and fast. They could be diverted to other duties, protecting airfields instead of escort or the other way around. It will depend on the circumstances. I am merely pointing out that these fighter units are the ones I have designated for Operation Oschenkopf."

"I understand," Kesselring nodded. He peered out of the window of his headquarters and then turned and scanned his officers. "It seems we have completed our business. The merchant ships will leave Messina at 0400 hours under escort of Italian destroyers and the transport planes will leave Naples at first light tomorrow for the flight to Sicily. Let us hope that we can deceive the Allies and get these ships, planes, men, and supplies safely into Tunisia."

By midnight, the 70 JU 52s at the Naples airfields, fully loaded with men, supplies, vehicles, and arms, were ready to take off. But Buchholtz continued to shuttle trucks in and out of the field in simulated loading chores. OSS agents in Naples were certain the aircraft would not leave the airfields before mid-day of 3 April.

Far to the south, in Messina, Sicily, at 0400 hours, 3 April, the surface ship convoy weighed anchor. The supply fleet included four large merchant ships, one transport and three freighters. The troop ship carried a battalion of men and the freighters carried 10,000 tons of supplies, including 37 big 88mm artillery pieces, 46 Mark IV Panzer tanks, and more than 100 motor vehicles. The fleet also included ten ocean going 500 ton Siebel ferries that carried a company of men each with their full equipment. Six Italian destroyers would accompany these merchant vessels.

Truly, if all of these reinforcements reached Tunisia, Field Marshal Rommel would have substantial help in his desperate battle with British and American ground troops that were closing in on him in northern Tunisia.

By daybreak of 3 April the fourteen ship convoy had cleared Messina and picked up its six Italian destroyers as escort far out to sea. By dusk, the convoy would clear the west tip of the triangular shaped Sicily, turn south, and start the dangerous run across the Strait of Sicily to Tunisia. On the second day out, FW 190s from JG 77 would escort the ships over the narrow passage in the Mediterranean.

At dawn of April 3rd, Col. Walter Hagen, kommodore of KVT 16 met with Maj. August Geiger of the transport geschwader's I Gruppen. "You will fly directly south to Sicily. Staffels 1 and 2 will land at Comiso and Staffels 3 and 4 will land at Borrizo. You are to disperse the aircraft at once, and camouflage them well. The airfield kommandant has constructed many dummy planes that will be placed about the airfield as soon as your own aircraft are dispersed and hidden. In the event of an enemy attack on these fields, the enemy will not hurt our laden JU 52s."

"But if they send in low level fighters or light bombers, will they not detect the aircraft on the fields as being dummies?" Geiger asked.

Hagen grinned. "They always bomb our airfields with heavy or medium bombers from relatively high altitudes, never lower than five thousand feet."

"Yes, Herr Colonel."

At dawn, 0500 hours, even as more trucks rumbled onto the Naples airfields for the benefit of OSS spies, the first trio of JU 52s lumbered over taxiways and soon roared down the runway at Capodichino to take off. Similarly, at Pomigliano Field, other JU 52s lumbered to the head of the runway in threes and then roared down the strip to take off. By daylight, the 70 Junkers were airborne and droning south to the Comiso and Borrizo Airdromes in Sicily.

The Junkers arrived at their Sicily bases by mid-morning and ground crews quickly scattered and hid the 70 JU 52s. They then put the wooden dummy planes about the taxiways and runway. The ruse apparently worked because on the afternoon of 4 April, B-17 snoopers from the 3rd Recon Group reported the mass of JU 52s at Borrizo and Comiso.

By the wee morning hours of 5 April, meanwhile, the German ship convoy that had left Messina was well into the open sea. But the Americans were preparing their first Operation Flax missions. At Navarin, Algeria, Col. Fay Upthegrove led a parade of 28 B-17s from the 99th Bomb Group toward the main runway. The Flying Forts lumbered forward like huge crawling grubs, their engines screaming while pilots kept the planes braked. At 0530 hours, Upthegrove wheeled his lead B-17 onto the head of the Navarin runway.

While the 99th Group commander waited for the control tower signal, he called his pilots, all of whom answered in the positive: all planes okay. He then called his own crewmen who also gave positive responses. Soon a green light blinked from the control tower. Upthegrove released the brake and the B-17 roared down the runway before hoisting itself into the northern sky.

At 30 second intervals, other B-17s from the Ninety-Niner Group sped down the runway and took off. By 0610 hours, 28 Flying Forts were droning northward over the Mediterranean Sea, heading toward the German fighter base at Trapani. Out to sea, 42 P-47s of the 325th Fighter Group soon joined the B-17s to escort them to their Sicily target.

At Chateau-dum-ru-Rhumel, Algeria, Col. Fed Lauer led a parade of 22 B-17s from the 2nd Bomb Group toward the main runway. He too called his pilots and his own crews to make certain all was in order. At 0530 hours, Lauer saw the green light in the control tower. He revved the four big engines of his Flying Fort and then released the brake before the B-17 roared down the runway and hoisted itself into the air like a giant, struggling walrus.

Fred Lauer had been a flying officer in the U.S. Army Air Force more than six years, another of the young men who had joined the Air Corps in the late 30s. He had been stationed at various bomber groups about the continental United States and became a squadron commander of the Defender group in early 1942. Because of his ability and leadership, Lauer had risen rapidly in rank and by late October of 1942, he had risen to full colonel and assumed command of the 2nd Heavy Bomb Group.

The 2nd Group itself was among the oldest air units in the U.S. Army Air Force. The 11th Squadron of this group had served in France during the latter part of the World War I conflict in 1918. The group had then returned to the Texas airfields of Ellington and Kelly, where its airmen trained successively with LB 5As, B-10s, B-15s, and finally the B-17 in 1938. The group had carried out simulated heavy bombing group missions to demonstrate to the Army that such strategic bombing was feasible.

The Defenders had moved to Ephrata, Washington, shortly after the outbreak of war in the Pacific and its airmen had carried out anti-submarine duty off the Pacific coast. The group had finally moved to North Africa in March of 1943, one of the last of the heavy bomb groups to reach the MTO. In fact, the Defenders had only carried out six missions thus far. But Lauer and his crews expected to play a major role in Operation Flax.

After Lauer took off on this yet dark morning of 5 April, other planes followed. Again at 30 second intervals B-17s of the U.S. 2nd Bomb Group roared down the Rhumel runway and lifted themselves skyward. Soon, the 22 Forts were also droning north over the Mediterranean. A half hour later, 38 Thunderbolt fighters from the 350th Fighter Group met the 2nd Group to escort the bombers to Sicily.

At 0600 hours, 18 B-17s from the 301st Bomb Group took off from Donat, Algeria, while 23 B-17s of the 97th Bomb Group took off from their base at Chateau-dum-ru-Rhumel to attack the debarkation airfields at Sidi Ahmed and El Aouina in Tunisia. 44 Lightnings from the 1st Fighter Group joined the heavy bombers, 22 with the 301st and 22 with the 97th.

The 99th and 2nd Bomb Groups with their escorts soon reached Sicily and crossed the island in almost complete surprise. They were over the Trapani and Boco de Falco Airdromes while the German ground crews were preparing the 190s of JG 77 and the 109s of JG 51 for take off to escort the transport planes in the dash across the strait to Tunisia. Still, by the time the 99th and 2nd Groups arrived over these air bases, 15 planes rose to challenge the Ninety-Niners and 12 fighter planes rose to challenge the 2nd Bomb Group. But the German pilots seemed confused and uncertain, hardly aggressive.

The U.S. pilots of the 325th Fighter Group under Lt. Col. Gordon Austin quickly disposed of the 15 Folke-Wulf fighters coming after the 99th Group's Flying Forts at Trapani. Austin himself quickly shot down two German fighters and Capt. James Simmons of the 319th Fighter Squadron also downed two FW 190s. Simmons caught one Folke-Wulf with a stream of 20mm shells that tore apart the fuselage and he got his second plane when he shot away the engine with exploding 20mm shells. Totally, the Checkertails of the 325th downed seven of the 15 German planes and scattered the rest, while losing only one plane of their own.

At Boco de Falco, the 350th Fighter Group pilots under Col. Marv McNickle did an equally quick job on the 12 Messerschmidts that had risen to attack the B-17s of the 2nd Bomb Group. McNickle and his pilots quickly knocked down nine of the 12 interceptors in a swift, devastating attack. The three survivors quickly flew off in different directions to escape the same punishment.

Thus the 99th and 2nd Bomb Group crews were free to hit the airdromes. They did run into AA fire, but from their 24,000 to 30,000 feet altitude the flak was ineffective and damaged only three Flying Fortresses, but downing none of them.

Col. Fay Upthegrove was delighted when he saw the horde of planes about the main Trapani runway. The FW 190s were bunched together since they were getting ready for take off. "Okay hit 'em in Vs!" Upthegrove cried.

"Yes, sir," Maj. Al Orance of the 416th Squadron answered.

Upthegrove dropped the first clusters of frag bombs from his lead plane "El Diablo" and the bombs hit squarely atop a trio of German fighter planes, blowing away two of them and setting the third afire. The rest of the 99th's 346th Squadron also dropped their bombs on the left sector of the airdrome, igniting more parked fighter planes. Then came the 348th Squadron that laced the same side of the airdrome to destroy still more German fighter planes.

Next, Maj. Al Orance led the first trio of B-17s over the right side of the airdrome and dropped a confetti of frag bombs that erupted like fire-crackers on the parked planes. More B-17s from the 416th Squadron and then the B-17s from the trailing 348th Squadron also hit the field with both thousand pounders and frag clusters. By the time the Ninety-Niners had droned away from the field, they had left behind them dense palls of smoke and countless fires.

The Ninety-Niners had found 70 to 80 planes on the field and the 99th Group airmen had knocked out at least half of them and damaged about fifteen more.

The same devastation prevailed at Boco de Falco Drome after the 2nd Bomb Group made its B-17 attack. The Defenders also caught hordes of German fighter planes on the ground. Col. Fred Lauer dropped the first load of bombs that erupted and smashed three ME 109s before other B-17 crews of his group laced the airfield. In the group's 20th Squadron, Lt. Thomas Lohr had put his clusters of frag bombs squarely atop a sextet of parked planes, destroying all six of them in numbing explosions and igniting fires.

"Goddamn, Colonel," Maj. Joe Thomas of the 20th Squadron called Lauer, "there can't be a goddamn plane left down there."

"We did a good job," Lauer answered. "Let's go home."

Meanwhile, at 0635 hours, the B-17s of the 301st and 97th Bomb Groups arrived over the Tunisian airfields where U.S. airmen could see ground crews apparently preparing the areas for the arrival of transport planes. The two heavy bomb groups sent whistling 1,000 pounders onto the Sidi Ahmed and El Aouina fields to chop huge holes in the runways. They struck the two airdromes with more than 100 tons of bombs, most of which had struck the runways. Besides wrecking the landing strips the Americans had destroyed installations and warehouses. The U.S. crews had left squares of destruction and fires in their wake. Neither Sidi Ahmed nor El Aouina would be in a position to meet and service German JU 52s.

As the B-17s droned homeward, Col. Sam Gormley of the 301st Group radioed Algiers that he had found the Germans preparing the Sidi Ahmed field for transport planes. Moments later, Col. Stan Donovan of the 97th Group radioed the same information to Algiers about the El Aouina airdrome.

Gen. James Doolittle had already digested reports from Colonel Upthegrove and Colonel Lauer on the mass of fighter planes they had found at Trapani and at Boco de Falco, German fighters apparently getting ready to take off to escort either ships or transport planes across the Strait of Sicily. Now, the the reports from the 97th and 301st Group commanders, the NASAF CinC was convinced that the Germans were preparing to send out their aerial transport fleet this morning. He ordered the 14th Fighter Group to make its sweep over the strait at once and he ordered the 310th Bomb Group to hit Borrizo Drome before the Junkers took off. He also ordered the 321st Bomb Group to attack Comiso

Airdrome before JU 52s could take off from there.

"I want our fighters from the 82nd Group to escort the B-25s," Doolittle barked. "I also want the 320th and 17th Bomb Groups on alert. If the German merchant ships have left Messina Harbor, these B-26s can hit the ships on the sea as soon as we locate them."

"Yes sir," the aide said.

Although the hordes of planes seen by U.S. recon pilots at Comiso and Borrizo were mostly dummies, the Americans would get a delightful break. The transport planes at Borrizo were just preparing to take off, moving in long lines toward the main runway, when Col. Tony Hunter arrived over the airdrome with the B-25s of the 310th Bomb Group. 18 Lightning fighters from the 82nd Fighter Group's 96th Squadron under Maj. Harley Vaughn were escorting the Mitchells.

The American bomber crews were elated as they dumped 2442 20 pound fragmentation bombs over the airfield, destroying about a dozen of the JU 52s and countless dummies. As Hunter led his B-25s away from the field, he got jumped by Lt. Herman Schneider with 15 ME 109s from the JG 51's 2 Staffel. However, Maj. Harley Vaughn quickly led his 18 Lightnings against the 109s.

The dogfight lasted about ten minutes, with the 96th Squadron pilots of the 82nd Group shooting down four of the German planes, while B-25 gunners shot down two of the Messerschmidts. The Americans suffered no aircraft losses, but two B-25s, badly shot up, ditched in the Mediterranean off Egadi Island. A British destroyer plucked the crews from the sea late in the afternoon.

The attack on Borrizo Drome prompted the Germans to act swiftly to get off the transports at Comiso. Maj. August Geiger rightly suspected that more U.S. bombers were on the way to Comiso. He turned to an aide before he flew off. "You will notify the fighter command that they must join us at once with fighters to escort us across the strait to Sidi Ahmed in Tunisia."

"Yes, Herr Major."

The Germans then hurried out of Sicily with their 58 Junker transports that carried 1800 men and nearly 2300 tons of supplies, arms, guns, and vehicles. Geiger was sure he would succeed. But he had underestimated the tenacity of U.S. fighter pilots.

Maj. August Geiger's I Gruppen from KVT 16 could not guess that his flights of JU 52s out of Borrizo and Comiso would become the first victims of the April massacres.

CHAPTER SIX

The Germans had endeavored to be cautious in forming up their transport planes on the morning of 5 April, but OSS agents had clearly seen the 18 JU 52s taking off from the damaged Borrizo Field and the 40 Junkers taking off from the Comiso airfield. The OSS spies, always on 24 hour alert, quickly reported these take offs to OSS headquarters in Algiers.

"Large numbers of JU 52s leaving Borrizo and Comiso. They will probably be over the Strait of Sicily at about 0900 hours."

A third Pilgrim group also sent a message out of Sicily: "German fighters forming up at Boco De Falco and Trapani Airdromes, possibly flying off to escort transport aircraft or surface ships."

OSS aides in Algiers were disappointed in

these messages. They knew that American bombers had hit the airfields at Trapani, Boco de Falco, and Borrizo. The U.S. airmen had presumably wiped out the three airfields of their parked fighter and transport planes and they now realized that the attacks had not been as total as reported. When aides reported the information from Sicily, General Donovan was piqued. The American bomber crews had obviously exaggerated their claims. He had not realized that many of the destroyed planes at Borrizo were dummies.

But the airmen of the 2nd and 99th Bomb Groups were not far off in their claims. Actually, Lt. Col. Johannes Steinhoff could only get off 20 FW 190s from his JG 51 airbase at Trapani and Maj. Herman Grasser could only mount 14 ME 109s from his damaged base at Boco de Falco.

Meanwhile, coast watchers on the southern coast of Sicily had spotted the German surface ship convoy moving south toward North Africa and they quickly sent messages to Algiers: "Surface ship convoy may be crossing Strait of Sicily to North Africa."

Other clandestine Allied observers in Sicily had also sent a message to OSS headquarters: "Huge air transport fleets are flying across the island toward the Strait of Sicily, obviously going to Tunisia. Suggest you alert fighter and bomber units at once."

NASAF wasted no time and radio messages went out to the 14th Fighter Group that was on the way to Sicily to make the armed recon sweep.

NASAF also contacted the 321st Bomb Group and their 82nd Fighter Group escorts that were on the way to bomb Comiso just as the 310th Group had hit Borrizo Drome earlier.

The 14th Fighter Group Avenger pilots drew first blood. Lt. Col. Tony Keith sent out pairs of P-38s to scour the southern coastal area of Sicily and at 0930 hours, Maj. Lou Benne of the 49th Fighter Squadron spotted the formation of JU 52s, 18 of them from the Borrizo Airdrome, under escort by 32 ME 109s of II/JG 27 under Maj. Gustav Rodel. Benne quickly called Tony Keith.

"Colonel, about twenty miles west of you, a line of transport planes with ME 109 fighter escorts."

"We're on our way; meanwhile, you may as well engage."

"Yes sir."

Soon, the next air clash in Operation Flax ignited over the Strait of Sicily. Benne waded into the ME 109s with his 14 planes and within moments, the Avenger pilots had knocked six of the German fighters out of the air, despite the two to one odds. The Germans had sorely miscalculated in considering the American pilots too inexperienced to deal with combat honed Luftwaffe pilots. Major Benne got two Messerschmidts when he shot the engine off one plane and ripped the tail from a second with chattering machine gun fire. Capt. Jim Griffith also got two planes when he tailed one ME 109 and shot off the wing, while he shattered the cockpit of a second to send the

Messerschmidt tumbling into the sea.

Meanwhile, Lieutenant Colonel Keith soon arrived with the other P-38s of the 14th Fighter Group. And while Benne and his pilots kept the ME 109s at bay, Keith led the Lightning pilots of the 48th and 37th Squadrons into the JU 52 formations.

"Hit 'em in pairs!"

"Yes sir, Colonel," Maj. Bill Levelette of the 48th Squadron answered.

The P-38 pilots then opened on the JU 52s, Junker survivors from the Borrizo Drome attack by the U.S. 310th Bomb Group. Within moments, the Americans knocked 14 of the 18 transport planes out of the air. Junkers blew apart from solid 20mm shell hits or exploded from other hits, or lost wings and tails before splashing into the sea. Four JU 52s got away but only because the 14th Group pilots had run out of ammo or had needed their guns to join Major Benne in fighting off the ME 109 pilots from JG 27.

By the time the air battle was over, surviving ME 109 pilots and Junker pilots were streaking back to Sicily. No supplies from this aerial flight would reach Tunisia. For their efforts in downing 14 transports and eight ME 109s, Lt. Col. Troy Keith had lost two of his P-38s.

NASAF quickly received a report from Keith on the battle south of Sicily. He explained that they had run into about 20 Junkers with escorts and had shot down most of them. General Doolittle rightly guessed that this formation was the Junker gruppen out of Borrizo that had been hit earlier by the 310th Bomb Group. He believed the larger JU 52 formation from Comiso had also left their airbase and was probably on the way to Tunisia. So he diverted the 321st Bomb Group and their 82nd Fighter Group escort squadrons from their flight to Comiso. NASAF aides told these airmen to also scour the Strait of Sicily for signs of more transport planes, or even perhaps the surface ship convoy that had left Messina two or three days ago.

In fact, the convoy of four merchantmen and ten ocean going ferries, with their six Italian destroyer escorts, had now sailed more than half-way across the Strait of Sicily. By the time this convoy approached the dangerous waters off the coast of Tunisia, the aerial transport convoy out of Comiso with escorting German fighter planes had caught up to the ships. The fighters would protect both the transport planes and the surface ships.

By 0930 hours, the 40 Junkers under Maj. August Geiger of KVT 16, along with 20 fighters from JG 77 under Lt. Heinz Berre had come more than halfway across the Strait of Sicily. Soon, Berre spotted the surface ship convoy and he sent ten of his FW 190s under Lt. Ernst Reinert to protect the convoy, while he took his other 190s to protect the aerial formation.

The surface ship convoy included four 7,000 ton merchantmen, ten 2,000 ton Siebel ferries, and six Italian destroyers of 1800 tons. The merchant ships included three freighters carrying guns, tanks, supplies, and more than 15,000 barrels of oil. The troop transport carried some 3,000 soldiers, and the Seibel ferries carried about 200 men each with their equipment.

The flotilla commander called Lt. Heinz Berre when he saw the fighter planes approaching. "Lieutenant, you do not have many escorts."

"We expect to have more," Berre answered.

"They must join us as soon as possible," the ship convoy commander said. "As we sail closer to the Tunisia coast there is danger of enemy interceptors from the Allied airbases."

The convoy commander had barely spoken when a new formation of German fighters, 14 Messerschmidts from JG 51's 3 Staffel, loomed from the north. A lookout aboard one of the Italian destroyers quickly called the flotilla commander, who hurried to the bridge and peered through his binoculars at the approaching planes. But, he frowned again when he saw the small number of ME 109s. The newcomers were under the command of Lt. Wolfgang Fisher.

The convoy admiral now called Lieutenant Berre, quite upset. "Is that all? Only another dozen fighter escorts?"

"I'm sorry, Herr Kommodore," Berre answered. "We have suffered some serious air attacks on our airdromes in Sicily this morning and we could only mount these thirty-four aircraft. Another flight of fighter planes is escorting the other aerial convoy that is flying out of Borrizo. However, we have been assured that more fighter planes will come out of Dejedeida in Tunisia to aide us in the escort duties."

"Good, good," the ship convoy commander nodded.

Meanwhile, Lieutenant Berre called Lt. Herman Schneider. "I am glad you are here. As you can see, we have both an aerial convoy and an ocean convoy that must be protected. I will keep the JG 77 fighters to escort the air transports, and you may escort the ships. Is that all right?"

"Yes, Herr Lieutenant," Schneider answered. The JG 51 staffel leader then scanned the skies before he spoke again. "I believe we have deceived the enemy quite well. There is no sign of an Allied aircraft."

"Let us hope so," Berre answered. "We cannot do much with thirty-four aircraft if they send out swarms of enemy fighters."

The Germans had indulged in wishful thinking. Thanks to recon planes, OSS agents, and Doolittle's intuition, the Americans were already aware of the location of both the surface ships and aerial transport convoys. Navigational analysts at NASAF headquarters, on the basis of these reports, had concluded that the transport planes would probably rendezvous with the fighters and surface ships near a position of 36° north and 14° degrees east at about 0930 hours. The German ships and planes were now about 75 miles southwest of Sicily.

The information went quickly to NASAF's radio room whose operators quickly called the commanders of both the 82nd Fighter Group and 321st Bomb Group. The operators directed the two American air units to divert their mission from an attack on Comiso to a possible attack on German surface ships and transport plane formations at the probable 36° north by 14° east location.

As soon as Colonel Covington of the 82nd Fighter Group got the information from NASAF headquarters, he altered his course and headed swiftly northwest. "We should reach that aerial convoy in about ten minutes," he told his pilots. The Blue Gulls group commander then called Lt. Col. Ed Olmstead of the 321st Bomb Group. "Colonel, you can alter course with us and attack the surface ships."

"I read you," Olmstead answered.

Lieutenant Colonel Olmstead then called his B-25 group airmen. "We'll attack in three plane elements. The last report says there are four large merchant ships and at least eight ocean going ferries. They've got a half dozen destroyers with them as escorts. The 82nd Group fighters will attack the aerial transport fleet."

"How about escorts for us?" Maj. Ellis Cook asked.

"Let's hope the 82nd can do a good enough job so we won't need any," Lieutenant Colonel Olmstead answered his 446th Squadron leader.

Within minutes, the 18 bombers were speeding toward the German convoy, with the P-38s above and around them and ahead of them.

Covington called his pilots again. "Keep your formation tight and stick with your wingmen. German interceptors could jump us at any moment."

"I hear you, sir," Capt. James Lynn of the 95th Squadron answered.

The American formations droned on for about five minutes before Covington spotted the German aerial convoy. The formations of 40 Junker transport planes had about 20 FW 190 fighters above and around them.

"This is Starbird Leader!" the 82nd Group commander cried into his radio. "Starbird I will accompany me to attack the transports. Starbird II will go after the escorts."

"Yes, sir," Captain Lynn of the 95th Squadron answered.

Moments later, the 36 P-38s from the Blue Gulls group peeled off, with Covington leading 18 planes from the 97th Squadron after the Junkees; while Lynn led the 18 planes from the 95th Squadron toward the German fighter planes.

Lt. Heinz Berre of JG 77 soon enough saw the American P-38s coming after the German aerial formations and he too cried into his radio. "We will attack these interceptors. I will lead the first element of 2 Staffel to attack the enemy fighters flying toward the transport planes. The second element will attack the enemy aircraft flying toward our fighter escorts."

"Yes, Herr Berre," Lt. Ernst Reinert answered.

Soon enough, the 20 FW 190s waded into the 36 Lightning fighters heading toward the German planes. However, the 95th U.S. Squadron under Capt. Jim Lynn quickly jumped the Folke-

Wulfs to thwart the German attempt to interfere with the 97th Squadron going after the transports. Whining, screaming aircraft engines echoed above the Mediterranean Sea as combating fighter planes arced and dipped about the sky.

Lynn quickly downed an FW 190 with chattering machine gun fire from his six forward guns, while Lt. Frank Lawson got himself two FW 190s. Lawson chopped off the tail of a Folke-Wulf with machine gun fire before the German fighter plunged into the sea. He then shattered the fuselage of a second FW 190 with solid 37mm cannon shell hits, killing the German pilot, before the JG 77 plane plopped into the sea.

The Germans, however, also scored. Lieutenant Berre got two P-38s when he blew open the fuselage of one plane with accurate 20mm cannon fire, and he chopped off the tail of a second Lightning with more accurate cannon fire. Lieutenant Reinert got a kill when he literally cut off a wing of a Lightning with chattering machine gun fire before the U.S. plane plopped into the sea just off Cape Sarrat in the Strait of Sicily.

The dogfight between the JG 77 and 82nd Fighter Group pilots had ended in the loss of four U.S. P-38s and damage to four more Lightnings, while Lynn and his American airmen had downed six Folke-Wulfs, about an even exchange. But strategically, the American Blue Gull squadron had stopped Lieutenant Berre from interferring with other 82nd Group pilots that attacked the transports.

Col. Bill Covington and his 17 pilots from the 97th Squadron waded into the hordes of JU 52s. The slow moving transport planes, dropping to almost deck level, became helpless targets for the speedy, heavily armed P-38s, especially since Lt. Herman Schneider had taken most of his 14 ME 109s from JG 51 to help out the FW 190s of JG 77 against the Lightnings from the 95th Fighter Squadron.

"Pick your targets and hit 'em in pairs," Covington cried into his radio.

"Yes sir," Capt. Richard McAuliffe answered.

Then the slaughter began. In pass after pass, pairs of P-38s from Captain McAulliffe's sector bounced the slow moving transport planes, blasting away with chattering machine gun fire and whooshing 37mm shellfire. One after another of the JU 52s dropped from the deck level and plopped into the sea. The American pilots shot away wings, tails, fuselages, and engines. Within ten minutes, the U.S. 97th Squadron pilots had downed eight JU 52s and damaged four more Junkers.

Meanwhile, Col. Bill Covington attacked the forward JU 52s with ten P-38s from the 82nd's 97th Squadron. Again in pairs, the heavily armed Lightnings made pass after pass against the German transport planes with chattering .50 caliber incendiary and dum dum machine gun fire. Once again, Junkers exploded, fell apart, caught fire, or lost engines before plopping into the sea.

The horrified Maj. August Geiger, who led the transport gruppen, tried frantically to keep his formation tight and close to the surface of the sea. But, with his escorting fighters neutralized, his transport planes became helpless victims against the P-38 pilots. He lost 12 more transport planes and suffered severe damage to nine others before the 82nd Fighter Group broke off its attack.

Meanwhile, the 321st Bomb Group Mitchells arrived over the German surface ship convoy that included its four merchant ships, ten Siebel ferries, and six Italian destroyer escorts. The ships were practically unprotected because most of the ME 109 fighters had gone off to help out Lt. Heinz Berre in the futile attempt to stop the 82nd Group attack on the aerial transport fleet. As soon as the B-25s loomed from the south, the convoy commander ordered his ships to scatter, while AA gunners took positions.

About ten ME 109s under Lt. Herman Schneider had now returned to cover the convoy after the unsuccessful efforts to the west. He cried to his pilots: "Enemy bombers approaching the surface vessels. We will climb high and attack them in pairs."

The JG 51 pilots would not interfere with the B-25 skip bomb runs because Colonel Covington, now finished with the aerial convoy, had now zoomed eastward with more than 20 Blue Gulls pilots. He soon tangled with the few ME 109s out of Boco de Falco and quickly routed Lieutenant Schneider and his Luftwaffe pilots. The 82nd Group pilots, their appetites whetted from earlier successes, quickly downed four of the German fighter planes in the uneven dog-fight. Only Schneider and one other pilot survived and they flew swiftly back to Sicily. No German fighter pilots would harass the 321st Bomb Group crews when the Mitchells made their numbing strafing and skip bomb attacks against the surface ships.

Lt. Col. Ed Olmstead cried into his radio. "Hit the ships in pairs!"

"Yes sir," Lt. Hank Bell of the 321st Group's 445th Squadron answered.

Then, the Mitchells dropped low and assailed the zigzagging German vessels and their Italian warship escorts. The B-25s skimmed at almost surface level to attack the ships with skip bombs and strafing fire. Covington and wingman Lt. Hank Bell singled out one of the destroyers, came right on top of the ship, and unleashed heavy strafing fire that scattered the shipboard sailors. Then the 321st Group pilots from close range hit the destroyer with three solid 500 pound delayed fuse bombs. The warship blew up and quickly sank.

The next 321st Group pilots pounced on a pair of Siebel ferries and blew both of them out of the water with more close range skip bomb hits.

"Nice job, boys," Covington cried into his radio.

"Yes sir," Lt. Hank Bell answered.

As Covington and Bell arced away, a pair of ME 109s that had escaped the 82nd Fighter Group attack sent heavy machine gun fire into the Mitchells, damaging Bell's plane. However,

Sgt. Bill Martin, the turret gunner on the B-25, sent a hail of .50 caliber machine gun fire into one of the 109s and downed it.

The 321st Group strafing and skip bomb attack continued. Maj. Ellis Cook of the 446th Squadron got two solid hits on another escort warship to leave the vessel burning and dead in the water. Capt. Frank Schwane of the 447th Squadron scored one hit and two near misses on a merchant vessel and left the ship afire and listing. Other 321st Group pilots scored hits amidship and near misses on two more of the merchant ships.

By the time the 321st Bomb Group air crews had left the target area, two escort ships, two merchant ships, and four Siebel ferries were on their way to the bottom of the sea, with two more escort warships, another merchant ship, and three more ferries badly damaged. Only one 7,000 ton freighter, three ferries and four destroyers would reach Tunis Harbor.

And still the NAAF air groups continued the morning assaults. The U.S. 12th Bomb Group from Col. Ken Cross's 211 Group made attacks on German airfields and harbor installations at Bizerte and Tunis. Col. Ed Backus led the Mitchells in these attacks. German anti-aircraft gunners downed two of the 12th Group B-25s, but German fighters had failed to intervene. U.S. 31st Fighter Group Spitfires from NATAF under the command of Col. Fred Dean waded into 17 Messerschmidt fighters under Lt. Heinrich Perzina of III/JG 51 out of Dejedeida, Tunisia.

The American pilots downed six of the ME 109s to a loss of two Spitfires. B-25 gunners also scored against the German interceptors, knocking down three 109s, with Sgt. Bill Gardner aboard Col. Ed Backus' plane getting two of them.

Two squadrons from the 12th Group decimated an airdrome outside of Tunis with whistling 500 pound bombs and heavy strafing fire, destroying several buildings and punching holes in the runway. The other two 12th Group squadrons pasted installations in the Bizerte and Tunis harbors to thwart any attempt of unloading the ships coming from Messina. Of course, the medium American Mitchells from the 321st Bomb Group had already decimated the convoy.

Thus on this 5 April morning, airmen from the NAAF air groups had dealt the Germans a harsh blow. In the multiple strikes and heavy dogfights against airfields, German transport planes, and German fighters, the Americans had destroyed or damaged 174 German planes, 57 of them being knocked out of the air, and the others caught on the ground at El Aouina, Sidi Ahmed, Borrizo, Trapani, Boco de Falco, and Tunis. Meanwhile, the 321st Bomb Group had sunk more than half of the surface ship convoy heading for Tunis, while the NATAF planes had brought heavy damage to the Tunis and Bizerte harbor facilities and the Tunis airdrome facilities.

By early afternoon, Maj. Gunther Unger of the German KG 26 bomber group swept low over the Strait of Sicily and into Tunisia with sixteen medium bombers to hit the Theleple and LeSers airfields of 211 Group. The Dorniers struck swiftly, before adequate interceptors could intervene. Unger and his crews knocked out seven planes on the ground between the two fields and damaged 16 other Spitfires while destroying two buildings. The cagey Unger got away before the RAF or American pilots could pounce on him.

However, Unger's quick strike was little consolation to the Germans. When Kesselring received the report that only 15 of the 70 JU 52s had reached Tunisia, he was flabbergasted. And in fact, the Junkers needed to land at scattered airfields in Northern Tunisia because NAAF bombers had worked over the transport airfields quite thoroughly. Among the survivors of the KVT 16 transport gruppen was Maj. August Geiger.

The rampant destruction by U.S. airmen on this 5 April morning was only the first of the April massacres against Germany's Operation Bulls Head.

CHAPTER SEVEN

On the evening of 5 April 1943, Field Marshal Albert Kesselring called his commanders to a meeting and he began by angrily berating Gen. Hannes Trautloft at OB Sud headquarters in Naples. Only 16 of the 70 transports had reached Tunisia, and only one merchant ship and four of the Siebel ferries had entered Tunis Harbor.

"What happened to your fighters? You said that Fleigerkoros II's pilots were among the best airmen in the Luftwaffe. Yet they failed miserably to protect the air transports and the surface ship vessels. How could this be? How?"

"I regret to say, Herr Field Marshal, that the enemy attacks on the staging airfields badly hurt our ability to mount enough fighters to protect the convoy," Trautloft said. "The American pilots showed exceptional aggressiveness against the few fighters that did get airborne. They effectively neutralized our escorts while other enemy gruppens attacked the JU 52s. They also mounted a full gruppen of medium bombers that attacked the surface ships with equal impunity, while our own fighters were kept at bay."

"We must use more fighter planes," Kesselring barked. "On our next escort mission, you will send out a full geschwader of fighters if necessary."

"Yes, Herr Kesselring."

The Luftflotte 2 kommandant now looked at General Hammhuber. "And what of your bombers? They were supposed to attack and destroy the enemy airfields in Tunisia, especially the fighter bases. Yet you only launched one attack."

"We did not have enough bombers," General Hammhuber said, "nor did we have fighters to escort these bombers over the Strait of Sicily. Only KG 26 could get aircraft off on this long and dangerous mission, but even this bomber attack came too late."

"But the plan called for your bombers to take off an hour before the transport planes," Kesselring scowled. "They should have been over the enemy airfields by the time the transport planes were crossing the Strait of Sicily."

"There was a lapse in communications," Hammhuber said sheepishly. "Captain Dinort's orders were to wait until he received such communication before he flew off his bombers. But the order did not come to KG 26 headquarters until noon."

"Terrible, terrible," Kesselring shook his head. "How can we help Field Marshal Rommel when there is such inefficiency in Luftflotto 2?"

No one answered the field marshal.

Kesselring then leaned forward and looked at General Buchholtz. "We must now consider the flight of a new air convoy, and without suffering the disaster we suffered today."

"We will plan more carefully, Herr Field Marshal," Buchholtz said. "We will need to make certain that we are more secret with our next aerial convoy into Tunisia."

"How soon can a new convoy leave for Tunisia?" Kesselring asked.

"Perhaps in four or five days," Buchholtz said. "We expect the large ME 323 transport aircraft to begin arriving in Naples tomorrow, and we will send at least twenty of these to Tunisia on the next flight."

"Then it is most important that we protect these huge transport planes," Kesselring emphasized with a gesture. He shuffled through some papers on his desk and he then scanned his subordinates again. "I must tell you that the Fuhrer is incensed over this serious loss today and I must face his wrath in two days at a meeting in Salzburg. There will be consternation for there are those on the OKW general staff who agree with Field Marshal Rommel that we should abandon Tunisia. But the Fuhrer is adamant. I hope that I can tell Herr Hitler that such a disaster as occurred today will no be repeated."

"Yes, Herr Field Marshal," Trautloft answered.

On 7 April 1943, Adolph Hilter held his meeting at Klesshein Castle in Salzburg, Germany. The conference included Axis leaders of the highest rank. Dictator Benito Mussolini himself had come to the conference, along with his Italian military chief of staff Gen. Guiseppe Mancinelli, the Italian naval chief Adm. Arturo Riccardi, and the Italian air chief Gen. Vittorio Marchese.

Among the Germans besides Kesselring were Gen. Alfred Jodl, the OKW chief of operations; Field Marshal Wilhelm Kietel, chief of the OKW, Marshal Herman Goring, CinC of the German Air Force; Field Marshal Erwin Rommel, CinC of the Afrika Korps, and Gen. Heinz Schmidt, Hitler's German intelligence chief.

Without doubt, never during the war in Europe had so many high ranking German and Italian leaders come together in one conference. But the situation in Tunisia was desperate and the Axis military commanders needed to make some important decisions.

Among those here, at least four men wanted to abandon Tunisia: Field Marshal Irwin Rommel, Gen. Alfred Jodl, Gen. Heinz Schmidt, and Adm. Artuoro Riccardi of the Italian navy.

Hitler stood behind a long table and glared at those in front of him. The Fuhrer was obviously upset, his neck red. He seemed angry with everyone in the room. He especially scowled at Erwin Rommel because he knew the field marshal wanted to give up Tunisia. The Fuhrer remembered well his praising communication to Rommel only several weeks ago when the Afrika Korps had hurled back U.S. troops in the Kasserine Pass, administering heavy losses against the green American GIs.

"The German people join me in expressing full confidence in your leadership and in the bravery of the German and Italian troops under your command," Hitler's telegram to Rommel had begun. "In your present situation, you must continue to hold on, not to yield a step, and to throw into the battle every weapon and every fighting man who can still shoot. Strong reinforcements will be sent to OB Sud within the next few days. Il Duce and the Italian Commando Supremo will do their utmost to provide you with added means to carry on the struggle. I am confident that you will exhaust the enemy in your fight, despite his superior forces."

Such was the praise from Hitler in February of 1943. But now, less than two months later, the campaign in Tunisia had badly deteriorated in the face of increasing Allied air, ground, and naval strength, and in the failure to keep Rommel's troops and air units adequately supplied. Several surface ship convoys had been horribly mauled by Allied naval and air units, with escorting Italian destroyers unable to cope with British and American assaults.

As early as mid-March, Rommel had sent messages to Hitler, urging the Fuhrer to abandon Tunisia and thus save the bulk of experienced German and Italian troops in the Afrika Korps.

His suggestions had infuriated Hitler and the Fuhrer's admiration for Rommel had turned sour. Hitler, in his madness to continue a campaign that was no longer sound, refused to learn any lesson from the debacle at Stalingrad, where he had lost 300,000 combat troops because he had refused to allow the Wehrmacht soldiers to retreat. Despite the warnings of OKW chief Jodl that Germany could suffer a similar defeat in Tunisia, Hitler had refused to consider an evacuation of North Africa.

In fact, the conference here at Klesshein Castle would not deal with the possibility of evacuating North Africa, but with a strategy to hold in northern Tunisia.

After the Fuhrer leveled his piercing dark eyes on Rommel for nearly a full minute, he scanned the others in the room before he spoke. "I cannot tell you how grieved I felt after the disastrous loss of these ships and transport aircraft two days ago. Yet one such defeat does not mean the end of the battle. Tunisia must be held at all costs."

"Mein Fuhrer," Field Marshal Rommel spoke, "you must understand the situation we face in North Africa. We cannot hold Tunisia against the vastly superior Allied forces. They continually throw newly arrived, fresh infantry and armored divisions against us. They have inexhaustible supplies of arms, while our own forces find themselves with fewer and fewer provisions each day. The enemy's air forces grow stronger daily. In the last week alone, they opened six new airbases in southern Tunisia, and they reinforced their air force with at least another ten gruppens of fresh aircraft and crews. Meanwhile, our own Fleigerkorps Tunisien loses more and more aircraft and men each day, with little or no replacements in pilots, crews, fuel, or supplies."

"Luftflotte Tunisien is well experienced in combat," Hitler gestured angrily, "and they can deal with ten times their number against these inexperienced American airmen. The same is true of Luftflotte 2. The pilots in this command have a long record of combat." Hitler looked at Kesselring. "I cannot possibly understand how your experienced Luftwaffe fighter pilots could not deal easily with these Americans so that the air and sea convoys could reach Tunisia inact."

"There were too many enemy planes, mein Fuhrer," Kesselring said. "Experience alone cannot compensate for superior numbers."

"Then use more aircraft," Hitler barked. "Send out five hundred or even one thousand planes, if necessary, to assure the safe arrival of reinforcements to Tunisia."

Kesselring did not answer. He did not have 1,000 planes in his entire Luftflotte 2, and he had seen few replacements. And worse, the few pilots and crews he did get were green, hastily trained men who could not compete with Allied airmen. But Kesselring did not express these opinions to Hitler, whose wrath would only intensify if he did.

"Please, Don Fuhrer," Admiral Riccardi now spoke, "we can say the same thing of our navy. We simply do not have the means to any longer deal with the powerful enemy naval forces. Their ships have reached several times our number and we do not have a fraction of their numbers in submarines and aircraft. I must tell you that the Mediterranean has become an Allied Lake, where they dominate both the sea and the air."

"I was told that the Italian navy was the best in the world," Hitler glared at Riccardi. "Perhaps Il Duce should put someone else in command of his navy, someone more aggressive; someone who can better inspire his sailors to fight."

Riccardi did not answer and the Fuhrer raved on. He made clear to everyone present that under no circumstances would he abandon Tunisia. When the Italians here looked at Il Duce, the Italian dictator squeezed his face slightly. His army, navy, and air forces needed more help in order to stop the British and Americans, and Mussolini knew that his Italian commanders wanted Il Duce to plead for more German aid.

"Don Hitler," Il Duce said, "I agree that we should hold Tunisia. There is no doubt that the enemy is looking beyond North Africa to Sicily or Italy. But they will not attempt an invasion of our shores until they have settled matters in Tunisia. I would say then that if Tunisia can be held until at least autumn, we can rob the enemy of using the summer months for an invasion of Sicily or Italy. To do this, we need more aid from the Third Reich, much more aid, Don Fuhrer."

"We have been giving you aid for two years, but your commanders have not used such aid wisely. I am willing to extend more, Herr Duce, but only if you make certain changes in your leadership so that further aid is not squandered."

Mussolini did not answer.

"Mein Fuhrer," Rommel spoke again, "you must reconsider your decision to hold Tunisia. The military situation is hopeless. We are only wasting our critically needed supplies and losing too many good men. I beg you to allow us to evacuate to Sicily. The loss of North Africa is only a matter of time, and better that we should be well armed and fully manned in Sicily and Italy with our experienced Afrika Korps, so we can repel any further Allied advance in the Mediterranean. Even General Schmidt would agree."

Hitler looked at Schmidt who did not answer at once. The German intelligence chief unrolled a map on the table before he spoke. "Mein Fuhrer," he pointed to several maps on the table, "the enemy now has some fifty airdromes scattered through Algeria, Tunisia, Libya, and Malta, with at least a full gruppen of American or British aircraft based on each one. Also, the enemy has several naval bases in the same area. These bases are jammed with every type of warship and submarine. The day is not far off when they will completely control the Strait of Sicily cutting off all hope of sending further reinforcements to Tunisia either by air or by sea."

"We cannot allow that to happen," Hitler gestured.

"There is no way of stemming the swelling strength of the Allied Forces," Schmidt continued. "Our agents throughout the Mediterranean and North Africa itself have reported new arrivals in enemy aircraft, ships, tanks, and men almost daily. These reinforcements dock at Algiers, Oran, and Cairo. Our agents see no hope of holding Tunisia, and all of them agree with Field Marshal Rommel — our best course at this time would be to evacuate Tunisia."

"Your agents are dummkopfs, like yourself," Hitler sneered at General Schmidt. "Il Duce is the only one among you who speaks wisely. We must hold Tunisia until at least the fall, so the Allies cannot mount an invasion of Italy or Sicily during the favorable summer months. They will need to wait until at least the spring of next year, by which time Sicily and Italy will be so well defended that no enemy, no matter how powerful he may be, will be able to make successful landings on these shores."

Those in the room did not answer Hitler and he rambled on. He said he would strengthen the Italian navy by the addition of more German destroyers in the Mediterranean. He made a number of further promises: new planes, pilots, and crews for Luftflotte 2, more combat troops, tanks, and supplies into Tunisia, and enough transport planes to blacken the skies over the route between Naples and Tunisia. Field Marshal Kesselring could send a continuous parade of men and supplies to Tunisia by air. He would also send two more squadrons of U-boats into Mediterranean waters to sink the Allied navy. He also assured Rommel that more merchant ships would reach Italy so that the Afrika Korps would get more than enough supplies and arms to hold fast in Tunisia.

Few of these there were convinced, least of all Rommel. The Afrika Korps commander spoke again. "While none of us doubt the sincerity of your words, mein Fuhrer, I believe that it will not be possible to send enough reinforcements into North Africa to hold Tunisia. The men of the Afrika Korps are utterly spent. They have been sapped of strength and they can no longer contain the enemy. Fleigerkorps Tunisien is exhausted. The pilots have fought hard and bravely, but they have been overwhelmed. All of them suffer from flying fatigue. To send more men, planes, and supplies into Tunisia is to invite an additional waste of our resources. I implore you again, mein Fuhrer, let us evacuate Tunisia and build strong defenses in Sicily and Italy."

Hitler did not chastise Rommel this time. Instead, surprisingly, he looked at the Afrika Korps commander with a hint of sympathy in his dark eyes. "Herr Field Marshal, there was a time when your advice and suggestions were of the utmost importance to me. But it is obvious that the strain of these North African battles have taken a toll. We can easily see that you are emotionally and physically ill from directing this harsh campaign. I can see that you need rest to regain your strength."

Rommel only stared at the German dictator.

"All of Germany is grateful to you, Herr Field Marshal, for you have done well and we are proud of you," Hitler continued. "But even the

best of us cannot go on indefinitely. I am therefore relieving you of your command of the
Afrika Korps. I would ask that you return to
your home, to your wife and son, and to worry
no more about battles, supplies, and strategies —
at least for the time being. When you have enjoyed a good rest I will give you a new
command."

Those in the room gaped in shock. Hitler had
just fired the most popular and cunning military
leader in the Axis camp. But no one, nobody
from Il Duce on down, made any comment.

"The rest will do you good," Hitler continued.
"We cannot afford to lose a man of your caliber.
And, since this war will go on for some time, you
can be certain that we will need your services
again when you are well."

Rommel did not answer and Hitler merely gestured. He repeated his earlier comments. Every
kind of necessary reinforcement would be fun-
nelled into Tunisia so that the last Axis bastion in
North Africa could be held until at least the fall.
He urged those present to show courage and resolve against their enemies, and he assured them
that if each man did his job, the enemy would not
drive the Afrika Korps from Tunisia. He urged
Mussolini to whip up more fervor in his sailors
and his airmen so they would succeed in escorting supply ships to Tunisia and in protecting the
Italian airfields, especially those around Naples.
He asked that the Italian air force join the German air force in defeating the Allied air forces
and thus assure a steady flow of supplies into Tu-

nisia.

When the conference ended, the participants left the room in silence. They were still stunned by Hitler's decision to fire Field Marshal Irwin Rommel, and they wondered whom the Fuhrer would call upon to replace the Desert Fox. They could not mull for long the precarious decision to hold Tunisia. Both the German and Italian commanders knew they must now find ways and means to keep Tunisia supplied with men, arms, and provisions, a seemingly impossible task.

On the morning of 8 April 1943, Gen. Jurgeon von Arnim, the deputy commander of the Afrika Korps, got a message from Berlin from the OKW chief of staff, Gen. Alfred Jodl. The memorandum stunned von Armim:

"The courageous, esteemed Field Marshal Rommel was obviously in need of rest because of his exhausting efforts in North Africa," the memo began, "and he has been ordered by the Fuhrer to take a well deserved period of recuperation. For the time being, you will assume command of the Afrika Korps. You will continue to carry out the battle strategies of the field marshal, with further orders to hold Tunisia at all costs. You will get ample supplies and reinforcements to carry on the Tunisian campaign."

Von Arnim quickly met wtih Gen. Hoffman von Waldau of Fleigerkorps Tunisien and with the division commanders of the Afrika Korps ground troops. The German officers listened in amazed silence when von Arnim explained what had happened. Most of them had faith in von Arnim's ability, but they were shocked by the loss of their beloved field marshal who had led them for more than two years in the North Africa campaign. They knew, however, that Rommel had been at odds with Hitler for the past several weeks and they should have expected the Fuhrer to strip Rommel of his command, even though the Desert Fox had been Germany's most admired and popular military commander.

"I can only say," von Arnim told the assembled officers, "that we must redouble our efforts to hold Tunisia. You will all meet with your kommandants and tell them that Field Marshal Rommel became ill during his visit to Germany for the conference at Salzburg. You will also tell them that for the time being, I will be directing operations in Tunisia."

"Yes, General," Hoffman von Waldau said.

"Meanwhile, Field Marshal Kesselring has assured me that he will send new supplies to Tunisia, by both air and sea. You can expect new reinforcements and more provisions quite soon."

And, in fact, right after the Klessheim Castle conference, Kesselring, Mancinelli, Riccardi, and Marchese flew back to Naples to initiate plans to send new reinforcements into Tunisia. Admiral Riccardi would again muster Italian destroyers to escort a new supply ship convoy from Naples to Tunisia. General Marchese met with General Trautloft and promised to supply several Italian fighter squadrons to help the German air force in protecting the Naples airfields and Naples harbor. Luftflotte 2 could then release more German fighter units to escort supply ships and aerial transports to Tunisia. And finally, Gen. Ulrich Buchholtz had once more mustered a horde of transport planes at Naples, nearly 50 JU 52s and over 20 of the new, giant six engine ME 323s.

By 9 April, General Buchholtz had loaded 22 ME 363s and 34 JU 52s. The huge air fleet would carry an entire regiment of troops along with 10,000 tons of supplies that included 88mm guns, Panzer tanks, bombs, ammunition, medicine, food, motor vehicles, and fuel.

"We will fool the Allies this time," Buchholtz told Field Marshal Kesselring. "We will take off at 0300 hours in the morning, at dark, and fly directly to Tunisia. The enemy will no doubt expect us to again stage out of Sicily, and we will surely deceive them."

"Ulrich, it is imperative that we do not fail again," Kesselring said. "When will you leave?"

"We intend to send out this aerial convoy tomorrow," the Lufttransport Mittelmeer CinC said. "The enemy will not expect another aerial convoy this soon, so we should have the element of surprise on our side."

"Good," Kesselring nodded.

"Of course," Buchholtz gestured, "it is imperative that we have ample fighter support."

"We have assigned JG 77 and JG 27 as escort," the Luftflotte 2 CinC said. "General Trautloft has assured me that both Colonel Neumann and Colonel Steinhoff will mount as many aircraft as possible, perhaps more than one hundred fighters. I was also told by General Marchese that his 5th Aero Squadron from the Italian 12 Gruppo will supply a minimum of fifty MC 202 fighters to protect the harbor and airfields at Naples. So we can use most of our own Luftwaffe fighters for escort duties."

"The transport pilots will be happy to learn that," Buchholtz said.

But Gen. Wild Bill Donovan's OSS agents had again kept U.S. intelligence well informed on German activities. They had reported the new buildup of German transport planes at Naples, including the nearly two dozen ME 323s. The agents had also reported the large number of surface ships in Naples Harbor, a merchant fleet that included three transports, four freighters, an oiler, and eleven Siebel ferries.

Donovan, from his OSS headquarters, wasted little time in contacting NAAF on these latest developments in Italy. In turn, General Spaatz asked Gen. James Doolittle to act and the NASAF CinC immediately put his bomber and fighter units on alert. A Roman message could come at any hour and the groups would need to scramble in a hurry. Doolittle had also singled out several of his air groups to deal with the potential air and sea convoys.

The U.S. 14th Fighter Group would again make a recon sweep in the Sicily area. The 99th and 97th Bomb Groups, meanwhile, would attack the Maddelena Harbor in Sardinia and the Naples Harbor in Italy, where, Doolittle hoped, the Flying Fortresses could catch the Italian destroyers and German merchant ships by surprise before they left port. NASAF assigned the 325th Fighter Group to escort the 99th Group and the 350th Fighter Group to escort the 97th Group. The 82nd Fighter Group with their P-38s would also escort the 321st Bomb Group to attack the German transport staging areas at Comiso and Borrizo in Sicily

Col. Fred Lauer's 2nd Bomb Group had been assigned to hit the transport airfields in Naples on 10 April in the hope of catching the German transport planes on the ground before they left Naples. The 1st Fighter Group with their P-38s would escort the heavy bombers to Naples. Finally, the 310th Bomb Group would attack the German airfield at Reggio de Calabria to thwart JG 77 fighter planes that might escort the German aerial convoy. The borrowed 214 RAF Wing would furnish escort with its Spitfires

Doolittle, through NAAF, had also requested the NATAF attack the German transport fields at Sidi Ahmed and El Aouina in Tunisia. Air Marshal Arthur Conningham complied and he assigned the B-25s of the 12th Bomb Group for the attack, with the P-40 fighters from the U.S. 57th Fighter Group as escorts.

Thus thirteen air groups from NAAF would be directly involved in Operation Flax on 10 April, while the RAF 211 Group planes that included U.S. air units would maintain strong CAPs over the Strait of Sicily and off the North Africa coast. Both Lt. Col. Tony Keith of the 14th

Fighter Group and Col. Bill Covington of the 82nd Fighter Group made certain that the strafing guns on their P-38s were loaded with ammo belts and their cannons were loaded with 37mm shells. Both Lt. Col. Gordon Austin of the 325th Fighter Group and Col. Marvin McNickle of the 350th Fighter Group also made sure they had ample fuel and ammo for escort duty with the 99th and 97th Bomb Groups.

Among the bomber units, both Col. Fay Upthegrove of the 99th and Col. Stan Donovan of the 97th had loaded their B-17s with 20 pound incendiary clusters and HE thousand pounders for shipping in Maddelena and Naples Harbors, while Col. Fred Lauer of the 2nd Bomb Group had loaded his own B-17s with the same kinds of bombs. All three bomb group commanders hoped to catch their targets before they left the harbors or airfields. The B-25s of the 310th Group also carried bombs, all of them HEs to gouge big holes in the runways at Comiso and at Reggio de Calabria.

However, the Germans had also readied themselves. At Reggio on the boot of Italy, Col. Edu Neumann had readied 55 fighters from his JG 27 to escort the JU 52 transport planes across the Strait of Sicily. At Trapani, Col. Johannes Steinhoff had mustered 53 Folke-Wulf fighters to escort the ME 323 transport planes to Tunisia.

In Sardinia, a squadron of Italian MC 202s were on the ready to protect the destroyers. At Naples, two squadrons of MC 202, Miachi fighters, 54 aircraft, had been sitting on full alert at the Aquino airfield. These fighters, along with a staffel of German ME 109s at the Montecervino airfield, also at Naples, would take off at once if or when German radar teams picked up blips of enemy bombers coming toward Naples. Kesselring was determined to protect the Naples airfields and the ships in Naples Harbor until the transport planes and merchant vessels were on their way to Tunisia.

In Tunisia itself, at the Fleigerkorps Tunisien base at Dejedeida, Maj. Erich Rudorffer suspected that U.S. bombers would surely head for Sidi Ahmed and El Aouina again if or when the Americans learned that a formation of German transport planes was on the way to Tunisia. So he mustered 44 ME 109s and kept them on full alert to intercept any American planes that came toward the transport plane airfields.

Thus had the Americans and Germans again set the stage for a new confrontation. Bedlam would again erupt over the central Mediterranean on 10 April 1943, only five days after the first melee in which the Germans had suffered disaster. Field Marshal Albert Kesselring believed that he had planned more wisely this time, and that he would be as successful tomorrow as he had been unsuccessful on 5 April. Conversely, Gen. Carl Spaatz of NAAF hoped that his Allied airmen would deal the Germans another numbing blow tomorrow.

Gen. Carl Spaatz (L) and Gen. James Doolittle (R) who directed
Operation Flax during April of 1943.

Gen. William "Wild Bill" Donovan, head of the OSS. His agents in Italy and Sicily kept Allies informed on departures of Axis ships and planes.

Capt. Richard McAuliffe (L), Col. Bill Covington (C) and Lt. Bob Schilde (R) of the 82nd Fighter Group. This unit had a field day against German transports.

Maj. Harley Vaughn of the 82nd Group's 92nd Squadron downed six transport planes.

Lt. Col. Troy Keith of 14th Fighter Group that shot down more than 37 German fighters during Operation Flax.

Maj. Lou Benne of 14th Group, got four transport planes on one mission.

Lt. Col. Ed Olmstead, CO of 321st Bomb Group. This unit decimated a German resupply convoy on 5 April 1943.

321st Group B-25 crew, L to R: Sgt. Pete Franklin, Lt. Mike Zordin, pilot Lt. Hank Bell, Lt. Carl Reiser, and Sgt. Ed White.

Crew from 310st Group B-25s: L to R: Lt. Joe Gilbert, Maj. Pete Remington, Lt. Ralph Howe, Sgt. Ed Blake, and Sgt. Tony DeMarco.

Col. Anthony Hunter of 310th Bomb Group. This unit helped to destroy air transport fleet on 5 April 1943.

Col. Fay Upthegrove of 99th Bomb Group. His B-17 unit caused untold damage against German air and sea bases in the Mediterranean.

Maj. Al Orance of the 99th Group's 416th Squadron.

Maj. Harry Burrell (C) of 99th's 347th Squadron poses with men from his squadron. Lt. Dean Shields, "Yankee Doodle" pilot, is 5th from left.

Capt. James Curl and pilots of his 66th Squadron who scored multiple kills during the Palm Sunday Massacre.

Capt. Ray Whittaker of 57th Group gets DFC for his Palm Sunday efforts.

Maj. Neville Duke and pilots of his RAF 92 Squadron did exceptional job during Palm Sunday massacre. Duke is second from left.

Col. Ford Lauer, CO of 2nd Bomb Group that ruined Naples airfields.

Lt. Tom Lohr of the 97th Bomb Group that sunk merchantmen in Naples Harbor.

Col. Arthur Salisbury (R), CO of the 57th Fighter Group, glee-
fully discusses Palm Sunday Massacre with pilots Lt. Frank Cleveland, Lt. Ed Campbell, Lt. Frank Ryan, and Lt. Tom Smith.

Maj. Arthur Knight of 57th Group won DFC for his efforts on Palm Sunday.

Lt. Col. Dan Loftus of the 7 SAAF Wing. His South African unit mauled German air convoys on both 19 April and 22 April of 1943.

Maj. Ed Parsonson of 7 Wing's 5 Squadron got five kills during Operation Flax.

Field Marshal Albert Kesselring, CinC of German OB Sud Ost planned Operation Bullshead to reinforce Afrika Korps in Tunisia.

Gen. Ulrich Buchholtz (L), Gen. Hannes Trautloft (C) and Gen. Erich Hammhuber (R) had responsibility for carrying out Operation Bullshead.

Field Marshal Erwin Rommel of Afrika Korps desperately needed supplies to hold in Tunisia.

Gen. Jurgeon von Arnim took over Afrika Korps when Hitler fired Rommel. But Operation Bullshead failed and he surrendered in Tunisia.

General Schmidt (R) points out to Hitler (C) and Mussolini (L) that it would be impossible to hold Tunisia. Hitler would not listen.

Lt. Heinz Berre of JG 77 was one of lucky German fighter pilot survivors during the heavy April air battles over the Mediterranean.

Col. Edu Neumann of JG 27 tried hard to defend transports, but failed to do so.

Maj. Gustav Rodel of JG 27 scored high against Allied fighters, but his efforts were not enough.

Col. Johannes Steinhoff of JG 77. His air unit took a beating when U.S. 99th Bomb Group destroyed some of his planes on the ground.

Major Ehrler of JG 77 got five kills in one air battle but to no avail.

Maj. Hartman Grasser had the responsibility of escorting 100 transport planes to Tunisia on Palm Sunday. His JG 51 pilots failed to do so.

Maj. Erich Rudorffer of III/JG 51 kept his gruppen in Tunisia, but he and his German pilots were hard pressed against hordes of Allied planes.

Lt. Heinrich Perzina of JG 51 was wounded during last dog fight in April.

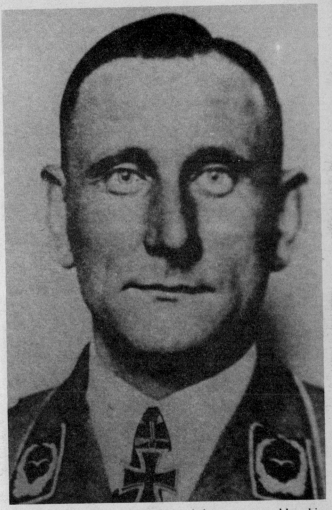

Lt. Col. Bruno Dinort of KG 26 carried out some good bombing raids against Allied bases in Tunisia, but could not stop Operation Flax.

Maj. Gunther Unger and his crew of his DO 17 bomber from KG 26.

OSS agents in Sicily radio information to OSS headquarters in Algiers.

Col. Walter Hagen (L) and Maj. August Geiger (R) of the KVT 16 transport plane geschwader. Geiger was killed during Palm Sunday massacre.

Col. Heinz Jost of the SS Gestapo effectively stopped OSS agents in Italy.

B-17s of the 99th Bomb Group drone over the Mediterranean toward Trapani airdrome.

Wrecked German planes at Boco de Falco after 99th Group attack.

Ninety-Niner bombs macerate German runway at Boco de Falco, Sicily.

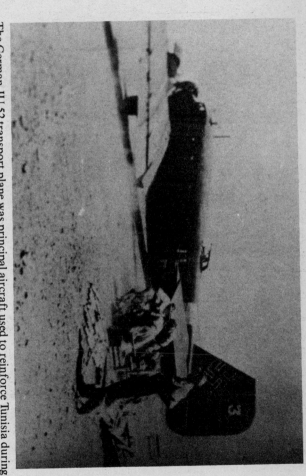

The German JU 52 transport plane was principal aircraft used to reinforce Tunisia during early 1943.

German ground crews load up a DO 17 light bomber for attack on Allied base.

Mitchells from the 321st Bomb Group drone over Sicily before a bombing attack.

B-17 from the 99th Group leaves Maddelena Harbor after air attack on destroyers.

Bombs from the U.S. 12th Bomb Group sail into German airfield at El Aloina.

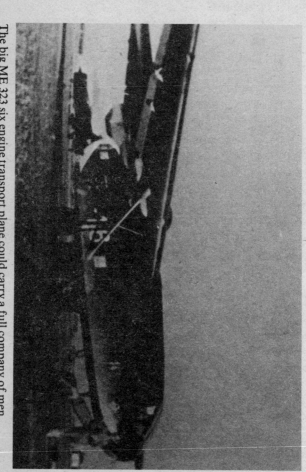

The big ME 323 six engine transport plane could carry a full company of men.

The huge mouth of the ME 323 enabled plane to load big Mark IV German tanks.

Loading a vehicle into an ME 323 Giganten transport plane.

A wrecked 12th Bomb Group B-25 after attack on Madeline by German KG 26 bombers.

Smashed hangars at Trapani airfield after attacks by U.S. B-17s.

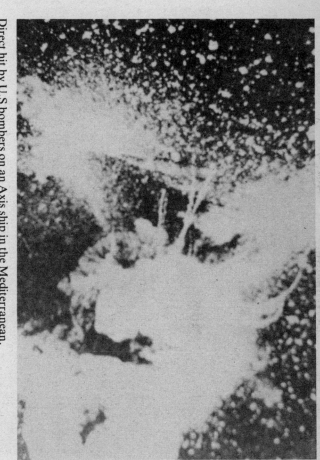

Direct hit by U.S bombers on an Axis ship in the Mediterranean.

American planes strafe a formation of JU 52 transports during Operation Flax.

American fighter plane strafes a huge ME 323 transport plane during Operation Flax.

FIGHTER GROUP VICTORIES

DESTROYED	PROBABLE	DAMAGED
2 Me 109 2 Me 202 3 Ju 87 4 Ju 52	5 Me 109	20
34½	5	22½
14 Me 109 3 Me 202 12 Cr 42 12 Ju 52 2 Me 110	2 Ju 52 4 ME 109	25
36	6	25
1 Me 202 28½ Ju 52 1 Cr 42 20 Me/202	4 Me 109 1 Me 202 1 Ju 52	23½
30½	6	23½
23 Ju 52 2 Me 109		7
25		7

Score card for the 57th Fighter Group after the Palm Sunday massacre.

Wrecked German planes at Tunisian airfield, grim evidence of Germany's final loss in North Africa.

CHAPTER EIGHT

At the bomber base in Navarin, Algeria, Col. Fay Upthegrove met with his group airmen in the huge quonset hut operations tent. At 0200 hours, 10 April, the air was still cool along the coastal area of North Africa, and most of the Americans huddled inside their furlined jackets as they sat on hard benches. Upthegrove's aides had pulled down a huge map of Maddelena Harbor, with a light over the map. Upthegrove waited until the aide had finished. He then looked at some papers in front of him before addressing his men.

"We've got a mission to Sardinia this morning, and as you can see, it's the Maddelena Naval Base. The Germans have been loading ships at Naples for the past couple of days and they've been readying Italian destroyers at Maddelena to obviously escort these merchant ships. We want to hit the destroyers before they get a chance to pull out; intelligence tells us there's about six destroyers in Maddelena and maybe six merchant ships and a half dozen Siebel ferries at Naples. If we can get these vessels before they can pull out of the harbors we can do a lot of damage."

Upthegrove paused momentarily when the sudden whine of aircraft engines echoed from the airfield about two miles from the operations tent. Ground crews were preflighting the B-17s. The colonel waited until the sound of screaming engines had diminished somewhat before he continued.

"We'll be taking off at about 0300 hours so we can reach Maddelena Harbor just before daybreak at 0600. We'll be carrying both HEs and incendiaries. We'd like to start fires as well as blow holes. If you'll look at your sheet, you'll see that I'll be leading the 348th myself, Major Lowry will lead the 346th, Major Burrell the 347th and Major Orance the 416th. We'll fly in the usual box formation patterns, 348th at twenty-eight thousand, 346th at twenty-five thousand, 347th at twenty-six five hundred, and the tail end 416 at twenty-three five hundred. Any questions?"

"That base is bound to have plenty of fighter planes around," Major Orance said. "What about escorts?"

"We'll have the 325th Fighter Group," Upthegrove answered. "They'll rendezvous with us southwest of Sicily at about 0400 hours and accompany us all the way in and out."

"Who's going in first, sir?" Maj. Leon Lowry of the 346th Squadron asked.

"You are," the 99th Group commander said. "The 346th Squadron will lead the attack. Then will come Major Orance's 416th Squadron. I'll follow with the 348th, and Major Burrell's 347th will be the tail end Charlie."

"What kind of fighter opposition can we expect?" Major Lowry asked.

"Intelligence believes that the fighter units at Maddelena are Italian. Some of these pilots are good, but most of them are quite squeamish. However, gunners will need to be careful because those MC 202 fighter planes are good. They're fast and highly maneuverable. With a good pilot that plane can do an awful job."

"Yes sir," Lowry said.

Upthegrove scanned his air crews again. "Any more questions?"

None.

"Okay, you can get to the mess hall. The cooks have prepared an early breakfast for us, and they've also prepared box lunches."

At Chateau dum-ru-Rhumel, Col. Stan Donovan of the 97th Bomb Group was also briefing B-17 crews. He too referred to a map behind him and some papers on the stand in front of him. He and his Flying Fort crews also listened when engines ignited at the airfields on this wee hour of 10 April.

Donovan told his crew essentially the same thing as Colonel Upthegrove told his 99th Bomb Group crews. The 97th would carry both HE

1,000 pounders and 20 pound incendiary clusters in the hope of sinking and burning ships at Naples harbor. He would lead his group with the 342nd Squadron at 28,000 feet. Maj. Paul Tibbets, who later led the atom bomb attack on Hiroshima, would lead the 340th Squadron at 25,000 feet. Capt. Ed Kane would lead the 341st Squadron at 26,500, and Maj. Frank Allen would lead the 414th Squadron at 23,500.

"Will we have enough escorts, sir?" Captain Kane asked.

"The entire 350th Fighter Group," Donovan answered.

"Who's going with us?" Major Tibbetts asked.

"Nobody," the 97th Group commander answered. "The 99th is going after the warship escorts in Sardinia and we'll be hitting the merchant ships at Naples. Any questions?"

"I guess not, sir," Maj. Paul Tibbets said.

"Okay, let's get an early breakfast and mount up. The mess cooks will also have box lunches for you."

The 97th Group would take off at 0315 hours and meet the P-47s of the 350th Fighter Group over the Mediterranean Sea before the B-17s and Thunderbolt fighters went on to Naples.

At this same Algerian bomber base, Col. Fred Lauer was completing his briefing with 34 B-17 crews of the 2nd Bomb Group. These heavies would attack the Capodichino airfield in Naples in the hope of knocking out German transport planes before the aircraft took off.

"We'll be flying out at 0300 and we should be

over target by dawn," Lauer said. "Let's hope those fields are crammed with German transport planes. The P-38s of the 1st Fighter Group will accompany us all the way in and out."

"What's the route in, sir?" Capt. John Summers asked.

"Right over Sicily," Lauer answered.

Summers nodded. He had flown the plane "Boomerang" that had carried Gen. Mark Clark, CinC of the 5th Army, and Gen. James Doolittle of NAAF to Gibraltar before the North African invasion in November of 1942. The B-17 had developed all kinds of mechanical trouble and it appeared the Fort might plunge into the sea. But Summers had successfully landed the plane in Gibraltar. Doolittle and Clark had congratulated Summers for his excellent efforts. Summers had been with the 97th Bomb Group but in March he had transferred to the 2nd Bomb Group to take command of the 2nd's 492nd Squadron.

The airmen of the 2nd Group also ate an early breakfast and carried box lunches.

At Berteaux, Algeria, Lt. Col. Tony Hunter of the 310th Bomb Group briefed his B-25 squadron leaders. "We'll be flying straight north, right over Sicily, and into Italy to hit the Reggio de Calabria airfield. The latest report says there's a swarm of fighter planes up there waiting to take off, presumably to escort transport planes. We'd like to catch those fighters on the ground if we can."

"What about escorts, sir?" Maj. Pete Remington asked.

"Thirty-four Spitfires from the RAF 214 Wing will take us in and out."

"Will one wing be enough?" Maj. Bill Plant asked.

"Let's hope so," Hunter answered. He paused. "Any questions?"

None.

"Okay, let's mount up."

By 0300 hours, 41 Flying Fortresses from the 99th Group, 37 Forts from the 97th Group, 34 B-17s from the 2nd Bomb Group, and 32 Mitchells from the 310th Group had left their bases in Algeria to begin the long flight over the Mediterranean Sea. They would pick up their 325th, 350th, 1st, and 214th fighter escorts halfway between North Africa and Sicily.

Earlier, at 0230 hours, Lt. Col. Tony Keith of the 14th Fighter Group met with 42 P-38 fighter pilots in the group operations tent at Telergma, Algeria. Keith too had a map on the wall behind him, and he too referred to some papers in front of him before he spoke. "Our mission is getting off pretty early this morning. We'll be making a sweep over Sicily and along the west and south coasts of that island. NASAF says the Naples Harbor is loaded with merchant ships and Naples airfields are jammed with transport planes. We'd like to knock out these ships and planes before they leave for North Africa. In case they're gone, we'd like to spot them as they're coming south toward Tunisia."

"What about fighter opposition, sir?" Maj. Lou Benne of the 49th Squadron asked.

"I'm sure we'll need to stay alert for ME 109s or FW 190s," Keith said.

"Yes sir," Benne answered.

"Any more questions?" When no one spoke, Keith nodded. "Let's get to the mess hall for early breakfast and then we'll mount up."

At Souk El Khemis, Tunisia, Lt. Col. Gordon Austin met with the P-38 pilots of his 325th Fighter Group. During this dark, cool morning on 10 April, he and his pilots also felt cold. They too hesitated when crew chiefs warmed up the engines of their Lightnings. Then Austin explained that the 325th Fighter Group would be escorting the 99th Bomb Group to Sardinia this morning. The pilots would take off by 0330 hours and rendezvous with the Flying Forts at about 0400 hours over the Mediterranean Sea at a position of longitude 13.4 east and latitude 37 north. They would take the Forts all the way in and out of Maddelena Harbor.

"I'll take the 317th Squadron on high cover," Austin said, "while Capt. John Simmons takes the 319th on the port lateral and Maj. Ben Emmert takes the 318th Squadron on the starboard lateral. They tell us that a couple of Italian fighter squadrons are on Sardinia. We've had experience with them and usually they're not very aggressive and not very good. But they do have some good pilots and those MC 202s are good fighter planes. So you'll need to be wide awake."

"No German fighters on that island, sir?" Captain Simmons asked.

"We don't think so," Austin answered.

"How about Sicily? Could the Germans mount fighters out of their Sicily airbases to intercept our flight to Sardinia?"

"We can't rule that out," Austin said. "We'll need to keep a few planes scouting off the east flank to keep a sharp watch for German fighter planes that might come out of Trapani or Catania, and maybe Gela." The 325th Fighter Group commander warned his pilots to take on any interceptors in pairs, with each pilot sticking with his wingman.

At Maison Blanche, Algeria, Col. Marvin McNickle of the 350th Fighter Group briefed his P-47 pilots on their escort mission with the 97th Bomb Group to Naples. At Rhumel, Algeria, Col. Ralph Gorman of the 1st Fighter Group briefed his P-38 pilots on their escort mission to Naples with the 2nd Bomb Group. Finally, at Le-Sers, Tunisia, the British 214 Wing prepared for their escort mission to Reggio de Calabria with the 310th Bomb Group.

By 0345 hours, the 14th Fighter Group had left its airbase and sped northward to reconnoiter Sicily. By 0400 hours, the other four Allied fighter groups had left North Africa to pick up their B-17 and B-25 charges far out to sea. In the darkness, the B-17s and B-25s looked like huge dark albatrosses. The P-47 fighters resembled black hawks darting about the sky and the P-38s looked like flitting black spiders.

By 0500 hours, the large 97th and 2nd BG formations were beyond Sicily and flying over the Tyrrhenian Sea toward Maddelena and Naples.

They would be over the harbor and airfield just after daybreak.

Meanwhile, the 97th Bomb Group had rendezvoused with the P-38s of the 350th Fighter Group high over the Mediterranean before the 34 Flying Forts and their 44 Lightning escorts droned swiftly toward Naples Harbor. And finally, the 310th Bomb Group and their Spitfires from the 214 Wing were flying directly over Sicily to hit the Reggio airbase on the boot of Italy.

At 0400 hours, in Naples, only OD men at the Italian fighter base in Aquino and the German fighter base in Montecervino were awake, and these men loitered in relative boredom at their stations. In Naples Harbor, the merchant ships were also quiet, lying at anchor in the dark. Loading would resume at daybreak so that the ships could leave the harbor at mid-day.

At Maddelena, Italian destroyers lay at anchor in the harbor, with only the night watch on stations aboard the darkened warships. They would weigh anchor at 0700 to meet the merchant ships and Siebel ferries west of Sicily. At the airbase on this island, a squadron of Italian MC 202s sat dormant on the field.

However, frantic activity prevailed at the KVT 16 transport fields at Capodichino and Pomigliano outside of Naples. The Germans had fully loaded 22 of the giant ME 323 six engine transport planes and 34 JU 52 three engine transports. Aboard the 56 aircraft were another 2,000 men of the 36th Grenadier Division along with 15,000 tons of supplies that included shells, ammunition, fuel, and provisions. Also on these planes were 20 of the 88mm artillery pieces, some 30 Mark IV tanks, and over 50 motor vehicles of all types. The Afrika Korps could surely use these reinforcements.

Col. Lenz Kumrey would lead the gruppen of ME 323s from KVT 5, while Col. Walter Hagen himself would lead the gruppen of JU 52s from KVT 16. Hagen met with Kumrey before take off.

"We will be flying directly south, across Sicily, and straight into Tunisia. Be sure to keep your transport planes in tight formation. Once we have left the southern coast of Sicily, we will fly low and we can thus avoid the enemy's radar as we come into Tunisia."

"Yes, Herr Colonel," Kumrey answered. "But we can be sure the enemy will not be aware of our flight? I have been told that enemy spies are all around us and they have surely seen the activities on our airbases. They will most certainly contact the enemy's headquarters in North Africa."

Hagen grinned. "We have issued a message that we are sure the spies will relay to the enemy. We have notified the kommandants at Comiso and Borrizo Airdromes in Sicily to expect us to arrive with these transport planes at 0700 hours. Thus the enemy will expect us to again stage out of Sicily. Before they realize this deception, we will be in Tunisia."

"Let us hope so," Colonel Kumrey said, "Still, we must have ample escorts."

"Most asssuredly," Hagen nodded. "Both JG

27 fighters out of Reggio and JG 77 fighters out of Trapani will rendezvous with us over Sicily. I am told we could have upwards of one hundred fighter escorts. And, if necessary, we will even have a gruppen of fighters from JG 51 out of Catania to join us as escorts. I will leave Naples first with the JU 52s and pick up escorts from JG 27 out of Reggio. You are to leave Capodichino and pick up your escorts from JG 77 whose fighters will fly out of Trapani. We will have ample escort, Herr Kumrey."

The KVT 5 kommandant nodded. However, he was not very confident. He had heard of the disaster a few days ago, when an equal number of American fighter planes had dealt effectively with an equal number of German fighter planes, while other American fighters had ripped the transport formations apart. Kumrey prayed that his ME 323s did not suffer a similar fate today.

At 0430 hours, while the American B-17s and their fighter escorts were droning over the Tyrrhenian Sea toward Naples, the German transport planes were taking off. 34 Junkers from Pomigliano were lifting off as were the 22 ME 324s from the Capodichino Drome. By 0445 hours, the 56 transport planes had cleared Naples and were droning south in tight formation toward Sicily. Ironically, the KVT planes flying south had passed the American B-17s flying north, with the German formations about 50 miles to the westward. Thus the Flying Forts from the 97th and 2nd Bomb Groups had missed the transport planes. The 2nd Group would find the Naples airfields void of JU 52s and ME 323s.

When Col. Fred Lauer of the 2nd Group arrived over the fields, he cursed. Still he did not want to waste his bombs. Two of the 2nd Group B-17 squadrons blasted the Capodichino airfield while the other Flying Fort squadrons plastered the Pomigliano Airdrome. The U.S. Defender group chopped up the runways and destroyed several service shops.

Other U.S. bomb groups, however, found their primary targets.

At about the same 0600 hours, 10 April, German dock and harbor crews at Naples were just sitting down to breakfast at their mess halls on the shoreline, while sailors aboard the five merchant ships and six Siebel ferries in the harbor had also sat down to breakfast. Within a half hour, the frantic activity would resume. Shore parties would load launch boats that carried supplies to the anchored ships before the sailors hoisted the provisions with winches to store the supplies in the holds. More German sailors would putter out from the shore with harbor craft jammed with troops. The Wehrmacht soldiers would board the three transport ships or the Siebel ferries. By noon, the 7 transports and 11 Siebel ferries would leave the harbor and head for Tunisia.

The Germans in and about the Bay of Naples had just eaten their morning meal and started to work when air raid alarms suddenly echoed over Naples Bay. Enemy aircraft approaching!

Shore parties darted for cover, while those

aboard the ships stiffened in fear, since they had nowhere to run. Civilians about the Bay of Naples shoreline also ran for cover while they once more cursed the Germans and Americans alike, the Germans for bringing this war to Naples and the Americans for dropping their bombs on this sunny Mediterranean city.

At the Aquino airbase, 22 Italian pilots hurried to their waiting MC 202 fighter planes to intercept these new American interlopers. At the Montecervino base, 12 German pilots rushed to their ME 109 fighters to take off. By 0610 hours the 34 Axis planes were zooming toward the approaching enemy bombers.

The airmen of the 350th U.S. Fighter Group waded quickly into the first formation of interceptors, the Italian MC 202s. The American P-47 pilots quickly shot down six of the Italian planes and scattered the remainder. The other Italian pilots zoomed away, unwilling to go after the bombers.

"Let's get the ME 109s," Col. Marv McNickle radioed his pilots.

Although the German pilots showed a willingness to fight, their 12 planes were no match for the more than 40 U.S. fighter planes. The 350th Group pilots waded into the German ranks and the odds more than three to one against them, the Luftflotte 2 airmen quickly lost eight of their planes to a loss of one P-47. The interceptors could not interfere with the 97th Group bomb run.

Soon, whistling bombs and clusters of incendiaries tumbled out of the B-17 bomb bays. The leading trio of 97th Group planes scored three hits, one on a transport and two on a 6400 ton freighter. By the time the first two squadrons of the 97th Group left the Bay of Naples, four of the merchant ships were either burning, sinking or badly damaged.

"Okay," Donovan yelled into his radio, "we've taken care of the merchant ships. 340th and 341st Squadron will go after those ferries."

"We read you, Colonel," Maj. Paul Tibbets said.

Then Major Tibbets led his squadron over the array of 500 ton Siebel ferries. "We hit in threes, in threes," he told his pilots.

When the trailing 97th Bomb Group squadrons dropped their bombs, most of them missed because the ferries were much more difficult to hit than the much larger merchant ships. Still, the 97th airmen made some damaging scores. Major Tibbets scored a hit on a ferry that left the vessel listing and burning. Other 97th crews scored two solid hits on a second ferry. The Siebel almost broke apart from the concussioning 1,000 pound explosions and the vessel quickly sank to the bottom of the Bay of Naples, taking half of the passengers and sailors with it. More 1,000 pounders damaged or sank six more of the Siebel ferries.

After the last 97th Group Flying Fortress left the area, total chaos prevailed in Naples Harbor. Only one merchant ship and two Siebel ferries were fit to sail. The Germans had suffered another severe blow. The all clear sirens brought German shore parties, Wehrmacht soldiers, and Italian civilians out of their shelters. They stared intently at the holocaust in the harbor. The Germans were depressed; all this work for the past two days had gone for nothing.

The Italians felt a little less angry. At least the Americans had been quite accurate this time, hitting only those targets in the harbor, with no errant bombs chopping up more of the city of Naples.

By 0700 hours, the B-17s of the 97th Bomb Group were far out to sea and droning back to North Africa. The P-47 cover from the 350th Fighter Group had jelled around and about these Forts for the long trip home.

Earlier, at Maddelena, the first streak of dawn had emerged from the east and shipboard cooks aboard the Italian destroyers in the harbor were getting ready to serve breakfast. They would start feeding the Italian sailors between 0630 and 0700 hours. But at 0600, sirens suddenly wailed across the naval base. Enemy bombers were approaching from the south. Sailors rushed to battle stations, while pilots at the Maddelena airbase hurried to their MC 202 fighter planes. Civilians, jerked from their sleep by the sudden air raid sirens, scooted into basement shelters and blasphemed the Americans for coming over so early to disrupt their sleep and possibly to tear up their town with errant bombs.

Lt. Col. Gordon Austin of the 325th Fighter Group soon enough saw the Axis planes coming toward the B-17 formations. The MC 202s were speeding toward the Forts at medium height. Austin called his pilots. "Bandits at twelve o'clock: high and lateral. Lead squadrons will challenge; tail squadrons will protect the bombers."

"Yes sir," Capt. John Simmons answered.

Austin took 30 of his P-47s to meet the enemy planes, while the remainder of the 325th Group Thunderbolts jelled around the bombers as the B-17s droned toward Maddelena Harbor.

Fortunately for the Flying Fortress crews, 34 U.S. fighter planes proved more than adequate to keep the enemy fighters at bay. The Italian pilots, despite their exceptional MC 202s, quickly panicked when the American P-47 pilots unleashed withering strafing fire and whooshing 20mm cannon shells. As soon as the U.S. airmen shot down a pair of the 202s, the other Italian pilots broke formation in uncertainty, hesitating, and leaving themselves vulnerable.

Maj. Bob Baseler of the 317th Squadron got three more quick kills, downing one MC 200 with shellfire that knocked off the tail of the Italian fighter. He got his next 202 with blistering machine gun fire that killed the Italian pilot, and he scored his third kill when he chewed away the wing of the enemy plane with 20mm shell hits.

With the half-hearted interception routed, the ships in the harbor below lay open to a high altitude attack. Italian warship commanders tried frantically to weigh anchors and get out of the harbor, but they would be too late.

Col. Fay Upthegrove looked intently at the destroyers below as the warships tried to work up steam. "We'll go over the harbor in threes," the 99th Bomb Group commander told his pilots. "Pick your targets and try to make every bomb count. We've got a break because our escorts have taken care of enemy interceptor planes."

The Italian sailors did unleash heavy AA fire from their destroyers and some of the flak proved quite accurate. Two 90mm shells blasted one Ninety-Niner B-17 out of the sky when the hits knocked off the left wing before the Flying Fort dropped like a jagged rock and plopped into the sea to explode. The burning, fragmented aircraft and its crew sank below the surface of the harbor. More AA fire hit a second B-17 and chopped off the tail before the heavy bomber tumbled downward toward the mountains beyond Maddelena Harbor. Three of the crew members bailed out to become German prisoners.

AA fire also damaged three more of the 99th Group B-17s, two of the planes seriously, while killing 17 crew members.

The 99th had not come over Maddelena unscathed. However, the Ninety-Niners soon took a heavy toll against the Italian warships. At 0600 hours, the bombardier on Colonel Upthegrove's lead plane cried into his radio.

"Bombs away!"

Whistling 1,000 pounders from the first trio of 99th Group planes fell into the bay. Among the dozen bombs, four of them struck home. One

1,000 pounder hit the destroyer *Crespi* on the bow and blew open a huge hole. Water cascaded into the forward area of the 2400 ton vessel. A second bomb, an incendiary cluster, struck the bridge area and set the topside afire. Sailors aboard the stricken vessel leaped over the sides and swam frantically toward shore.

The next wave of 99th Bomb Group planes, under Maj. Al Orance, unloaded another dozen thousand pounders, half of them incendiaries and half of them HEs. This time, four of the twelve bombs struck home. Within ten minutes, the 2700 ton destroyer *Monginevro* was aflame from bow to stern and settling rapidly to the bottom of Maddelena Harbor. Then more whistling bombs from the 99th sailed into the harbor, damaging two more of the Italian warships.

Maj. Harry Burrell, leading the 347th Squadron, came in next and kept his eye on a skimming destroyer that was trying to steam out to sea. But his quartet of bombs all scored, two direct hits and two near misses. The destroyer burst into flames, listed quickly to port, and would soon settle to the bottom of the bay. Other 347th Squadron planes caught a second destroyer, badly damaging the Italian warship with two hits.

By the time the 99th Group's B-17s droned away they had sunk three destroyers and damaged two more. The American airmen were satisfied.

At 0700 hours, the day of combat had just begun. Two U.S. medium bomb groups from NA-

TAF, the 12th and 320th made their runs over the Sidi Ahmed and El Aouina Airdromes. The B-25s gouged out holes in the two runways with 1,000 pound bombs. Their escorts, P-40s from the 57th Fighter Group under Col. Arthur Salisbury, had effectively held off German interceptors from the JG 51s III Gruppen out of Dejedeida, Tunisia. Salisbury and his Black Scorpion pilots quickly downed six of the fifteen ME 109s that had risen to challenge the B-25s.

At the same 0700 hours, 10 April, 37 FW 190s under Col. Edu Neumann of JG 27 were ready to take off from the Reggio de Calabria airdrome on the boot of Italy, while 22 FW 190s from JG 77 under Lt. Col. Johannes Steinhoff prepared to leave Trapani Airdrome in Sicily. However, the U.S. 310th Bomb Group arrived over Reggio as the FW 190s were forming up for take off. Whistling incendiary bombs from the American B-25 group quickly destroyed 31 of the German fighters on the ground. The escorting British Spitfire pilots from the 214 Wing had no need to fight off German interceptors. Neumann could only get off 16 Folke-Wulfs to escort the JU 52s now droning southward toward Tunisia.

Word had reached OSS headquarters in Algiers on the departure of the massive aerial transport fleets from Naples. Word from OSS agents out of Sicily had also reached Algiers, telling them that neither the giant Gigantens nor the JU 52s had stopped to stage from Comisco or Borrizo. Wild Bill Donovan guessed rightly that these new German air fleets would not stage out of Sicily, but would fly directly from Naples to Tunisia. He quickly sent a coded message to NASAF.

"You may expect large enemy air fleets over the Strait of Sicily within the next hour. Suggest you send out interceptors and escorts at once."

NASAF headquarters quickly notified the 14th Fighter Group that was out on the recon sweep. The headquarters operations personnel also notified the 321st Bomb Group and their 82nd Fighter Group escorts to divert their attack on Comiso. Instead, they would look for German transport planes that were apparently flying south over Sicily toward Tunisia.

CHAPTER NINE

At 0715 hours, the droning aircraft engines of three U.S. air groups echoed in the skies over the Mediterranean Sea: the 14th Fighter Group, 82nd Fighter Group, and 321st Bomb Group. The American pilots and crews were looking for the German transport planes that were apparently heading toward the Strait of Sicily.

The German transport pilots, of course, knew that swarms of American air groups had already pasted the Naples and Reggio air bases, as well as the Naples and Maddelena harbors. As a result, the new surface ship convoy would not sail for North Africa and Col. Edu Neumann had only mounted 18 FW 190s from his JG 27 to escort the formations of JU 52s. Neumann met the Junkers just short of Sicily's southern coast and he then joined the transports as they began their flight across the Strait of Sicily.

"We will protect the JU 52s as well as we can," Neumann told his fighter pilots. "I will personally maintain the high cover with I Gruppen and Major Rodel will maintain lateral cover with II Gruppen."

"Yes, Herr Neumann," Maj. Gustav Rodel answered.

"We will keep scouts ahead of us to report the approach of any enemy aircraft," Neumann continued, "although I am quite sure the enemy expected to destroy the transport aircraft in Naples. I doubt if they are waiting for the JU 52s over the sea and I believed we can arrive in Sicily without difficulty."

"Let us hope so, Colonel," Rodel answered.

In the lead JU 52 transport plane of KVT 16's II Gruppen, Maj. August Geiger stared from his cockpit window. He watched some of the FW 190s from J7 27 dart about the sky above him. But Geiger felt uneasy. He had heard the confident speeches about fooling the Americans this time, and he had heard the assurances that plenty of fighter escorts would accompany the transports, but he had not seen more than a dozen FW 190s around his Junkers. The skies should have been filled with German fighters. The disaster of five days ago again preyed on his mind and he would not feel relief until he landed these Junkers on Sidi Ahmed. He called Colonel Hagen.

"Herr Colonel, I do not see many fighters around us."

"Do not worry," Hagen answered, "more will be on the way. Still, remain alert and keep your formation tight."

"Yes, Colonel."

To the rear of this first aerial parade, Col. Johannes Steinhoff, leading 42 FW 190s from JG 277, had caught up to the 22 ME 323s above the Sicilian skies. He then called his pilots.

"It is imperative that we protect these Gigantens. Some of these huge aircraft are carrying a full company of men in their cargo area and others are carrying up to ten tons of supplies. I will maintain high cover with III Gruppen and Major Ehrler will maintain lateral cover with I Gruppen."

"I will do so, Colonel," Ehrler answered. "I have already sent out scouts to the west and to the east to scour the skies for any sign of enemy aircraft."

"We do not expect to see interceptors," Steinhoff said, "for it appears the enemy expected to destroy the transport aircraft on the ground in Italy or at the staging bases in Sicily. They did not expect us to fly directly to Tunisia. Nevertheless, Major, you are wise to keep scouts on our flanks."

Meanwhile, in the lead ME 323, Col. Lenz Kumrey peered out of the port window of the cockpit and stared at the fighter planes that hung in the sky like a protective ring. He felt a measure of confidence. Surely, these FW 190 pilots would deal with American interceptors, if any such U.S. planes found the transports at all. He too hoped they had deceived the Allies by flying directly to Tunisia instead of stopping to stage out of Sicily. Nonetheless, he called his ME 323 pilots.

"Please keep the formations tight; keep them tight. Gunners must remain on full alert."

"Yes, Herr Colonel," someone answered.

Meanwhile, in Tunisia, Maj. Erich Rudorffer of III/JG 51 was giving final instructions to his own ME 109 pilots. "The transports are on the way," he told his staffel leaders. "It appears they have successfully deceived the Americans and they will cross the strait without interception by enemy aircraft. It is our duty to protect the airdromes at Tunis since the enemy has unfortunately caused serious damage to the El Aouina and Sidi Ahmed Airdromes. We must also help out in escorting the transport aircraft into Tunisia."

"Do they not have escorts, Herr Rudorffer?" Lt. Heinrich Perzina asked.

"Yes," the major answered, "but they can never have too much protection. We will mount thirty-four aircraft at once. I will take 1 and 2 Staffels to protect the Tunis airfields, while Lieutenant Perzina will lead the 3 and 4 Staffels out to sea and join the escort planes coming from Sicily. I realize that this give us less than twenty aircraft each for these missions, but it is all we can spare and we must do what we can."

"Very well, Herr Major," Lieutenant Perzina said.

"1 and 2 Staffels will remain on aerial patrol

over the Tunis airfields for as long as necessary," Rudorffer continued, "until the JU 52s and ME 323s have landed safely."

"Or find themselves at the bottom of the sea," Perzina said bitterly.

The lieutenant from III/JG 51 had fought in North Africa for more than a year and he had seen the fortunes of Fleigerkorps Tunisien go from bad to worse, especially with the arrival of U.S. air groups. He had been fighting a losing battle in Tunisia for more than two months and now he saw only a more deteriorating situation in the weeks ahead.

"We must do what we can," Rudorffer said again, glaring at Perzina. "We will surely do badly with a defeatist attitude, Lieutenant. I must remind you that two hundred thousand Afrika Korps troops are depending on us."

"I'm sorry, Major," the 3 Staffel leader answered.

"We will mount our aircraft," the major said. "Perhaps, if we are fortunate, the Dornier bombers will accomplish their air mission of destroying enemy airfields in Tunisia."

In fact, 30 DO 17 bombers from KU 26 under Col. Bruno Dinort were again crossing the Strait of Sicily to hit the American fighter bases at Les Sers and Theleple, and the U.S. bomber base at Medinine. When Dinort crossed the north coast of Tunisia at 0730 hours, he picked up as escorts a German fighter unit from Tunis, 30 planes. Dinort watched the ME 109s jell around his bombers and he then called his Dornier pilots.

"I will take 1 Staffel to LeSers, Major Unger will take 2 Staffel to Theleple, and Major Weiss will attack the American bomber base at Medinine with his 3 Staffel."

"Yes, Herr Colonel," Major Unger answered.

Dinort then called the fighter leader. "We will need escorts to three targets."

"Very well, Colonel."

Then ten ME 109s peeled off to join each of the Dornier staffels as the KG 26 units broke off to attack the three American bases. The German bomber pilots would be making their runs in about 20 minutes. But when the Dorniers reached their airfields, they found few parked planes. Long before the DO 17s had crossed the Tunisian coast, the B-25s from the 12th Bomb Group at Medinine had gone off on its bombing mission with the 57th Fighter Group out of Le-Sers as escort. More U.S. and RAF fighter planes of Les Sers and Theleple had gone off on CAPs over the African coast.

But the lack of planes on the ground may have been fortunate, for Dinort met little opposition. Only the RAF 92 Squadron from the 211 Group mounted planes to meet these bombers and while they downed four of the Dorniers, the other Dorniers made their runs over the Allied airfields.

Col. Bruno Dinort felt a mixture of disappointment and relief over Les Sers. He found few parked planes but no interceptors, either. He came in low with his 12 bombers, punching holes in the runway and destroying two service buildings, while Allied ground crews darted for cover.

At the Theleple field, American and British ground crews had similarly scattered and lived into foxhole shelters while Maj. Gunther Unger swept over the field with his 12 Dorniers to chop up the runway and to hit installations. Unger left three service buildings burning and two wrecked planes on the air base. And finally, KG 26s 3 Staffel raked the medium bomber base at Medinine where the Dornier pilots destroyed only four B-25s and a pair of C-47 transport planes on the ground, while setting afire a repair shop and chopping holes in the runway.

As the German bomber crews departed Tunisia and headed toward Sicily, most of the German airmen felt satisfaction. They had extracted vengeance against the Americans who had been pelting them so badly for the past couple of months.

Meanwhile, the two transport plane formations, about 15 minutes apart, had cleared Sicily and were flying on a 219° bearing and heading for Tunisia. NASAF had then ordered all U.S. air groups on alert, while radioing the 14th, 82nd, and 321st Groups to intensify their search for the German transport planes in the Strait of Sicily. Unfortunately for the German KVT 16 and KVT 5 transport formations, they were on a collision course with the three American air groups.

At 0800 hours, Lt. Col. Tony Keith of the 14th Fighter Group spotted the long line of JU 52s heading south. He could also see the handful of 190 fighters around the Junkers. The Avenger group commander quickly called his pilots.

"Targets are dead ahead. There must be thirty or forty Junkers in tight formation and flying low. 48th Squadron will take the escorts; 49th and 37th Squadrons will deal with the transport planes."

"We're on our way," Maj. Lou Benne of the 49th Squadron answered.

Moments later, Tony Keith took his 48th Squadron pilots upward and the Avengers waded into the German 190s with their 12 P-38s. Col. Edu Neumann of JG 27 stared at the oncoming Lightnings and he called his own pilots.

"Enemy fighters! We will attack in pairs!"

But 18 FW 190s could not cope with 36 Lightnings. While many of these German pilots were experienced combat airmen, most of them were hastily trained newcomers. JG 27 had lost many of their best pilots during the Mediterranean campaign. The Americans had been well trained and what they lacked in lesser combat experience, they made up in daring and aggressiveness.

For ten minutes, the din of machine gun fire, bursting 20mm and 37mm shells, and whining aircraft echoed across the sky. Not only had the Avenger pilots of the U.S. 14th Fighter Group mauled JG 27 in the aerial dogfight, but the Americans of the 14th's 48th Squadron had stopped any of Neumann's airmen from interfering with the American pilots who waded into the JU 52s.

In the diving, darting dogfight over the Mediterranean, the 14th Group pilots downed eleven of the German 190s, while losing four P-38s of their own. Maj. Bill Lovelette of the 48th Squadron got two Folke Wulfs. He caught one plane with strafing fire, blowing away the cockpit and killing the pilot. He got his second kill when a pair of 37mm shells blew off the tail of the 190 and the aircraft plopped into the sea.

Capt. Herb Ross and Lt. Carroll Knott of the same 48th Squadron also got a pair of kills. Ross knocked the engine off one 190 before the plane wobbled downward and crashed into the sea. He got his second kill when he chopped off the wing of the Folke Wulf with 37mm shell hits. Lieutenant Knott got his two kills in a single pass, shooting down one plane with heavy strafing fire and blowing apart the second German aircraft with 37mm shells that opened the fuselage and ignited the gas tanks.

Of the four American kills, Col. Edu Neumann got one when he caught a P-38 in his sights and chopped away the fuselage with chattering machine gun fire. The formidable Maj. Gustav Rodel got two of the German kills. Rodel downed his first Lightning when he deftly turned and tailed the unsuspecting American pilot before blowing away the tail of the American plane. The P-38 plunged into the sea. The major got his second kill when he roared down from above the chattering wing fire shattered the Lightning cockpit to kill the pilot. Lt. Wolfgang Fisher got the fourth JG 27 kill when he climbed high, then dove rapidly and caught a Lightning with three solid shell hits.

Still, the lopsided score forced Colonel Neumann to break off the fight. He took his surviving JG 27 pilots to the eastward, hoping to reform his ranks before taking on the American pilots again. However, before he could do so, other P-38 pilots from the 14th Fighter Group would ruin the transports.

"Hit those planes in pairs," Lt. Col. Tony Keith cried into his radio. "Stick with your wingmen and attack in tandem."

"Yes sir," Maj. Lou Benne of the 49th Squadron answered.

Maj. August Geiger, leading the forward Junker formation, stared at the oncoming U.S. fighter planes in horror. He knew at once that he would suffer the same kind of disaster that had befallen him five days ago. He could easily see that the escorting 190 fighters had failed to contain the Americans. Now, Geiger and the other I Gruppen transport pilots would become helpless victims of the P-38s.

In pairs, the Lightning pilots from the 14th Avenger Fighter Group zoomed into the transport ranks, unleashing chattering machine gun fire and 37mm shells. Again, one after another of the JU 52s fell from the sky. Some of the Junkers exploded from solid hits, others lost engines, tails, or wings from exploding shells, and still others burst into flames from incendiary tracer hits. For nearly 15 minutes the 14th Group pilots roared into the helpless Junker transport planes, shooting down 21 of them and damaging at least six more.

Some of the Avenger pilots enjoyed multiple kills. Maj. Lou Benne and his wingman shot down three of the Junkers as did Capt. Jim Griffith and his wingman. Lt. Dick Howe got one as did many of the other pilots from the 49th and 37th Squadrons.

Benne and his wingman caught the first Junker with exploding 37mm shells that ripped open the fuselage and both pilots gaped as they saw German soldiers tumbling out of the fractured plane and plopping into the sea before the plane itself splashed in the water. They got their second JU 52 with blistering machine gun fire that set the aircraft afire before the plane crashed into the sea in a sizzle of smoke and fire. On the second pass, Benne and his wingman came back in tandem, with blistering machine gun fire, chopping segments of the JU 52s three engines. The Junker plopped into the sea.

Captain Griffith and his wingman from the 37th Squadron got their first two planes on the first pass, chopping off the tail of one Junker with blazing machine gun fire and then igniting the gas tank of the second with exploding 37mm shells. Both planes plopped into the sea. On their next run, they cut off the wing of the JU-52 that simply cartwheeled and plopped into the sea.

Lieutenant Howe got his kill when he smashed the cockpit with 37mm shell hits, killing pilot and co-pilot. The Junker wobbled on for several hundred yards and then fell into the sea.

In the rear KVT 16 formation, Col. Walter Hagen had watched the attacks in the same horror as did Major Geiger. He too had seen one after another of his transport planes explode in mid-air, fall apart from 37mm explosions, or burst into flames before they fell into the blue Mediterranean. Hagen, like Major Geiger, had been among the few pilots to escape with their JU 52s.

Fortunately for the Germans, the American P-38 pilots had finally run out of 37mm shells and they needed to reserve at least some of the machine gun bullets in the event they got jumped by German fighters. The thirteen JU 52s that escaped the slaughter, some of them badly damaged, streaked on toward Tunisia. However Col. Walter Hagen would not get all of his 13 surviving planes safely down on Tunisian airbases.

A disappointed Tony Keith called his pilots. "There's nothing more we can do here, boys. Let's go home."

"Yes sir," Maj. Lou Benne answered.

Meanwhile, the pilots and crews of the U.S. 82nd Fighter Group and the 321st Bomb Group were still scouring the waters south of Sicily at 0930 hours, when a vanguard scout from the 82nd Group spotted the huge ME 323 formation with its fighter escorts. The pilot ogled at the gigantic planes and he then called Col. Bill Covington, the 82nd Group commander.

"Sir, only five minutes to the west, on a 211 bearing—a huge enemy aerial fleet is heading south. Damn it, Colonel, I never saw planes as big as those."

"Hang on, we're on our way," Covington answered.

Both the 82nd pilots and the 321st Bomb Group pilots sped westward. Only a few minutes later, Covington saw the huge ME 323s that were flying in formations of three plane Vs. The 82nd Group colonel ogled in fascination at the giant six engine planes. He had never seen anything like them. They looked big enough to carry a warehouse full of supplies or a whole company of men. The 82nd Group CO had also been the 190 fighters that seemed dwarfed alongside the ME 323s. Covington called Lt. Col. Ed Olmstead of the 321st Bomb Group.

"Colonel, the targets are straight ahead, and goddamn, they're the biggest things I've ever seen in the sky. You'll need to do a lot of shooting to knock one of those suckers down."

"We've got ten forward firing guns on these B-25s," Olmstead answered confidently. "We'll knock those bastards down."

"I'm sending my 95th Squadron after the escorts, while the rest of us deal with the transports," Covington said.

"Okay," the 321st Group Ruinator commander answered.

Col. Johannes Steinoff of JG 77 saw the squadron of American fighter planes coming toward his own fighter formation, while the other U.S. planes roared toward the transports. He called his pilots. "Enemy fighters! We must attack in pairs. They must not reach the transport aircraft."

"Yes, Colonel," Maj. Henrich Ehrler said.

The JG 77 airmen fared no better against these

P-38 airmen from the 82nd Group as had the JG 27 pilots agains the U.S. pilots of the 14th Fighter Group. The Americans were again more aggressive and eager than the German pilots, most of whom were inexperienced replacements, since JG 77 had also suffered the loss of many experienced pilots during more than two years of war in the Mediterranean. The whine of darting planes, the rumble of shells, and the chatter of machine gun fire echoed across the sky. Within a half hour, JG 77 lost 16 of its FW 190s and suffered damage to ten more. The Blue Gulls of the 82nd Group lost seven P-38s and sustained damage to five more planes. This second lopsided victory had again thwarted German pilots from interfering with the U.S. pilots who were speeding toward the transport planes.

Capt. Jim Lynn of the 82nd's 95th Squadron had scored one kill when he got a 190 with chattering machine gun fire that set the plane afire before the German plane plunged into the sea. Lt. Frank Lawson of the same Blue Gull squadron scored an astonishing three kills in a matter of minutes. Lawson got his first score when he came down on an FW 190 and laced the fuselage with incendiary machine gun tracers. The plane burst into flames but the German pilot luckily bailed out before the flaming aircraft plunged into the sea. The lieutenant got his second kill when a pair of 37mm shells hit and exploded to blow the 190 apart. His third kill came from chattering machine gun fire that ripped off the tail of the Folke Wulf.

Lt. Bill Schilde of the 82nd Group got two kills in the same pass. He had tailed one FW 190 and destroyed the fuselage with exploding 37mm hits. As the German fighter plane went down, Schilde got a second 190 in his sights and set the plane afire with short bursts of machine gun fire. The Blue Gull pilot then soared high and came down on another JG 77 fighter, ripping the FW 190 apart with machine gun fire before the German plane plunged into the sea.

Among the German pilots, Col. Johannes Steinhoff got two kills. He downed one P-38 when he hit the plane squarely with shellfire and tore apart the fuselage. He got the second kill with chattering machine gun fire that tore off the left wing of the Lightning

Maj. Henrich Ehrler also got two kills when he barrel-rolled out of sight from one tailing P-38 and he then came down into the rear of a second Lightning. He chopped off the tail of the American plane with exploding shells. Ehrler then jinked his plane away from two American pursuers, made a sharp turn, and tailed a prey of his own. He knocked down the plane with machine gun fire that cut away the tail of the Lightning. Lt. Heinz Berre got the fifth U.S. plane when he deftly escaped two American pilots, climbed high, and came down on a surprised U.S. airmen. He shattered the cockpit of the P-38, killing the pilot.

The seven German kills had been small consolation for the loss of 16 planes and the disabling of ten more. Despite the odds of more than two to one against the 82nd Group's 95th Squadron, the Americans had again proven themselves and their P-38s superior to the German pilots and their FW 190 fighter planes.

Colonel Steinhoff, like Neumann, took his surviving JG 77 pilots out of the fight in the hope of regrouping them to battle the American Blue Gull pilots again. But he would also be too late.

The P-38s of the Blue Gull group's 96th and 97th Squadron, along with the 18 B-25s of the 321st Ruinator Group, were now wading into the giant ME 323 transport planes, sending streaking shells and chattering machine gun fire into the huge aerial monsters. However, the German transport planes were not only big, but quite strong and durable. The P-38 pilots made several passes at the same plane, attacking in pairs, before they could finally drop one of the ME 323s into the sea. But the tenacious Blue Gull pilots came back again and again with their P-38s until they had exhausted shells and ammunition.

"We were probably stupid," Col. Bill Covington admitted later. "If we got jumped by bandits over the battle area or on the way home, we couldn't fight back."

However, the dangerous tactic of using up all ammunition paid off for the Blue Gulls of the 82nd shot down nine of the huge ME 323s and damaged more.

The B-25s of the 321st Ruinator Group, however, proved much more effective. Like the 310th, the 321st had also switched over from medium bombing to low level attack bombing. The

321st had also begun using skip bomb strategies at low level, replacing the navigator compartment in the nose with ten forward firing machine guns. The Ruinators had been out today to bomb an airfield so they had carried 500 pounders instead of skip bombs, and these bombs were no good against the droning ME 323s. However, the heavy armament of ten forward guns carried much more firepower than the P-38s.

Lt. Col. Ed Olmstead took his B-25s into the droning six engine transport planes in tandem pairs, with the first Mitchell slamming the target with murderous multiple machine gun bursts before the tandem B-25 followed with more heavy strafing fire to finish off the plane. The 321st Group soon knocked down eight of the huge Gigantens with their blistering fire.

Lieutenant Colonel Olmstead and his tandem wingman got two of the huge transports as did Lt. Hank Bell and his wingman downed two of the Gigantens. Further, Bell's gunners, Sgt. Joe Stanton and Sgt. Glen Mays, downed two of the attacking FW 190 escorts. Maj. Ellis Cook, Maj. Dick Smith, Capt. Frank Schwane, and Lt. Jim Martin of the 321st Group had also downed one of the big transport planes, while Schwane's gunner, Sgt. Larry Rider, downed an FW 190.

When their assault had ended, Covington called Lieutenant Colonel Olmstead. "We did a good job on those giants. We got most of them, but our P-38s haven't got many bullets left, or shells. We'll need the rest of our strafing ammo in case we run into more bandits. I think we better return to base."

"You'll need to stick by us like parasites," Lieutenant Colonel Olmstead said.

"Will do," Covington answered.

Thus did this second massacre end over the Strait of Sicily. The four surviving ME 323s and 14 JU 52s droned on toward Tunisia. Both Col. Lenz Kumrey, one of the lucky Giganten survivors, and Col. Walter Hagen hoped they could reach their transport airfields without further assaults by American planes. But the limping transport planes would find more trouble before they reached safety.

The 12th Bomb Group under Col. Ed Backus had already decimated the El Aouina and Sidi Ahmed airfields and even now, Lt. Col. Dan Loftus with 36 Spitfires from his 7 SAAF Wing had streaked toward the Gulf of Tunis to intercept the surviving JU 52s and ME 323s. Loftus and his South Africans had been on CAP when they learned that the German transport planes had been intercepted by the American air groups, and that remnants of these aerial convoys were droning on to Tunisia. The 7 SAAF Wing leader had thus altered course.

Fortunately for Colonel Hagen of KVT 16 and Colonel Kumrey of KVT 5, Maj. Erich Rudorffer had mustered 24 ME 109s from III/JG 51 out of Dejedeida, Tunisia to intercept the Spitfires. Rudorffer had not broken the 7 Wing completely but he had stalled them. In the dogfight over the Tunisian desert, the Germans downed six of the Spitfires to a loss of six of their own. But the 7 Wing pilots could afford these losses, where Rudorffer could not. Nonetheless, Rudorffer had disorganized the 7 SAAF Wing badly enough to reduce their effectiveness against the German transport planes.

However, at least 24 of the 7 Wing fighters reached the battered transport formations and Loftus cried into his radio. "Hit them in tandem!"

"Yes sir," Maj. Edward Parsonson of 5 Squadron answered.

"We'll take the Junkers," Loftus said, "and 5 Squadron can take on the monsters. 4 Squadron will stay upstairs to keep an eye out for Jerry fighters."

"Yes sir," Lt. John Green said.

The 16 Spitfires under Lieutenant Colonel Loftus hit the transport planes. Unfortunately, the South African Wing had expended most of its ammunition in the dogfights with III/JG 51. So they were only able to bring down two of the ME 323s and two of the JU 52s. But even the Lufttransport Mittelmeer survivors did not fare well. Colonel Kumrey belly-landed on a North African beach and thus only one ME 323 out of 22 landed safely at Tunis without damage.

However, 12 of the JU 52s landed safely in Tunis without damage, including the aircrafts of Walter Hagen and August Geiger.

Thus did the Germans suffer another disastrous day. They had lost a horde of vessels in the harbors, most of the transport planes heading for Tunisia, serious destruction at El Aouina, Sidi Ahmed, Naples, and Sicily airfields, and major installations. And finally, American and 7 Wing airmen had destroyed 117 German and Italian planes in the air and on the ground during this 10 April 1943 morning.

CHAPTER TEN

Field Marshal Albert Kesselring found himself in a most unenviable position by the evening of 10 April, with heat from Berlin searing the communication lines between Germany and Naples. Gen. Alfred Jodl had drawn the job of scolding the Luftflotte 2 CinC for this second debacle within five days. The OKW chief severely chastised Kesselring with a deluge of questions: How could this kind of disaster recur? Why hadn't Kesselring taken better precautions? What happened to the Luftflotte 2 fighter pilots who were supposedly the best in the world?

Kesselring reminded Jodl that enemy spies were rampant throughout the Mediterranean and Jodl concurred. "We know that these spies have had considerable influence on these disasters. Therefore, we intend to do something about them. We are sending a team of SS men to OB Sud to deal with these agents who have been reporting your every move to the Allies."

"Yes, Herr Jodl."

"Col. Heinz Jost, a most capable intelligence man, will soon arrive in Naples to take charge of security measures," Jodl said.

After the reprimand from Berlin, the Luftflotte 2 CinC called a conference with his subordinate Luftwaffe commanders: General Buchholtz of Lufttransport Mittelemeer, General Trautloft of Fleigerkorps II fighter command, and General Hammhuber of Fleigerkorps Sud-Ost bomber command.

"I'm sure I need not tell you that Berlin is infuriated," Kesselring said. "The Fuhrer is enraged with these disasters. OKW chief Alfred Jodl has warned me that severe changes would come if we do not avoid further defeats such as the one we suffered today. We must do more to assure a flow of supplies to Tunisia. General von Arnim must have men and provisions."

None of the subordinates answered.

"Berlin is sending an SS Gestapo unit into Naples under one Col. Heinz Jost," Kesselring continued. "This man will make every effort to find these spies and do something about them."

"Herr Field Marshal," General Buchholtz said, "the last thing we need is a Gestapo purge. We have enough problems with partisans and up to this point, the Italian populace has been at least indifferent. They have not interfered with our activities. If the Gestapo conducts harassments here, hordes of Italians will defect to the partisans to make our position more difficult."

"I agree with General Buchholtz," General Trautloft said. "We do not need the Gestapo in Italy or Sicily to cause problems among the civilians and perhaps from our own airmen. Morale is low enough and an SS nuisance would only make things worse."

"I have no control in this matter," Kesselring said. "My orders are to give this Colonel Jost every cooperation, and I warn you all to do the same."

"When will the Gestapo be here?"

"Within the next day or two," Kesselring said.

"Herr Field Marshal," Buchholtz said, "What of the aerial convoy that is due to leave tomorrow? We have loaded 34 JU 52s that carry badly needed medicine, ammunition, and foodstuffs."

"They will fly out as scheduled," Kesselring said. "We will also send out oil tankers from Trapani Harbor, four vessels. The fighters from JG 77 will furnish escort for the tanker convoy, although Colonel Steinhoff will need at least two staffels of aircraft to protect Trapani Harbor. Colonel Neumann at Reggio plans to mount fighters from his jagdgeschwader to escort the transport aircraft." He looked at General Trautloft. "Is that not correct?"

"Yes," the Fleigerkorps II CinC answered. "JG 27 will mount two staffels of fighters for escort duty."

Kesselring nodded. "Please return to your

units and alert your subordinates that Gestapo SS may come into their camps to question them. While they should be discreet, your airmen must cooperate."

"Yes, Herr Field Marshal," Trautloft said.

Whether or not the Gestapo could stop the Allied spy network in Axis held islands of the central Mediterranean was mere conjecture. However, on the evening of 10-11 April, Wild Bill Donovan's OSS agents were as active as ever. They had observed the loading of four big tankers in Trapani Harbor until the oilers lay low in the water with countless tons of vitally needed oil for the Afrika Korps. Other Allied spies had accurately guessed that JG 77 could only mount 20-25 planes as escorts, all that were available at Trapani after the losses in aerial dogfights and the losses in the Allied air attacks on the Trapani airfield.

Donovan's spies had also concluded correctly that about 30 to 40 tri-engine Junker transport planes were preparing for take-off from the Capodichino Airdrome in Naples. The JU 52s would probable leave in the pre-dawn, before any high level American heavy bombers could attack the airfield. The agents also reported that FW 190 fighter aircraft had been loading up at Reggio de Calabria, perhaps 20 or 30 of them, to apparently escort these transport planes into Tunisia.

When OSS headquarters in Algiers relayed these agent reports to NASAF, Gen. James Doolittle assigned four of his air groups to deal with these apparent new German attempts to reinforce Tunisia. He ordered the 99th Bomb Group to knock out the tankers in Trapani Harbor, with the 14th Fighter Group escorting the B-17s. The NASAF CinC then ordered the 82nd Fighter Group to make a recon sweep in Sicily and along that island's coast to report any Junker transport formations. He then ordered the 1st Fighter Group to also make sweeps in and around Tunisia. Finally, Doolittle once more called on NATAF to beef up its CAPs from 211 Group off the coast of Sicily.

By 0300 hours, 11 April, U.S. group commanders were briefing their airmen. At Navarin, Algeria, Col. Fay Upthegrove outlined the target at Trapani Harbor, referring to a map pinned on the wall behind him.

"As you can see," he told the Ninety-Niner airmen, "there are four good sized oilers in the harbor, along with a few other ships and some harbor craft. Our job is to hit the tankers. According to intelligence reports, the Germans have finished loading these oilers and the ships will probably sail tomorrow. NASAF doesn't want any of these vessels to reach Tunisia."

The Ninety-Niner airmen listened.

"Now," Upthegrove gestured, "please study the recon reports carefully because it shows the location of each target vessel in the harbor. The 346th Squadron will attack the first tanker, here," he tapped the chart. "Major Burrell's 347th Squadron has this tanker, and Major Whitmore this one here. Major Orance's 416th will attack this last one," Upthegrove tapped a lower part of the map.

"Are we carrying incendiaries?" Major Orance asked.

"Both," the colonel answered. "Two thousand pound incendiaries and two big HE thousand pounders. That should give us plenty of weight to set the targets afire and to knock them apart."

"Yes sir," Orance answered.

"The 14th Fighter Group will furnish escort," Upthegrove continued, "and I'm told they'll have over fifty planes. Intelligence says the Germans have about thirty FW 190s around Trapani, so the 14th should be able to deal with them quite easily." He sighed. "Okay, unless there are questions, let's mount up."

At Telergma, Algeria, at the same wee morning hour of 11 April, Lt. Col. Tony Keith briefed 51 Lightning pilots of his 14th Fighter Group. "We're going to Trapani this morning as esscort for the 99th Bomb Group. These B-17s are hitting some oilers in the harbor, and we've got to protect them against any German interceptors. Fortunately, the Germans only have two or three dozen available fighters at Trapani so we should be able to contain them during the B-17 bomb runs."

Maj. Lou Benne of the 49th Squadron frowned. "Colonel, are you sure the Germans only have that few planes in the area? It's my understanding that they have a full geschwader there."

"They did have," Keith grinned, "but that geschwader has suffered a lot of attrition. According to OSS agents, the German fighter unit at Milo/Trapani has not received any replacement aircraft or pilots to replenish their losses."

Major Benne nodded.

Lieutenant Colonel Keith now referred to a map on the wall behind him. "As usual, we'll rendezvous with the bombers at latitude 35.60 north and longitude 12.60 east over the Strait of Sicily. We'll take the B-17s all the way in and out." He then looked at Capt. Jim Griffith of the 37th Squadron. "Captain, your squadron will take the high cover and scout positions."

"Yes sir," Griffith answered.

Keith looked at his watch. "You have time for breakfast. We'll be taking off at about 0400 hours, meet the bombers at 0500, and reach IP at about 0600. Please synchronize your watches."

The airmen of the Avenger fighter group responded. When the briefing ended, the 51 U.S. fighter pilots moved off to breakfast.

At Berteaux Field, Algeria, 52 pilots from the 82nd Fighter Group had been on the ready all during the evening of 10 April and into the wee hours of 11 April. OD men at group headquarters had remained alert for messages from Roman to send off their P-38s on armed recon sweeps. Similarly at Rhumel, Algeria, OD men of the 1st Fighter Group had been on alert for a Roman message. The call came at 0300 hours

181

to make sweeps in and around Sicily and both American fighter groups prepared for take off.

At 0400 hours, far to the north at Trapani, Col. Johannes Steinhoff felt uneasy. He knew that the four heavily loaded tankers sat in the harbor and would leave for Tunisia at mid-morning. He also knew that Allied snoopers had no doubt relayed information on these oil-ers and the JG 77 kommandant rightfully sus-pected that the Americans might send a bomb group to Trapani before the big tankers left port with their precious fuel.

Steinhoff took count in his badly decimated geschwader and he found only 32 FW 190s in combat ready condition. These few planes were not much to defend against a U.S. bomber for-mation and a probable full fighter group as es-cort. Nonetheless, at 0500 hours, he met with Maj. Heinrich Ehrler of his I Gruppen and Maj. Kurt Uben of his II Gruppen.

"Do not be surprised if enemy bombers come over Trapani Harbor at daylight today," he told his subordinates. "The enemy would no doubt like to sink these tankers before the ships can sail for Tunisia. Therefore, we must be on alert."

"But we have only thirty fighters fit for com-bat," Uben said.

"They will have to suffice," Steinhoff an-swered. "We were promised replacements. But such new aircraft and crews cannot be deliv-ered overnight."

"Herr Colonel," Major Ehrler said, "surely,

Luftflotte 2 must realize that the tankers in the harbor are inviting targets for enemy bombers. Could they not send at least a few reinforcement staffels to Trapani while we await new planes?"

"I asked for some," Steinhoff said, "but I was told that none were available."

Ehrler did not answer.

"We must be ready," Steinhoff continued. "We will mount our aircraft if or when our radar picks up any approaching enemy aircraft."

To the northeast, at Reggio de Calabria, on the heel of Italy's boot, Col. Edu Neumann also held a conference with his gruppen kommandants at 0500. While not as badly depleted as JG 77, JG 27 only counted about 40 FW 190s available for combat. Neumann had received word at 0400 that 40 transport planes would leave Naples at 0500 hours. His Folke Wulfs would pick them up over the Strait of Sicily and escort them into Tunisia. The Junkers were carrying medicine and other vitally needed supplies for the Afrika Korps.

Neumann now gave his gruppen kommandants last minute instructions. "Major Rodel will take the fighters of his II Gruppen as high cover and as scouts. I will lead I Gruppen on the starboard lateral and Hauptman Fisher will assume the port lateral with the aircraft of III Gruppen."

"I only have twelve available aircraft, Herr Neumann," Capt. Wolfgang Fisher of III Gruppen said. "Will this be enough?"

"It will have to do," Neumann answered. He shuffled through some papers in front of him before he spoke again. "Please return to your units and make sure your pilots are ready. We will get a call as soon as the transport planes leave Italy. They will endeavor to fly directly south to Tunisia, without staging in Sicily."

"Yes, Herr Colonel."

To the north, at Capodichino Field in Naples, the 34 JG 52s had been fully loaded by 0400 hours. The transport planes carried over 100 tons of provisions that included medicine, food, ammunition, clothing, and other supplies.

Gen. Ulrich Buchholtz himself gave last minute instructions to his 34 transport pilots because both Colonel Hagen and Major Geiger were luckily somewhere in Tunisia after the rout yesterday. "I realize that the KVT 16 geschwader has suffered serious losses in recent days and no doubt there are many among you who are quite uneasy this morning. Still, we must remember that our soldiers of the Afrika Korps are suffering terribly, and they need every pound of provisions we can send them. Therefore, we must do all we can to deliver whatever we can. These JU 52s will leave Naples at 0500 hours. You will rendezvous with forty fighter escorts over Sicily to continue the flight into North Africa."

"Only forty escorts, mein General?" somebody asked.

"Unfortunately, these are all that are available," Buchholtz answered. "But the fighters are from JG 27 and these pilots are very good. If anyone can protect you, it will be the airmen of Colonel Neumann's jagdgeschwader." The Lufttransport Mittelmeer CinC then gestured. "You flight leaders, be sure to keep a tight, close formation. I can only say, good luck to all of you."

At 0500 hours, just before dawn, the first trio of JU 52s wheeled into the head of the Capodichino runway before zooming down the strip and into the air. By the time the first hint of daylight emerged from over the Alpinine Mountains to the east, the last of the 34 Junker transport planes had taken off. Before the JU 52s were out of sight, Franklin agents had sent their coded messages to OSS headquarters in Algiers: "34 loaded, tri-engine transports have left Capodichino between 0500 and 0515 hours."

As soon as the reports arrived from Italy, Wild Bill Donovan contacted agents in Sicily regarding the transport airfields. Were ground crews at these German fields in Borrizo and Comiso preparing the airdromes for the arrival of transport aircraft? Pilgrim agents in both areas reported negative: did not appear that JU 52s would land in Sicily. Donovan then sent a coded Roman message to NASAF headquarters. In turn, NASAF sent coded messages to the 82nd and 1st Fighter Groups.

"Prepare to intercept enemy transport planes over the Strait of Sicily at about 0800 hours."

185

At 0700 hours, Col. Bill Covington of the 82nd Fighter Group scrambled his 51 Lightning pilots and by 0720 hours all of the P-38s had taken off from Barteaux Field and droned north, northeast toward the Strait of Sicily. At 0730 hours, Col. Ralph Gorman scrambled 49 pilots from his 1st Fighter Group at Rhumel, Algeria. By 0750 hours, the 49 Lightnings were off and also heading north, northeast toward the Strait of Sicily.

Meanwhile, by 0700 hours, 34 B-17s of the 99th Bomb Group were approaching Trapani on the western tip of Sicily. 52 Lightnings of the 14th Fighter Group hung around and above the Flying Fortresses. At 0710 hours, sirens wailed across the Sicily seaport: enemy bombers approaching from the south. German ack ack gunners hurried to their gun pits, while pilots from JG 77 rushed to their waiting FW 190 fighter planes.

By 0730 hours, 30 German fighters were streaking south to meet the enemy bombers. Soon enough, Col. Johannes Steinhoff saw the B-17s in the distance, but he also noted the horde of P-38s above and around the Flying Forts. The JG 77 kommandant scowled. From his observations, he believed the American escort unit outnumbered his interceptors by close to two to one. He knew instinctively that a hard time lay ahead and that he and his pilots were not likely to break the Lightning screen to reach the bombers. Nonetheless, Steinhoff called his airmen.

"I Gruppen will attempt to reach bombers, while II and III Gruppen will attack the enemy escort planes."

"Yes, Herr Colonel," Maj. Kurt Oben answered.

But Lt. Col. Tony Keith of the 14th Fighter Group had also seen the oncoming FW 190s. He called his own pilots. "Bandits straight ahead at twelve o'clock high. 48th Squadron will maintain lateral protection of B-17s; 49th and 37th Squadrons will attack the interceptors."

"Yes sir, Colonel," Maj. Bill Lovelette of the 48th Squadron said.

"Will do, sir," Maj. Lou Benne of the 49th Squadron said.

While Lovelette tightened the ring of P-38s from his squadron around the B-17s, Lieutenant Colonel Keith and Major Benne roared forward with the remaining 37 Lightnings of the Avenger group's 49th and 37th Squadron. Moments later, the rumble of gunfire rattled across the sky as the U.S. P-38 pilots and German FW 190 pilots clashed in still another dogfight over the Mediterranean Sea.

In a replay of earlier battles in this Operation Flax vs Operation Bulls Head campaign, the German airmen again came out second best. Lt. Col. Tony Keith got a 190 when he dove down on the unsuspecting Folke-Wulf pilot and sliced off the left wing of the German plane with chattering machine gun fire. Maj. Lou Benne got two German fighters, tailing the first

190 and ripping apart the tail with machine gun fire. He got his second kill when he shattered the cockpit of the Folke-Wulf with bursting 37mm shell hits. The explosion killed the Luftwaffe pilot before the 190 tumbled into the sea.

Even Capt. Jim Griffith got two kills among the few 190s that broke through the fighter screen. He shattered one German plane with two 37mm shell hits that blew away the fuselage. He got his second when he tore off the engine of the 190 with exploding 37mm shells. Meanwhile, Sgt. Joe McKirk, aboard Maj. Al Orance's B-17, also got an FW 190 with chattering machine gun fire from his top turret position.

The Germans downed four of the P-38s. Col. Johannes Steinhoff got a Lightning as did Maj. Heinrich Ehrler. Maj. Kurt Uben and Lt. Edgar Berre, along with Lt. Ernst Reinert, also downed American planes. Steinhoff downed his P-38 when he chopped the Lightning's tail apart and the plane tumbled into the sea. Ehrler got his kill when he blew away the wing of the Lightning with exploding shells. Uben riddled to pieces the tail section of a P-38 with heavy machine gun fire. Berre, after eluding two pursuers, came down and blew open the fuselage of a P-38 with exploding 20mm shells. Reinert got the last kill with shell hits that knocked off the twin tails of the Lightning before the P-38 spun into the blue Mediterranean below.

However, the dogfight had cost JG 77 14 FWs lost and several 190 damaged. Steinhoff had no alternative but to break off the interception.

Meanwhile, the B-17s droned over Trapani Harbor from heights of 25,500 down to 24,500. The Flying Fortresses unloaded their 60 plus tons of bombs into Trapani Harbor. Among Colonel Upthegrove's lead trio of B-17s, they scored four hits that left a tanker completely engulfed in fire and dense smoke. The tanker was finished. Maj. Harry Burrell scored two hits on another ship, opening holes in the prow. The tanker then listed badly. In the next trio of B-17s, Capt. Dean Shields, bombardier aboard "Yankee Doodle," hit the listing oiler squarely with two bombs and the battered tanker began settling to the bottom of the harbor.

From the 416th Squadron, Maj. Al Orance's lead trio of planes scored five hits on a third tanker, blowing open the hull and igniting huge oil fires. Lt. Carl Mitchell, the bombardier on Orance's "Bad Penny," had scored two of the hits himself. The 400 foot tanker then slowly started down. The next trio of B-17s scored more hits on the victim to accelerate the oiler's plunge to the bottom of the harbor.

The last squadron over the harbor, Maj. Warren Whitmore's 348th, also scored, making two hits on a fourth tanker. Although they did not sink the ship, they left the vessel burning and listing. Thus, with oilers down or going down and other tankers unseaworthy, none of this precious oil would ever reach the Afrika Korps in Tunisia.

German ack ack gunners, spewing up deadly 88mm shells, shot down one of the 99th Group B-17s, damaged four other bombers, killed 11 crew members, and wounded 20 more Ninety-Niners. But despite these losses, the 99th had dealt still another murderous blow to Germany's Operation Bulls Head.

"We did okay, Colonel," Maj. Al Orance radioed the 99th Group CO.

"Good show," Upthegrove answered. "Keep the formation tight. We could get jumped by bandits on the way home."

To the west, the 34 Junker transports were now droning over the Strait of Sicily with 31 FW 190s from JG 27 hanging around and above them. At 0750 hours, Col. Edu Neumann saw the horde of American fighter planes coming toward the German air formation. He called his pilots.

"Enemy fighters ahead. We must keep them away from the transport aircraft. Attack in rotte pairs; rotte."

The Americans were ready. As soon as Col. Bill Covington saw the formation of German planes ahead of him, he called Maj. Harry Vaughn of the 96th Squadron. "Bandits ahead. We'll take them; you go after the Junkers."

"Roger, Colonel," the 96th Squadron CO answered.

The 38 Blue Gull pilots zoomed off and

waded into the formation of FW 190s. Still again, a dogfight erupted over the Mediterranean. Colonel Neumann's JG 27, with only 30 planes, could not deal with the superior number of P-38s from the 82nd Fighter Group. Within minutes, the Blue Gulls downed 14 of the German fighters.

Among the 82nd pilots, Colonel Covington and Capt. James Lynn got two kills each. Covington got his first kill when he came into the FW from the lateral with streaking machine gun fire that riddled the 190s fuselage and nearly cut the plane in half. He scored his second hit when he ripped open the underbelly of the 190. Lynn got his two kills in a single pass, downing the first with blistering machine gun fire and dropping the second with 20mm shells.

After the maceration of JG 27 and the exodus of the geschwader's surviving planes, Colonel Covington called Captain Lynn. "Keep your squadron here in case we see more more bandits. I'm taking the 97th Squadron to help out Vaughn against the transport planes."

"Yes sir," Capt. Jim Lynn answered.

Again, a formation of German transport planes found themselves exposed to U.S. fighter planes. The Americans showed no mercy, pouncing on the Junkers like hawks on helpless doves. This 11 April 1943 morning would be the worst yet for Germany's Lufttransport Mittelmeer.

In the two plane tandem attacks, the P-38 pilots of the 82nd Blue Gull Group waded into the transport planes with chattering machine gun fire and whooshing 20mm shellfire. The 37 Lightnings roared into the German aerial convoy again and again, ripping off wings, tails, and engines; shattering cockpits, fuselages, and cargo areas; igniting engines, gas tanks, or entire planes. The attack resembled an assault by predatory dragonflies descending on flying beetles. One after another the JU 52s fell from the sky to plop into the sea, some as battered wrecks, some as flaming coffins, some in disembowled fragments. The debris of the German aerial convoy lay along a 40 mile length of sea.

Eight of the Blue Gull pilots scored multiple kills: Col. Bill Covington, Capt. John Lynn, Lt. Ron Kinsey, and Capt. Richard McAuliffe with two each. Lt. Frank Lawson and Lt. Paul Cochrone got three each. Lt. William "Dixie" Sloan, a soft spoken young man from Richmond, Virginia, got an astonishing five planes to raise his kill score to 12 German planes. Sloan had been a staff sergeant pilot with the group in early 1942 and he had been awarded a lieutenant's rank when the U.S. Army Air Force ordered all combat pilots to hold officer's rank.

Sloan's five kills on this 11 April 1943 day had made him the top ranking U.S. air ace in the MTO. His kill score of 12 would last for nearly a year, well into 1944, by which time the incredible Sloan would be back in the States with a kill score of 15.5.

Of the 34 Junker transports that had left Naples three hours earlier, all but two had become victims of the murderous Blue Gulls machine gun fire and 37mm shells. The two surviving Junkers had somehow managed to lose themselves in rare cumulous clouds above the Mediterranean Sea. Covington made no attempt to find them. He was more than satisfied with his efforts today. The 82nd Blue Gulls Fighter Group would earn a DUC for these outstanding accomplishments.

Besides the horrifying catastrophe against the 34 plane aerial convoy, this 11 April day had brought other discouraging damage to the Germans. Both the famed JG 27 and JG 77 jagdgeschwaders had been all but wiped out by the evening of 11 April. Steinhoff counted only 11 serviceable planes at Trapani and Neumann found only 9 serviceable planes in his Reggio air base force. Finally, the destruction of the four tankers at Trapani Harbor had just about eliminated the Axis merchant fleet in the Mediterranean.

The Germans surely needed some strategy changes to avoid further disaster in the central Mediterranean. German commanders of OB Sud Ost bickered among themselves, blaming each other for these serious losses. However, all of them agreed on one point. The American OSS spy system had played a major role in helping the Allies and they now welcomed the expected efforts by the Gestapo SS.

CHAPTER ELEVEN

Col. Heinz Jost was no doubt a harsh man. This Gestapo officer saw disloyalty, traitors, spies, and saboteurs in every dark cellar, remote patch of countryside, or obscure apartment. No one had ever seen Jost without his friendly smile, a smile that was quite deceiving in the tall, robust man. Those around Jost never knew when he was angry or happy, disappointed or satisfied, unsure or confident. Further, no one had ever detected any kind of emotion in his constant monotonous voice that never rose or fell in decibel levels. But every staff officer in OKW knew a certainty about Col. Heinz Jost: he was ruthlessly determined and efficient.

Jost had spent most of his career in exposing spies who relayed important information to the

Allies, or in running down partisans who carried out sabotage activities in Nazi occupied Europe, or in identifying Germans who were disloyal to the German hierarchy. His record had been excellent, so that few Germans in the Wehrmacht or Luftwaffe looked forward to any kind of investigation by the colonel and his SS team.

Yet every man in OB Sud-Ost in the central Mediterranean now agreed that something needed to be done about enemy spies. While some of Kesselring's subordinates had occasionally nabbed an Allied agent or a clandestine radio in Italy or Sicily, they had barely dented the OSS network. The officers and men of OB Sud-Ost were either administrators or fighting men, with little training in intelligence or counter intelligence.

Col. Heinz Jost arrived by plane in Naples on the late morning of 12 April 1943, the day after the latest German debacle in Operation Bulls Head. Sixteen Gestapo men arrived with Jost aboard the JU 52. Two other Junkers had arrived with another 40 agents so the Gestapo colonel had brought with him from Berlin nearly 60 men. Apparently, Gestapo Chief Himmler had not spared any effort to wipe out the spy nests in Italy and Sicily.

Jost had barely settled himself and his staff in the Hotel de Napoli at about noon when he called OB Sud-Ost headquarters for an audience with Field Marshal Kesselring and his commanders. Generals Buchholtz, Trautloft, Hammhuber, and even the visiting General von Arnim from

Tunisia wore sober faces when they showed up for the afternoon conference. Nobody liked the Gestapo. The SS used extreme methods for getting information out of people, while they often harassed the innocent in the process.

Jost scanned the solemn faced officers about him, with a twinkle in his blue eyes and a warm grin on his face. Despite the SS colonel's pleasant look, however the OB Sud-Ost officers felt uneasy. Finally, after looking through some papers in front of him, the Gestapo colonel looked at his audience.

"You are all very fortunate to be so far from Berlin," Jost began, "since even the wrath of our beloved Fuhrer cannot radiate this far south. Those of us in the Reichstaff have felt the very chancellory shudder from the Fuhrer's anger over these disasters. There is, of course, every reason for outrage. I do not claim that incompetence prevails among the officers and men of OB Sud-Ost, but I must tell you in all frankness that there are those in Berlin who believe that the entire staff here should be relieved of command."

The officers said nothing.

"However," Jost continued with a gesture, "I was able to convince certain leaders of the OKW staff that the problem here stemmed from the widespread Allied spy network that operates in Italy, Sicily, and other islands of the Mediterranean. It is quite obvious that too many Italians and most of the North African populace has shifted their allegiance to the Allies. I would also say that you would be foolish to any longer depend on the Italian military for anything. If most of them are not outright traitors, they are at best indifferent, unconcerned, and cowardly. All of our intelligence reports tend to show that the Italians have become unreliable."

"Please, Colonel," General von Arnim finally spoke, "I have found many of these Italians quite courageous in the Tunisian campaign."

"Perhaps," Jost said, "but they are the exceptions and not the rule. In any event, there will be no more surface ship or aerial convoys to North Africa until we have completed our work."

"No more convoys?" von Arnim gasped. "But that is impossible. We are locked in a violent struggle in Tunisia. We cannot possibly expect to stop the enemy there without a continuous flow of reinforcements and supplies."

"Up to this point in Operation Bulls Head, Herr General, you have received few reinforcements and even fewer supplies," Jost said. "All we have seen are disastrous losses in ships, aircraft, men, and provisions. The debacle yesterday was an excellent example. Do you propose that we give the enemy the opportunity to carry out more shooting duck exercises?"

"But we must have reinforcements."

"You shall have them," the SS colonel said, "but not until we are certain that the enemy can no longer get knowledge of these aerial convoy movements so they can again pounce on you like wolves on helpless deer. The OKW is fully aware of the enemy's superior resources in ships and aircraft. Only if you can send out new surface ship and aerial convoys under the most secret conditions can you expect to bring reinforcements safely into Tunisia."

"What do you suggest, Colonel?" Kesselring asked.

"My men will move throughout Naples, Sardinia, and Sicily to find these Allied spies whom I suspect may number in the hundreds. We have brought with us the latest detection equipment to locate and destroy clandestine radio receivers and transmitters. The next time reinforcements leave Italy or Sicily, there will be no spies to notify the Allies in Algiers."

"How long will this take?" von Arnim asked. "We already suffer from a severe shortage of men and supplies and we can hardly expect to contain the enemy in Tunisia without help."

"If we are lucky, we should complete our work in a week," Jost said.

"I am not sure we can wait that long for more supplies," von Arnim said. "Perhaps Field Marshal Rommel was correct to suggest that we evacuate Tunisia."

"Impossible," Jost cried sharply. "The Fuhrer insists that you hold. As of now, the OKW plan is to maintain your positions in North Africa until the fall. You must simply urge your men of the Afrika Korps to make an ultimate effort in a stubborn defense, despite the odds against you."

"It is easy for you to say that, Colonel," the acting Afrika Korps commander said. "You are not in Tunisia. You do not face the daily air attacks by hordes of enemy planes that blacken the skies. You are not subjected to the daily artillery bombardments and the unceasing attacks by countless enemy tanks. You have not seen soldiers with a small ration of bullets for their guns and an even smaller ration of food for their bellies, and no medicine when they are wounded. Never in the history of war have so few men done so well under such circumstances as has the Luftwaffe and Wehrmacht soldiers of the Afrika Korps."

"I appreciate all you have said, General," Jost gestured again, "but I must repeat — there will be no more convoys into Tunisia until we have cleaned out the nest of spies in Italy and Sicily." He scanned the officers again. "I hope I will have the cooperation of all of you and of the men in your commands."

"Rest assured, Colonel, you shall have it," Field Marshal Kesselring said. "Just tell us what you want us to do."

"I will divide my men into sixteen teams, three or four men on each team. Two of these teams will cover the Naples airfields area, another pair will conduct its work at the Naples harbor area. More teams will cover the harbors and airfields in Sicily and southern Italy. I want at least a half dozen Wehrmacht or Luftwaffe specialists to work with each SS team. They should include radio men, radio technicians, and communications personnel. I would also like a minimum of four vehicles for each team, including a mobile radio-radar detection vehicle. Each team will cover a wide geographic area, at least five miles in circumference around the ports and airfields. Can you furnish these men and vehicles, Herr Field Marshal?"

"Yes, of course; whatever you want," Kesselring said.

"I must also ask that beginning tomorrow and until you send out your next convoy, no Italian civilian employees should be allowed to leave his work area in the airfields and harbors. From now on," Jost said, "the Italians must remain totally uninformed of all your activities."

"That is impossible, Colonel," General Trautloft said. "How could we feed and house the hundreds of civilians who work for us? Besides, if we keep them virtual prisoners, their complaints would reach the highest echelons of the Italian government, and no doubt bring severe protests from many of the Italian authorities."

"General Trautloft is correct," General Buchholtz said. "There is already a growing animosity between many of the Italian and German military officers. To suggest that we should now restrict Italian civilians would only widen this mutual mistrust."

"Then you must dismiss all Italian employees," Jost shrugged, "at least until you have seen new convoys safely to North Africa. The point is — no Italian civilian must be in a position to report to anyone the activities in the harbors and airfields of Sicily and Italy."

"What you ask cannot be done," General Trautloft insisted. "We would create more problems than we solve."

"I must insist, I'm afraid," Jost said. "Perhaps you can tell these civilians that because of severe gasoline shortages you cannot take them back and forth to their jobs. You can give them the option of continuing to work and live on the airfields and port areas until the shortage is alleviated, or they can seek employment elsewhere."

"That may be a way out," Kesselring said. "Very well, Colonel."

"Good," the Gestapo officer nodded. "I would like to activate these teams as soon as possible, and I would like all of them at their stations quickly, so that we can begin our operations by tomorrow morning at the latest."

"Yes, Colonel," Kesselring said.

By the evening of 12 April, the 16 teams had been organized, with each unit including three to four Gestapo men, six specialists, and four vehicles. Those in the Naples area quartered themselves in barracks on the airfields or in naval accommodations about the harbor. During the evening hours, Junkers flew other teams to their destinations: Salerno and Reggio in Italy; Palermo, Trapani, Catania, Borrizo, Comiso, Cerbino, Messina, and Boco de Falco in Sicily. Two teams went to Sardinia and three teams went all the way to North Africa to operate in the Sidi Ahmed, El Aouina, and Tunis areas.

The sudden arrival of Col. Heinz Jost's Gestapo teams had not gone unnoticed in Algiers. Nor had the formation and distribution of these special anti-spy teams gone undetected. By midnight of 11 April, radio messages came from Pilgrim and Franklin agents in Sicily and Italy, along with a warning that new reports from OSS agents might be curtailed. Gen. Wild Bill Donovan scowled irritably when he got these messages, although he surely must have suspected that the Germans would not allow his agents to operate with near impunity forever. He met with Gen. Carl Spaatz on the morning of 13 April.

"I've got distressing news, Carl," Donovan said. "The German Gestapo is making an all-out effort to break up our intelligence network. It's possible that we may not get any more reports on the movement of German ships and supply planes. I suspect the Gestapo will make widespread use of radio detection instruments and they could well pinpoint the locations of our transmitters. Since our agents have been invaluable, I don't want to jeopardize their safety by asking them to continue sending radio reports."

"Are you suggesting that we can't depend on your agents from now on?" General Spaatz asked.

"Not for a while," Donovan answered.

"But they've been vital to the success of Operation Flax," the NAAF CinC said.

"Captured agents sure as hell can't help us," the OSS chief said. "I think that for the time being you'll need to depend on reconnaissance planes."

Spaatz shook his head. "That's bad. Recon

planes do help, of course, but they can't take the place of people who are making on the spot observations."

"I can only tell you to keep your air groups on continued full alert," Donovan said. "Maybe you should also increase your recon activities, and beef up your CAPs over the Strait of Sicily. As I said, Carl, our agents are too valuable to get killed or captured. We'll need them quite badly when we invade Italy or Sicily."

"I understand," Spaatz nodded. "We'll just have to do the best we can without OSS help."

"I'm sorry," Donovan apologized.

For the next several days, Col. Heinz Jost and his Gestapo teams scoured the southern areas of Italy and most of Sicily. The teams covered the mountain and valley terrain, the surrounding grounds of the Naples airfields at Capodichino, Pomigliano, Aquino, and Montecervino. They searched homes, apartments, store buildings, and commercial structures within a two mile radius of Naples harbor, while their detection trucks growled up and down the streets of Naples to locate and expose any radio transmitters. The Germans did find three radios and they arrested several suspected agents inside the city.

A similar dragnet went on in Salerno and Reggio, also in southern Italy, while other SS teams worked tirelessly in Sicily. The Gestapo units had cleared civilians for a radius of two to five miles from the major island airfields especially Comiso and Borrizo, while they searched buildings all about the harbor areas of Messina, Palermo, and

Trapani. The Germans had claimed a measure of success in Sicily, where they found and destroyed seven clandestine radios, while arresting 17 suspected spies. The bulk of the OSS agents had escaped the probing German anti-spy teams, but these secret agents could no longer make radio transmissions without the certainty of detection.

By 17 April, several days after the massive Gestapo operation began, no more radio messages reached Roman in Algiers. The U.S. agents had to hide themselves and their equipment, and they dared not send new messages from Sicily or Italy. By mid-day of 17 April, Col. Heinz Jost called on Field Marshal Albert Kesselring. The colonel wore a smug look on his face that enhanced his perpetual grin. Jost had reason to gloat.

"The enemy spy network is finished, Herr Field Marshal. You may resume your resupply operations without fear of enemy agents reporting such movements to Tunisia. While we captured only a small number of radios and operators, we have effectively frightened the others into silence, and they will not dare to send reports to North Africa. Our team will remain in strategically located areas while you carry on with Operation Bulls Head. We have especially placed two strong teams about the airdromes where you are massing many of your transport and fighter aircraft."

"I am glad to hear this, Colonel," Kesselring said, "for it was General Buchholtz's intent to send a new aerial supply convoy out of Naples for a direct flight into Tunisia. In fact, this formation will be the largest aerial convoy yet. We are massing fighters from several geschwaders at Boco de Falco in Sicily to escort these transport planes. If the enemy does not learn of the buildups in Naples and Boco de Falco, General von Arnim will get a welcome mass of new supplies."

"I can promise you," Jost said, "that no enemy spies will be close enough to observe your activities tomorrow; nor will they be able to transmit messages to North Africa."

"Good," Kesselring nodded.

True enough. The Afrika Korps, between 12 April and 17 April was fighting a desperate battle to hold the line in North Africa. However, the German defenses had begun to crumble. The British had broken German defenses at the Mareth Line and Afrika Korps troops had been evacuated, thus allowing New Zealand troops to occupy these strong positions. Other British troops had captured the key highway junction at Gabes and the rail head at Djebel. And now, the Britishers and New Zealanders of the British 30th Corps were pounding new German defense lines that stretched from Wadi-Akarit on the west to Wadi-Zigzago on the east, a distance of 15 miles.

If the 30th Corps could break this new German defense perimeter, they would be in the open plains to the north for a dash to Tunis. The Americans, meanwhile, had overrun El Guettar and had reached the defended Chensi Pass as well as occupying Beja. If the GIs broke through here, they too could barrel over open plains to their ojective, the seaport city of Bizerte.

By 17 April, British troops on the right and American troops on the left had continued to pressure the Afrika Korps, whose Tunisian hold gradually shrank. The Germans were now defending a diminished bridgehead, anchored by the towns of Enfidaville, Pont-du-Fahs, Medjez-el-Bab, and Sedjenane. The Allies now planned a final assault on these key bases, with elements of the British 8th Army opposite Enfidaville, the French XX Corps in the area of Pont-du-Fahs, the French V Corps at Medjez-el-Bab, and the American II Corps to the north at Beja near Sedjenane.

The hard pressed Gen. Jurgeon von Arnim had encamped the German 20th and 21st Korps to hold desperately on the western lateral of their bridgehead until reinforcements in men and supplies arrived. His 15th Panzer Division and elements of the Italian Commando Supremo, meanwhile, hung on along the eastern lateral of the contracted defense line. All of these forces, about 200,000 men, would get supplies from Tarhuna, just north of the line, if a new aerial convoy or surface ship convoy could reach Tunisia.

Only a trickle of supplies had been arriving in Tunisia during the past couple of weeks because for the Allied Operation Flax and by mid-April fuel supplies alone were almost exhausted. Reserves of the Afrika Korps had reached their lowest point since the Germans first came into North Africa in 1941. On the morning of the 17th, General von Arnim met with his Fleigerkorps Tunisien commander Gen. Hoffman von Waldau, Gen. Fritz Bayerlin of the 21st Korps, and Gen. Wilhelm Borowietz of the 20th Korps.

"I must tell you that I am grateful for the determination of our troops. Without a doubt, our brave soldiers and airmen have performed beyond all expected human endeavors, with little food, ammunition, and equipment. These efforts are unusually remarkable when we consider the recent disasters to our merchant ship and air convoys. Such news could have utterly destroyed their morale. But," he gestured, "I can offer you good news for a change. Luftflotte 2 is preparing to send the largest aerial transport fleet that ever flew on a single flight — one hundred aircraft. They will bring to us countless tons of supplies that include more than ten thousand barrels of gasoline. These supplies will surely enable us to hold fast on the Enfidaville and Sedjenane Lines."

"That sounds fine and we should be filled with joy," General Bayerlin said, "but I feel no enthusiasm in view of the recent disasters to other convoys."

"I too suspect that this new aerial convoy will only be more fodder for Allied aircraft," General Borowietz said bitterly.

"Not this time," von Arnim grinned. "Some very efficient SS teams have choked off the Allied spy system in Italy and Sicily and our enemy has no idea that we have prepared this aerial fleet. The transports will leave Naples tomorrow afternoon and will arrive in Tunisia at dusk. The

208

unloading process can take place at night, when we are relatively safe from the Allied air forces."

"I am not sure," Bayerlin shook his head.

"Tomorrow is Palm Sunday," von Arnim said. "The Americans will send out their usual patrols tomorrow morning. By noon, they will be confident that we are not sending transport planes to Tunisia from Italy and they will relax their vigil. By the late afternoon they will be completely complacent and probably suspend aerial patrols for the remainder of the day. We can thus expect the convoy to reach Tunisia without interference."

"Still, one hundred transport planes represents a sizable air fleet," General von Waldau said. "What about escorts?"

Von Arnim fumbled through some papers, scanned one of them, and then spoke again. "Unfortunately, after the series of dogfights, both JG 77 and JG 27 are all but spent. However, I am told that a gruppen from JG 53 and a gruppen from JG 51 will furnish about fifty to sixty Messerschmidt fighters. And as the convoy approaches the North African coast, III/JG 51 of Fleigerkorps Tunisien should mount fighters as an added protection."

"I see," von Waldau said.

"Let us hope you are correct, Herr General," General Bayerlin said.

"I am confident," the Afrika Korps acting CinC said. "I ask that you meet with your subordinates and tell them to continue their stalwart defense; help is on the way. By mid-week next your ground units will have all the supplies they need."

On the same 17 April day, Field Marshal Albert Kesselring stood in the control shack at Capodichino Airdrome in Naples and watched the array of trucks move in continuous parades toward the mass of KVT 16 Junker transport planes. The trucks arrived in endless lines before service troops transferred materiel inside the Junker cargo areas. Combat troops also scrambled out of trucks and boarded the JU 52s. The varied types of supplies included gasoline, artillery shells, ammunition, medicine, food, clothing, incidentals, small vehicles, and 23 artillery pieces.

All day the trucks carried troops and supplies to the tri-motor transport planes, and the work continued with order and efficiency. Next to Kesselring stood Colonel Jost and General Buchholtz. After the trio watched the activities for some time, Jost finally spoke.

"You are fortunate today, Herr Field Marshal. Our SS teams have cleared the area surrounding the field within a five mile radius. No unauthorized person knows what is going on here. The same can be said for the areas around the Pomigliano Drome. When the transport aircraft take off tomorrow only we and those on these airfields will know they have left Naples."

"You are certain, Colonel?" Kesselring asked.

"Absolutely," the Gestapo officer answered. He then turned to Buchholtz. "You are to be congratulated, Herr General. Your men appear quite efficient and enthusiastic in their work."

"They realize as well as anyone the critical needs of the brave Afrika Korps," Buchholtz said, "and they do their duty."

"Of course," Jost said.

While the heavy activity prevailed at the Naples transport fields, a similar burst of activity prevailed at Boco de Falco Airdrome in Sicily. General Trautloft himself had flown to the airfield to direct preparations of fighter escorts for the transport convoy. He had brought in 30 ME 109s from JG 53's II Gruppen at Catania under Capt. Wolfgang Tonne to join the 36 ME 109s of JG 51's II Gruppen that was already based here at Boco de Falco under Maj. Hartman Grasser. Trautloft had also brought in a squadron of Italian MC 202 fighters to join the escort formation.

By the evening of 17 April, activities at Boco de Falco had ceased. 66 ME 109s and 18 MC 202s were fully loaded with strafing belts and 20mm cannon shells. After the evening meal, General Trautloft met with Major Grasser.

"Is all in readiness?" the Fleigerkorps II CinC asked.

"Yes, mein General," the major answered. "It is our hope that eighty-four fighters will be sufficient to escort the transport planes. Both our own Luftwaffe pilots and the Italians are eager to succeed in this mission."

"If the transports reach Tunisia," Trautloft nodded, "not only would the Afrika Korps get needed supplies for their valiant defense, but such a successful flight would surely raise the

211

morale of every man in OB Sud-Ost."

"If, as the Gestapo colonel says, we have eliminated the spy network," Grasser said, "then we should carry out this operation successfully."

"I'm sure the Gestapo has done its job."

"Still, we will keep our eighty-four escort plane pilots on full alert," Grasser said, "and I hope that this many fighters will be enough to contain enemy interceptors, should we meet any."

Thus the Germans had prepared their biggest aerial transport fleet yet for Operation Bulls Head. They had indeed enjoyed the advantage of secrecy, for no messages from OSS agents had come out of Italy or Sicily to inform Wild Bill Donovan that the Germans had massed another huge transport fleet in Naples and massed a fighter plane force in Boco de Falco in Sicily. On the evening of 17 April, the Americans were unaware that the Germans were planning to send their biggest aerial fleet yet into Tunisia.

But fate sometimes intervenes. NASAF had planned only routine missions for 18 April, Palm Sunday, and even these missions were quite few because tomorrow was an important holiday for the Christian world. Most of the Allied airmen in Africa expected a day of rest. However, one of the scheduled missions for this holy Sunday was a B-17 strike on Boco de Falco.

CHAPTER TWELVE

At 0600 hours, 18 April, church bells echoed across the desert from St. Bartholomew's Church in the village of Navarin. The peals came in a steady, metronome cadence. Today was Palm Sunday in the predominantly French influenced area and Arab and French civilians would attend mass this morning. Occasionally, crew chiefs who preflighted B-17s revved the Flying Fort engines on the American airfield and the screaming pitch intermittently drowned out the sound of church bells.

From the 99th Bomb Group orderly room, the night OD personnel, finishing their last hour on the graveyard shift, watched the broken lines of shuffling Arabs who plodded toward the pealing bells. Other Arabs heading for the village had jammed themselves aboard rickety carts pulled by oxen. As the Ninety-Niner operations officer peered from his hut and watched the stream of church goers, he felt a wistful nostalgia. Back in the States, he too would have been going to church today. But here, in the desert of North Africa, he had no time for mass. He had been too busy preparing the FO for today's mission, and he would need to have copies of the directive ready for a 0630 briefing.

In the mess halls, Ninety-Niner bomber crews occasionally paused and listened to the church bells in the distance. Most of these combat crews felt the same nostalgia. Today was a major Christian holy day. But instead of dressing in their Sunday finery for church services, they had attired themselves in combat gear for a mission to Sicily.

By 0615 hours, the church bells had ceased and the first of five Palm Sunday masses had begun at Navarin's St. Bartholomew Church. At the same hour, Col. Fay Upthegrove mounted the podium in the huge 99th Group operations hut. He waited until the operations officer had passed out copies of today's mission FO and he then pulled down the quite familiar map of the Central Mediterranean from the wall behind him. Then the colonel spoke to his men.

"I know that a briefing seems inappropriate on Palm Sunday. It is true that a lot of men in this group will get an opportunity to attend church services today, but unfortunately, we will not be among them. However, the war can't wait." He

214

slapped a point on the map. "Here, the airfield at Boco de Falco in Sicily. Recon plans say the Nazis have been massing fighter planes at the base, although we don't know exactly why. At any rate, we'll be hitting that airdrome this morning with a mixture of HEs and incendiaries."

"Colonel, sir," Maj. Al Orance of the 416th Squadron asked, "if that's a big fighter base, how about escorts?"

"The 14th will take us in again," Upthegrove answered. "They'll furnish a full group of fifty-four Lightnings."

"Will that be enough?" Maj. Harry Burrell of the 347th Squadron asked.

"We hope so," the 99th Group CO answered. "Squadron leaders should study the FO carefully. I'll come in first with the 346th Squadron at twenty-four thousand. The 347th Squadron comes in next at twenty-five, five, then the 348th at twenty-seven, and Major Orance's 416th Squadron will come in last at twenty-eight, five. We'd like to knock out the runway and as many parked aircraft as possible. Any questions?"

None.

"Okay, jeeps and command cars are waiting outside to take us to the field. Let's mount up."

At Telergma, Algeria, no church bells pealed across the rocky desert terrain surrounding the American airfield. The French had not been as successful here in converting the Arabs to Christianity. Only a small mission church sat amid the adobe structures of the small village and a mere handful of Catholics, mostly French nationalists, would go to mass this morning.

However, at the 14th Fighter Group base, the Americans had constructed a chapel. This morning, a majority of the men from this group would jam the chapel for services. Catholics would attend an early mass and Protestants would attend later services in the same structure. However, as in Navarin, some of the airmen here would not attend religious services today—54 Avenger fighter pilots. These 14th Group airmen who sat in the briefing quonset hut at 0700 hours on this sunny morning, loitered on benches and listened to Lt. Col. Tony Keith.

"I wish I could tell you that our mission this morning was routine, but I'm not sure. Ordinarily, an escort run to an enemy airfield doesn't cause us much trouble, but recon reports say that Boco de Falco is jammed with German fighter planes. The heavies of the 99th Group will try to knock out that base this morning, and we may get jumped by a skyful of FW 190s and ME 109s. So we'll need to be especially alert."

"Who'll take high cover?" Maj. Lou Benne asked.

"You will, Lou," Keith answered, "your 49th Squadron. The 48th will take the starboard lateral and the 37th will take the port lateral."

"Yes sir," Capt. Jim Griffith of the 37th Squadron said.

"You'll find the instructions on the FO sheet pretty clear," Keith said. "We'll rendezvous with the bombers at latitude 37.1° north and longitude 10.2° east. If there are no more questions, let's mount up."

A moment later, the 54 fighter pilots from the 14th Group boarded jeeps for the ride to their waiting Lightnings. By 0730 hours, the Avenger airmen began taking off in pairs, zooming down the Telergma runway. By 0745 hours, the P-38s had disappeared into the northern sky. By 0800 hours, they had crossed the coast of Africa and droned over the Mediterranean Sea to rendezvous with the B-17s coming out of Navarin.

Most of the other bomber and fighter units of the Allied air forces in Africa remained quiet on this Palm Sunday holiday, except for flights of 211 Group patrol units that flew two hour CAPs over the Strait of Sicily and off the North African coast. They would keep an eye out for possible German transport planes. However, by 0900 hours, no 211 Group pilots had seen a sign of a German aircraft over the Mediterranean Sea.

Both General Doolittle of NASAF and Air Marshal Conningham of NATAF were convinced that the Germans would not send any aerial convoys to Tunisia today. Although OSS agents had not sent messages to Algiers for the past week, Allied recon planes had been quite active. They had failed to note any sizeable buildups anywhere except at Boco de Falco. In fact, for the past several days, no one in Allied air or naval units had seen a sign of a German transport plane or surface ship. Gen. Carl Spaatz, CinC of NAAF, also thought that perhaps the Germans had given up on aerial transports to Tunisia, and he surely did not expect any German transport planes to make runs into Tunisia today, Palm Sunday, a holiday for most Germans also.

Still, as a matter of routine, Spaatz kept the CAPs over the central Mediterranean and he planned to keep the patrols out all day.

At 0815 hours, the 54 Lightnings of the 14th Fighter Group met the 33 B-17s from the 99th Bomb Group over the blue Mediterranean. The Ninety-Niner crews watched one fighter squadron assume high cover, while the other two P-38 squadrons settled alongside the formation of Flying Fortresses. Lt. Col. Tony Keith called Upthegrove.

"We'll be with you all the way in and out, Colonel."

"Stay alert," Upthegrove answered. "They tell us that Boco de Falco is jammed with fighter planes and we could see a sky full of bandits."

"We'll be awake," Keith promised, "but make sure your gunners stay alert. We may not be able to maintain a one hundred percent screen."

"Roger," Col. Fay Upthegrove answered.

At 0845 hours, sirens wailed through the German airbase at Boco de Falco. Luftwaffe pilots from II Gruppen JG 51 and from II Gruppen JG 53 hurried to their ME 109s, while flak gunners dashed to their anti-aircraft pits. Others at the base darted for cover to wait out the air raid. Unfortunately for the Germans, only two staffels of ME 109s got off before the attack, so that only 32 Messerschmidts were airborne to meet the interlopers.

Col. Fay Upthegrove, with General Doolittle

himself riding in the nose of "El Diablo," led the first trio of B-17s over the field and of the six HE 1,000 pounders and three tons of incendiary clusters that tumbled out of the Flying Fortresses, three-fourths of them hit squarely on the runway and on parked planes next to the strip. The HEs tore nine holes in the airstrip and the incendiaries smashed six planes. Before the German base commander could deter fighters to take off on secondary runways, more B-17s from the 346th Squadron punched holes in this subordinate airstrip.

"Your boys are sharp today, Fay," General Doolittle cried from the nose of the 99th Group's lead B-17.

"We're doing okay," Upthegrove answered.

As soon as the six Ninety-Niner heavy bombers unloaded on the runways, the eight planes from Maj. Harry Burrell's 347th Squadron scattered their clusters of 20 pound frag bombs atop parked aircraft. They smashed or set afire more than 20 ME 109s. Lt. Ed Ball, the bombardier on Lt. Dean Shield's "Yankee Doodle," scored solid hits that knocked out five planes on the ground.

Now came the ten Flying Forts from Maj. Warren Whitmore's 348th Squadron. The bombardiers sighted carefully, pinpointing hordes of parked German fighter planes. Tumbling bomb clusters descended on the array of Messerschmidts with most of the explosives hitting squarely. A staccato of concussions erupted across the west segment of the airfield to chop apart some 14 planes while igniting at least 11 more German fighters.

"Goddamn, Major," Whitmore's co-pilot grinned, "we sure did a job on them."

"Good show," Major Whitmore returned the grin.

Finally, Maj. Al Orance droned over Boco de Falco Airdrome with the nine Flying Fortresses of his trailing 416th Squadron. Again the American bombardiers sighted carefully. At 1010 hours, bombardier Ted Gutz on the squadron's lead B-17 "Bad Penny" cried into his radio.

"Bombs away!"

A confetti of frag bombs then tumbled downward and struck a cluster of parked Italian MC 202 fighters, knocking out four of them with shuddering incendiary explosions. Orance grinned and called his bombardier. "Goddam, Carl, right on target."

"Yes sir," Gutz answered.

Eight Flying Forts of the 416th Squadron followed, dropping more incendiary bombs. A new staccato of explosions left a new mass of fire and debris along a length of parked MC 202s. By the time this last 99th Group squadron had left the target, 16 more Italian fighters were either aflame or twisted into wrecks.

German AA gunners fired furiously at the attacking B-17s, but the high level bombers had escaped most of the exploding puffs of flak. However, the German gunners downed one B-17 from the 348th Squadron and damaged four more, two seriously. One of the badly damaged planes ditched in the sea on the way back to Navarin and a British destroyer fished them out of the Mediterranean. Seventeen Ninety-Niners had died during this raid on holy Palm Sunday.

While the B-17s wrecked Boco de Falco drome, Lt. Col. Tony Keith and his Avenger pilots from the U.S. 14th Fighter Group tangled with the German pilots of JG 53 and JG 51. Keith took the 35 pilots of his 48th and 37th Squadrons after the 21 planes from JG 53 under Hauptman Wolfgang Tonne, while Maj. Lou Benne took the 19 Lightnings of his 49th Squadron against the 11 ME 109s of JG 51 that managed to get airborne before the B-17 attack.

Keith's two squadrons waded swiftly into the JG 53 formations to ignite a heavy dogfight long before the Messerschmidts could reach the B-17 bombers. Keith himself got a fighter when he downed the 109 with chattering machine gun fire that cut the Messerschmidt in half.

Both Maj. Bill Lovelette of the 48th Squadron and Capt. Jim Griffith of the 37th Squadron got two kills each. Lovelette got his first score when he jinked away from a Messerschmidt, turned sharply, and came down on a second ME 109 with blistering strafing bursts that chopped apart the tail. The German plane plunged into the sea. The major got his second kill when he blew away the engine of the enemy plane with 37mm shell hits. The Messerschmidt tumbled downward and crashed on the airfield. Jim Griffith got his first score with chattering machine gun fire that ripped off the wing of his prey, and he got his second when he tore apart the tail section with more .50 caliber fire.

On the German side, both Captain Tonne and Oblt. Harti Schmeidel got a pair of kills. Tonne downed a Lightning with chattering machine gun fire that shattered the cockpit and killed the American pilot. He got his second score with streaking shells, three of which struck squarely and blew the American plane apart. Oberlientenant Schmeidel tailed a P-38 and chopped the plane apart with strafing fire. He downed the second Lightning with exploding shells that hit squarely and the P-38 burst into flames before arching downward. However, the pilot successfully bailed out. A British destroyer picked him up the next day.

The heavy dogfight above Boco de Falco Airdrome and off the coast of Sicily, however, had cost the Germans 16 planes and seven damaged to a loss of six American Lightnings and damage to four more U.S. planes. But worse, the Germans had failed to disrupt the B-17 attack on the Boco de Falco Airdrome. The Ninety-Niners had destroyed a phenomenal 80 planes on the ground and inside hangars.

By noon, the Germans had cleared away the wreckage at the airfield and filled enough holes to bring surviving JG 51, JG 53, and Italian planes into some semblance of order. At 1300 hours, Gen. Hannes Trautloft met with Major Grasser, Major Tonne, and Major Rodel who had brought some FW 190s to Boco de Falco from Reggio de Calabria on the heel of Italy.

"We have taken count after this serious air raid this morning," Major Grasser said, "and I have consulted with the base service chief. I must tell you that only 20 ME 109s, 14 FW 190s, and ten MC 202s are available for escort duty after losing so many parked aircraft to the bombers and quite a large number in the air battle. I must ask you, Herr General, are forty-four fighter planes enough to escort the one hundred transport aircraft that are scheduled to leave Naples this afternoon?"

Trautloft pursed his lips. "I do not know. I will consult with Field Marshal Kesselring by coded communications."

When Trautloft called Kesselring to report the damaging assault on Boco de Falco, the Luftflotte 2 CinC was stunned. He told Trautloft he would talk to General Buchholtz and Colonel Jost and then get back to the fighter chief.

When Buchholtz heard of the rout at Boco de Falco, he was quite dismayed but not discouraged. "Forty-four fighters may not be many," he told Kesselring, "but we may not need any fighters at all. Thus far, enemy reconnaissance planes have not detected the horde of transports at Naples since we have loaded them during the night and kept them hidden during the day. I would guess that the enemy has no idea that we have prepared one hundred transports for a flight to Tunisia."

"Guessing is not enough," Kesselring said. "We must be sure." He looked at Jost. "What is your opinion, Colonel?"

"I am inclined to agree with the general, Herr Field Marshal," the SS officer said. "I am sure there have been no radio transmissions to North Africa by Allied spies for at least the past four days. Our detector equipment would have picked up such transmissions within ten miles of the airdromes."

"Mein Field Marshal," Buchholtz said, "we have not sent aerial convoys to North Africa for a week, and the Allies can only believe that we have given up on such aerial flights after our severe earlier losses. True, the enemy has been patrolling the Strait of Sicily, but we also know that they are growing lax in this effort. I would think that by late this afternoon, they will not even have reconnaissance flights over the strait, especially on this Palm Sunday."

"I can see the logic of your thinking," Kesselring nodded. "But . . . only forty-four planes—I don't know."

"Please Herr Field Marshal," Buchholtz persisted, "we have planned too long and our men have worked too hard to call off the flight now. By tomorrow, the enemy's reconnaissance pilots may detect our hidden transport planes at the Capodichino and Pomigliano Airdromes. We should not hesitate."

"I too believe that you will never have a better opportunity to send this transport flight to North Africa than you have this afternoon," Jost said.

"Very well," Kesselring nodded. He looked at Buchholtz. "When do you intend to send off the aircraft?"

"At 1500 hours."

"I will notify General Trautloft at Boco de Falco so that these forty-four fighters can rendezvous with the transport formation south of Sicily."

The decision was made. 100 JU 52s would leave the Naples area at 1500 hours on this Palm Sunday afternoon, to arrive in Tunisia at dusk. German service troops could then unload the Junkers at Sidi Ahmed and El Aouina during the dark hours of night, when Allied air units would not likely make any air attacks.

General Buchholtz had apparently made the correct decision because by mid-afternoon, the Allies had grown weary of the CAPs over the central Mediterranean. All day, the 211 Group had sent out armed fighters to scour the blue sea between Tunisia and Sicily, but they had seen nothing. The U.S. 57th Fighter Group had gone out first early this morning and had returned with nothing to report. Then the U.S. 79th and 31st Groups went out to find nothing. Next, the RAF 285 Wing had sent out planes and then the South African 7 SAAF Wing. Not only had these Allied pilots probed the flight lanes over the sea, but they had searched along the Tunisian coastline to determine if transport planes might be coming in. All proved negative.

By 1500 hours on the 18 April Palm Sunday, Gen. Carl Spaatz, CinC of NAAF, called off further aerial patrols for the day.

"It's obvious the Germans don't intend to do anything today," Spaatz said. "Anyway, this is a

225

holy day for most of our airmen, so we may as well give them the rest of the afternoon off. As soon as the 79th Group ends its patrols, we quit until tomorrow."

But NATAF had already ordered the next patrol and the pilots were ready to go. So Spaatz merely shrugged and told his aide to allow the 57th Group pilots to make the final patrol of the day.

Meanwhile, in Naples, the transports began taking off in pairs. At Capodichino, the pilots brought their JU 52s onto the taxiways and lumbered toward the main runway in an endless parade. At precisely 1500 hours, Maj. August Geiger whirled his lead plane of KVT 16s II Gruppen to the head of the runway. Seconds later, he and his wingman roared down the airstrip and into the afternoon sky. More planes followed and by 1530 hours, 45 of the German tri-engine transport planes were airborne. The Junkers jelled into formation and then headed south.

Two miles away, at Pomigliano Airdrome, at the same 1500 hours, Col. Walter Hagen whirled his lead Junker of KVT 16s I Gruppen to the head of the runway and soon roared down the apron with his wingman. In the control tower, Field Marshal Kesselring, General Buchholtz, and Colonel Jost watched the planes taking off in pairs before hoisting themselves into the sky. By 1540 hours the last of the 55 Junkers were airborne.

Kesselring waited until the planes disappeared

to the south and he then turned to General Buchholtz. "Let us hope we are successful today."

"I am confident," Buchholtz said. "These aircraft are carrying nearly twenty thousand tons of supplies and two full battalions of troops that will surely be of inestimable value to the Afrika Korps."

Far to the south, at Boco de Falco, Maj. Hartman Grasser had mustered 23 serviceable ME 109 and FW 190 fighters, along with six MC 202s. He gave the pilots a final briefing. "We will rendezvous with the transports at 1630 hours, just south of Sicily in the strait. I will take the Messerschmidts of JG 51 on high cover. Hauptman Tonne will take the aircraft of his JG 53 on the port lateral and the MC 202s will join Major Rodel from JG 27 on the starboard."

"Major," Rodel said to Grasser, "in view of the heavy superiority in the enemy's aircraft complements, will twenty-nine aircraft be enough for escort?"

"We think so," Grasser said. He scanned his mixed German and Italian pilots. "If there are no further questions, we will man our aircraft."

At 1610 hours, the German and Italian fighter planes began taking off. They flew in single file because of the potholes in the runway, compliments of the U.S. 99th Bomb Group this morning. So Major Grasser needed more time to get his 29 fighters off the ground. Not until 1640 hours did all of the Axis planes take off and ten minutes later, Grasser and his fighter pilots met the huge formation of transport planes. He called Col. Walter Hagen.

"Herr Hagen, we will maintain both high and lateral covers and we will accompany you all the way to Tunisia."

"Good," the KVT 16 kommandant answered. "We do not expect interceptors this late in the afternoon, especially on Palm Sunday. Still, I ask that your fighter pilots remain alter."

"Most assuredly," Grasser answered. The JG 51 major sent a trio of ME 109s to the fore as scouts to keep a sharp watch for possible U.S. or British planes.

In Dejedeida, Tunisia, Maj. Erich Rudorffer of JG 51's II Gruppen got a call from Fleigerkorps Tunisien headquarters. The coded message said that transport planes had left Naples and had picked up fighter escorts out of Sicily. The Junkers were expected to arrive in Tunisia about dusk, around 1800 hours. III Gruppen of JG 51 should send out as many ME 109s as possible to meet the transport planes, since the transports had only about 30 escorts with them.

Rudorffer met with his staffel leaders as soon as he got the message from Fleigerkorps Tunisien. "The transports are expected to reach Tunisia at dusk. We have been asked to escort these JU 52s into Sidi Ahmed and El Aouina. We will mount thirty-four aircraft at 1700 hours, so that we can make a rendezvous with them at 1730 hours. I will take 1 Staffel to escort the planes going to Sidi Ahmed and Lieutenant Perzina will take the aircraft of 2 Staffel to escort those transport planes going to El Aouina."

"Do they not have escorts out of Sicily?" Perzina asked.

"Yes," Rudorffer said, "but unfortunately they could not mount many fighters because of an enemy bombing attack on Boco de Falco this morning. So the JU 52s have only about thirty escorts with them. Luftflotte 2 headquarters believes that these supply planes should have as many escorts as possible as they approach Tunisia, and they have called upon our gruppen."

Perzina did not answer.

In southern Tunisia, at Theleple, the 57th Fighter Group and its attached 314th Fighter Squadron from the 324th Fighter Group were preparing for the last combat air patrol of the day. Col. Arthur Salisbury had called a briefing of 53 airmen, 41 P-40 pilots from his own U.S. 57th Black Scorpion Group and 12 P-40 pilots from the attached U.S. 314th Hawk Squadron.

"I know this patrol seems foolish since CAPs haven't seen a thing all morning or this afternoon. But we're going out anyway as the last CAP of the day. We'll be carrying out routine patrol with twelve Spitfires from the RAF 92 Squadron giving us high cover. They'll join us just north of Soussa and over Hergla Island. We'll then proceed to the Gulf of Tunis and patrol easterly and westerly off Cape Bon. We come back when our low gas supply dictates. I'll lead the 65th Squadron, Major Knight will lead the 64th Squadron, and Captain Curl will lead the 66th Squadron. Lieutenant Colonel McKnown and his 324th Group pilots will take the tail end Charlie position."

"Goddamn, Colonel," Major Knight scowled, "we've already pulled one CAP today and we didn't see a damn thing. Nobody else has seen any Krauts either. Why go out again?"

"Actually, NAAF wanted to call off this last patrol," Salisbury grinned, "but then decided to go ahead because it was already planned."

"Yes sir," Knight answered somewhat bitterly.

At 1600 hours, the 12 Hawk pilots of the 314th Squadron and the 41 Black Scorpion pilots of the 57th Fighter Group boarded jeeps and rode out to their waiting Warhawks. By 1610 hours, the pilots had settled themselves into their cockpits and soon followed Colonel Salisbury's lead plane to the main Theleple runway. At 1620 hours, Salisbury zoomed down the airstrip with two wingmen and a half minute later, the next trio of P-40s took off. By 1635 hours, all 53 Warhawks were airborne.

The P-40s flew north, following the winding road that led to Soussa. When the formation crossed the shoreline, at an 8,000 feet altitude, they met 12 Spitfires from the RAF 92 Squadron under Maj. Neville Duke. The Spitfires rose upward to give the P-40s top cover since the RAF fighter planes were much better at high altitudes than were the P-40s.

"We'll stay upstairs all the way, sir," Major Duke radioed Colonel Salisbury.

"Okay," the 57th Group commander answered the RAF squadron leader.

The formations of planes, four abreast, soon turned northward and out to sea. The P-40s held at 14,000 feet with the Spitfires at 18,000. Soon the Cape Bon Peninsula, blotched by a late afternoon shadow, loomed ahead of them. The fighter pilots saw nothing on the cape as they droned on, skirting the North African coastal town of Korba where a small detachment of German AA gunners sent up ineffective flak. The Allies ignored the Germans because they were looking for bigger game — surface supply ships or an aerial transport convoy.

At 1650 hours, the formation made a wide turn near the town of Ras el Fortass and began its eastward swing on this late afternoon patrol. In patrol formation, the first quartet at 4,000 feet and ascending quartets of aircraft to 8,000 feet, the pilots continually scanned the sky, the sea, and the North African coast. But they saw nothing. Salisbury soon spotted the protruding tower of the cathedral in the battered town of Zombretta. This village represented the most easterly segment of the patrol area and the colonel called his pilots.

"Okay, left turn; one more westward swing and we return to base."

"That's what I like to hear, Colonel," Maj. Archie Knight answered. The 64th Squadron commander was hungry and he could not wait to return to Theleple for chow.

The quartet of P-40s swung into the setting sun, with the Spitfires still above them at 15,000 feet. The staircase formation droned on, while long shadows from the towns of Zebra and Al Hamine now jutting into the sea off the tip of the Cape Bon Peninsula. Salisbury looked at his fuel gauge. He had about 30 minutes of gas left. Good; they could make their last sweep and then return to Theleple, landing there in about 20 minutes.

The 57th Group CO had not guessed that as he flew westward, he would accidentally run into the most astonishing aerial target he had ever seen. At this very 1630 hours, 97 JU 52 transports (three had turned back with mechanical trouble) had almost reached the Cape Bon Peninsula, droning south at low altitude, with 29 escorting German and Italian fighter planes. The worst clash yet in the Flax-Bulls Head contest was only moments away.

Within the next hour, the Germans would suffer the worst aerial disaster of the war in the Palm Sunday Massacre.

CHAPTER THIRTEEN

No one in the 57th Group, 314th Squadron, or 92 Squadron knew who first sighted the long formation of German transport planes and their fighter escorts. The JU 52s were camouflaged in painted hues of dark gray, green, and blue to blend with the sea, while the 29 escorting German and Italian fighters weaved and darted about the Junkers. All of the Americans and Britishers, however, agreed that the two mile long German formation was about six miles off the Cape Bon shoreline and midway between the towns of Ras el Ahmar and Ras el Fortass. Ironically, the 97 Junkers were less than a half hour from their destinations at Sidi Ahmed and El Aouina. Further, the planes from Maj. Erich Rudorffer's III/JG 51 out of Dejedeida, Tunisia, had just taken off, but they would arrive on the scene moments too late to prevent the upcoming slaughter.

About half of the transport planes carried only cargo, another quarter of them carried mixed cargos and squads of men, and the remainder of the Junkers carried only soldiers, about a platoon of troops on each JU 52. The soldier passengers in the cargo areas carried burp machine guns to defend themselves against attacking Allied planes. However, the small weapons would prove next to useless against the driving, zooming P-40s and Spitfires.

Maj. Hartman Grasser of JG 51 saw the oncoming Allied planes and he gaped in astonishment. He quickly called Colonel Hagen. "Enemy aircraft, perhaps sixty or seventy fighters, heading for your formations. We will go off to intercept them. Please maintain your course and at maximum speed. We will make every effort to hold the enemy at bay while you complete your flight. We are expecting more fighters from Tunisia and perhaps they will arrive soon to help out."

"Yes, Major," the KVT 16 kommodore said. Then the colonel called his transport pilots. "Please maintain tight formation and remain at low altitude."

Meanwhile, Col. Arthur Salisbury cried into his own radio. "Major Knight's squadron will assist 92 Squadron against the enemy escort planes. 64th, 66th, and 314th Squadrons will attack transports. Make your attacks in tandem pairs."

"Yes sir," Capt. Jim Curl of the 66th Squadron said.

The planned attack, three squadrons against the transports and two fighter squadrons against the Axis fighters, never came off as expected. Within moments the action over the Mediterranean became a brawling melee of U.S. and RAF fighters attacking both German and Italian fighters and transports.

The vicious battle off the coast of Cape Bon on this waning Palm Sunday afternoon lasted only ten minutes, but in that time, the Americans and Britishers ran up the biggest and most lopsided aerial score of the MTO campaign thus far.

"Juicy, juicy," Capt. Jim Curl radioed his 66th Squadron pilots. "Let's get 'em, but watch out for fighters."

"Stay in pairs, boys; in pairs," Col. Arthur Salisbury again warned his pilots.

Then the first four Warhawks including Salisbury's lead plane, roared in high pitched howls before splitting in pairs to make a long, sweeping turn to the right. The second four plane element, under Capt. Jim Whittaker, followed the first four Warhawks.

Salisbury and his wingman, however, ran into a quartet of ME 109s and they needed to fight off these German fighters instead of attacking the JU 52s. Salisbury arced sharply upward as did wingman Lt. Joe Byrne. The 57th Group commander caught a Messerschmidt in his sights and chopped the plane apart before the fragments plopped into the sea. Lieutenant Byrne, meanwhile, got three German fighter planes in a minute. He caught one plane with a burst of .50

caliber fire that shattered the left wing. He tailed a second and ripped off the tail with more strafing fire from his six wing guns. Byrne then blew open the fuselage of a third 109 before the German fighter plopped into the sea.

Meanwhile, Lt. Tom Smith and wingman Lt. Frank Ryan tangled with a trio of 109s under Lt. Herman Schneider of JG 51. The five planes darted, zoomed, and turned about the sky to get an advantage against each other. The Americans prevailed. Smith got behind a 109 and blasted the fuselage, igniting the gas tank before the German fighter exploded. Lt. Frank Ryan cut off the tail of a second Messerschmidt with 20mm shell hits.

Lieutenant Schneider, however, got away to make a score of his own when the German fighter pilot laced the P-40 of Lt. Al Costanza of the 57th Group's 65th Squadron. Schneider caught the P-40 with raking machine gun fire and other U.S. pilots saw Costanza's plane skimming into the sea.

Meanwhile, Capt. Ray Whittaker and the three pilots of his flight reached the transport planes. Whittaker and his wingman from the 65th Squadron, Lt. Mark Stanfort, got a phenomenal six kills within a minute. Whittaker got his first plane with streaking 20mm shells that knocked off two engines of a JU 52 before the plane plopped into the sea. He got his next Junker with chattering tracer fire that hit the gas tank before the transport plane exploded, and he got his third when he shattered the cabin of a third tri-engine plane, killing the pilot and copilot.

Stanfort got his kills in similar fashion. He fired at the first two JU 52s that came into his sights with a short burst of machine gun fire that left the port and nose engines burning. Flames trailed through the entire length of the plane and the JU 52 splashed into the sea in a ball of fire and smoke. Stanfort then zoomed after a second Junker that was trying to reach land. The U.S. pilot ripped the plane apart with machine gun fire before the plane crashed on the beach and exploded. He got his third kill when he tore off the nose of the transport with murderous 20mm shell explosions.

More quartets of 57th Group P-40s also peeled off in pairs and raced into the helpless German transports. Capt. Jim Curl and his wingman, Lt. Ed Campbell, got five JU 52s and one ME 109 between them.

Curl attacked a pair of Junkers from astern, firing at two German tail end Charlies. The bursts of fire chopped away chunks of the cabin on one transport and sliced off a portion of a wing on a second Junker. Curl came back for a second attack, firing several more bursts of machine gun fire at the wobbling, damaged planes he had just hit earlier. This time both planes burst into flames and smashed on the surface of the sea. As Curl arced away, he saw an ME 109 dive through an element of four Warhawks and he tagged the underside of the German fighter before unleashing a long burst of machine gun fire into the belly of his adversary. The ME 109 burst into flames and crashed into the sea from a 1,000 feet height.

Lt. Ed Campbell roared into a formation of JU 52s where soldier passengers tried to respond with burp guns that did little or no damage.

"They looked like blinking red flashlights from the windows of the transport," Campbell said later.

The minor burp gun fire presented no problem for Campbell who promptly downed one Junker with shellfire that tore open the fuselage. He quickly downed a second JU 52 when he set the plane afire with blistering machine gun fire and he got his third score when he almost cut in half the fuselage with less than a half dozen 20mm shell explosions. All three Junkers plopped into the sea.

Lt. Frank Cleveland in Captain Curl's 66th Squadron got the biggest score against the Junkers on this waning Sunday afternoon. "When I peeled off to attack," he later told a foreign correspondent, "the enemy transport planes looked like a thousand black beetles crawling across the water."

Cleveland became too excited on the first pass. He fired bursts of machine gun fire too soon and the tracers came up short, with the slugs kicking up water. However, on the next pass, his burst of fire tattooed the tail area of a JU 52 and crawled up the fuselage. The ship went down, hit the water in a great sheet of spray, and then exploded. Cleveland pulled away and saw German soldiers struggling in the water. The 66th Squadron pilot then waded into a trio of Junkers, cutting loose with streaking 20mm shells and chattering machine gun fire. One Junker exploded, the second fell apart, and the third lost a wing before the trio of enemy planes plopped into the sea. Less than a minute later, Lt. Frank Cleveland came down on still another Junker and tore the fuselage open with his last half dozen shells. Five quick kills.

However, as Cleveland arced away, he suddenly saw his cockpit shudder and he felt a sting in his left arm from a grazing bullet. A German 109 pilot had caught him in his sights before unleashing a burst of machine gun fire. Luckily for the American pilot, he managed to escape, but he now wobbled away with his arm bleeding and his plane shuddering. Still, he got back to Theleple where he crash landed.

Lt. Dick Hunziker of the 65th Squadron was on his first mission, flying as wingman for Maj. Ralph Thomas. As soon as the melee began, he lost Thomas. Hunziker then felt isolated and confused as he saw American and Axis fighters climbing, diving, and attacking each other. Then he heard somebody cry over his radio.

"MC 202s up here; come on up and help out."

Hunziker climbed to 5,000 feet where he again saw the confused sight of arcing planes all over the sky. He finally got on the tail of a 202. However, he gaped in horror as he saw golf balls streaking past him on both sides of the fuselage. An Italian pilot was on Hunziker's own tail and firing 20mm shells.

Hunziker quickly took evasive action that brought him over the shoreline of North Africa. Here, he hooked onto a German fighter on his first chatter of wing fire chopped away the nose of the FW 190. Pieces of the German plane flew in all directions before the Folke-Wulf crashed into a green field and exploded.

Hunziker now turned in a wide arc and spotted a Junker transport sputtering toward the shoreline, alone and helpless. The young lieutenant and his first combat mission almost felt guilty. But then he remembered that the men and supplies aboard the JU 52 could mean death to the ground fighting GIs. The 57th Group pilot quickly came down to unleash his last cluster of 20mm shells that riddled the Junker into fragments, before the battered transport smashed onto the beach. The U.S. pilot saw a few German soldiers crawl out of the smashed plane.

The pilots of the 314th Squadron did equally well. Lieutenant Colonel McKnown and his wingman, Lt. MacArthur Powers, had become separated from the other pilots and found no opportunity to take on any ME 109s, FW 190s, or MC 202s. But they surely scored high against the long column of JU 52s that droned at their 100 to 200 foot altitude above the surface of the Mediterranean Sea. McKnown peeled off to hit one three plane V, while Powers arced off to the right to attack a second V of Junkers.

McKnown, a burly, outgoing man from Lawrence, Kansas, opened with spraying .50 caliber machine gun fire that prompted the trio of JU 52s to scatter. However, McKnown caught up to one of the Junkers and ripped open the fuselage. The JU 52 cartwheeled and plunged into the sea.

The Kansas native chased another Junker at deck level, only a few feet above the surface of the sea. He continually sent short bursts of machine gun fire into the tri-engine transport that finally exploded and plopped into the sea.

MacArthur Powers, a former photographer from Inwood, N.Y., and an ex-RAF pilot, got three Junkers when he jumped the V of transport planes. Chattering machine gun fire set the first victim afire and the plane wobbled on for several hundred yards before plopping into the sea. He caught the second Junker with solid 20mm shell hits that chopped the left wing off. The Junker flipped over and splashed into the sea. The New Yorker then nailed his third victim when he shattered the cabin with machine gun fire and killed pilot and copilot. The plane skidded along the sea, hit the Cape Bon shoreline, and then exploded.

Powers then went after a second trio of JU 52s, also chasing them at deck level. He got one of them with 20mm shell hits that battered the tail before the Junker crashed into the sea. However, before he got the second Junker, he felt his own Warhawk shudder from a tattoo of machine gun fire from an FW 190 that was on his tail. Powers quickly turned and zoomed high and away from the predator. The 314th Squadron pilot then saw a pair of FW 190s that were jinking eastward below him. The lieutenant opened again with stafing fire, blowing one of the Folke-Wulfs apart and damaging the second. He thus raised his score to 12 planes during his combat career in the MTO with the USAAF and RAF.

Lt. Richard Duffy of Detroit, Michigan, made the highest score on this Sunday afternoon. He downed five JU 52s and one MC 202. Duffy was zooming toward the German transports when he caught an Italian fighter plane in his sights. He sent the MC 202 spiraling downward with telling 20mm shell hits. Duffy then pounced on the JU 52 formations. He bounced the first V of Junkers with 20mm shells that blew one plane apart, machine gun fire that set a second JU afire, and more shells that ripped open the fuselage of the third transport. Duffy arced away and then came down on a second trio of Junkers, downing two of them before the third got away. One flaming plane fell into the sea and the second battered Junker skidded onto the beach of Cape Bon and fell apart.

Duffy could do no more for he had now expended all of his ammunition, machine gun bullets as well as 20mm shells.

The Spitfire pilots of 92 Squadron also took a heavy toll. The Britishers had supposedly held the job of holding off the Axis fighter planes but in the melee, the Britishers also shot up Junkers as well as enemy fighter planes. The RAF airmen downed seven German and three Italian fighter planes, along with four Junker transport planes. Maj. Neville Duke and his pilots had done an effective job to allow the Americans to decimate the transport formations.

While the Americans and Britishers carried out their slaughter against the German transports and Axis fighters, some of the German and Italian pilots managed to cause damage. Maj. Gustav Rodel got two P-40s when he caught U.S. pilot George Blakely with shattering fire that set the plane afire. Blakely bailed out and plopped into the sea where a U.S. destroyer rescued him the next day. Rodel caught another Warhawk with shattering 20mm shells. The P-40 bellied into the water and the pilot scrambled out of the plane. The JG 27 fighter pilot got his third kill when he ripped away the tail of a P-40 that skidded up the Cape Bon shoreline and exploded.

Maj. Hartman Grasser got two kills, a P-40 and a Spitfire. He shattered the Warhawk with chattering machine gun fire and the U.S. plane arced into the sea. Grasser got his Spitfire when he came down on the unsuspecting 92 Squadron flyer and killed the British pilot with withering machine gun fire.

Four other German pilots also scored kills, three P-40s and one Spitfire. The Italians from 12 Gruppen downed two Spitfires and a P-40, but lost seven of their MC 202s. The Axis flyers thus downed eleven U.S. and British planes while damaging four more Allied aircraft. However, these kills were little consolation for the massacre against the German transport formations.

Besides the multiple kills by Colonel Salisbury, Lieutenant Byrne, Lieutenant Smith, Captain Whittaker, Lieutenant Sanfort, Lieutenant Campbell, Captain Curl, Lieutenant Cleveland, Lieutenant Colonel McKnown, Lieutenant Powers, and Maj. Neville Duke, 21 other U.S. and British pilots had also scored two kills or more.

The ten minute air battle had left the sea littered with the debris of destroyed and burning ME 109s, FW 190s, MC 202s, and JU 52s. Thirteen other Junkers crash landed or smashed up on the beach or in the open fields beyond the town of Ras el Ahman or the Cape Bon Peninsula. Most of these downed German planes were burning. 18 more German and Italian planes made belly landings further inland.

Maj. Erich Rudorffer finally arrived off Cape Bon at about 1745 hours, but the battle was over. The III/JG 51 kommodore could only ogle in horror at the debris floating about the sea, the burning planes along the beach, and the smashed aircraft scattered about the Cape Bon Peninsula. The skies were empty and silent now. The German major cursed under his breath before he called his pilots.

"There is nothing we can do here; we will return to base."

"Yes, Herr Major," Lt. Heinrich Perzina said.

Not until midnight, the last hour of Palm Sunday, 18 April 1943, did the U.S. operations officers finally verify the claims of Allied pilots. The startling total was 60 JU 52s and 16 Axis fighters down, seven JU 52s and nine enemy fighters probably destroyed, 17 transports and 11 fighters damaged. The American and British pilots had expended 40,000 rounds of ammunition and 15,000 rounds of 20mm shells in 156 sorties on this Palm Sunday afternoon.

Predictably, after the astonishing success of the Palm Sunday massacre, all three squadrons of the

57th Fighter Group, the 314th Fighter Squadron, and the RAF 92 Squadron won DUCs and Victoria Citations. Among the participating pilots, Lt. Joe Byrne, Capt. Ray Whittaker, Col. Arthur Salisbury, and Capt. Jim Curl won DFC's. Lt. Frank Cleveland, Lt. MacArthur Powers, Lt. Bill McKnown, Lt. Jim Whiting, and Lt. Ed Stout won Silver Stars. 20 other U.S. pilots won the Air Medal and 16 more won Bronze Stars. Never in a single engagement thus far in the European war, had so many American airmen won so many decorations in a single engagement.

Of course, celebrations prevailed throughout the night of April 18-19 at the Theleple airbase. Both Allied pilots and ground crews were ecstatic over the stunning aerial victory. The partying did not end until the wee hours of the morning of 19 April.

Conversely, in Sicily and Italy an ominous gloom prevailed. Only ten Junkers out of 97 had reached the Sidi Ahmed and El Aounia airbases in Tunisia to deliver still another trickle of supplies and men. The Germans had suffered their worst aerial debacle yet in their Operation Bulls Head. In Sicily, only a handful of Axis pilots returned to Boco de Falco. Among them were Maj. Gustav Rodel, Capt. Wolfgang Tonne, and Maj. Hartman Grasser. Missing and presumed lost were Lt. May Winkler and Oblt. Walter Zellot, two German fighter aces who had scored 67 and 74 kills respectively during their illustrious combat careers in the Luftwaffe.

Among the transport formations, 80% of the

supplies and men aboard the 97 JU 52s had been lost. Also missing was Maj. August Geiger whose JU 52 had apparently been among the 83 transport victims. Col. Walter Hagen, among the German wounded, had escaped his JU 52 that had belly landed on one of the Cape Bon beaches.

When news of the Palm Sunday massacre reached Berlin, Dictator Adolph Hitler was infuriated as was OKW chief Alfred Jodl, Luftwaffe chief Herman Goring, and other VIPs of the OKW and OKL. But no one could do anything about losses.

"Our Christian God favored the Americans and British instead of the Germans on that holy day," Gen. Ulrich Buchholtz would say to an interpreter two years later when he became a U.S. prisoner at the end of the war in Europe.

The next day, 19 April, the persistent Germans sent out 23 transport planes with a mere 12 ME 109s as escorts to make still another dash across the sea to Tunisia. Unfortunately, they suffered still another disaster. At 0530 hours, the 7 SAAF Wing was on CAP, finishing up the first morning patrol with 36 Kittyhawks. 5 Squadron flew at the 4,000 feet low station, 2 Squadron at medium height, and 4 Squadron as top cover at 8,000 feet. Lt. Col. Dan Loftus, the 7 Wing air commander, smelled pay dirt when he heard from pilots of the RAF 22 Squadron that had made a sweep out of Malta and had run into some JU 88 twin engine fighters near Pantelleria.

"They're escorts for transports," the 22 Squadron leader radioed Loftus. "Junkers are flying south of us toward Tunisia."

"We'll take them," the 7 Wing leader said.

Fifteen minutes later, Loftus and his South African pilots spotted the formation of 23 JU 52s and 16 Italian tri-motor transport planes just south of the island of Pantelleria. The Germans were obviously scraping bottom if they elected to use the slow, cumbersome Italian Fiat G-12 transport planes.

"Okay, hit 'em in tandem," Loftus radioed his pilots.

"Yes sir, Air Commander," Maj. Ed Parsonson of 5 Squadron answered.

The Axis had only mounted eight MC 200 and eight MC 202 Italian fighters from 12 Gruppen with a mere five 109s from II/JG 27, indicating that the Germans were also suffering a severe shortage of German fighter planes. 7 Wing's 5 Squadron quickly shattered the rather squeamish and inexperienced Italian fighter pilots, quickly downing seven of them and chasing off the rest. The 109 pilots proved more formidable, but 5 Squadron shot down three of them, However, Lt. Ernst Reinert downed a Kittyhawk, his 150th kill.

Still 7 Wing had little interference while attacking the Junker and Fiat transport planes and the South Africans downed 16 JU 52s and 11 Fiats. Lieutenant Colonel Loftus downed two JU 52s and Maj. Ed Parsonson got three Axis transport planes. Only 16 of the transports escaped, with some of these damaged. These surviving JU 52s and Fiat C-12s made it to Sidi Ahmed.

However, just after dawn on the morning of 23

April, B-17s from the 99th Bomb Group droned over the Sidi Ahmed Airdrome and dropped over 40 tons of bombs. The Ninety-Niners chewed up the runways, service buildings, and taxiways, while destroying ten of the transport planes on the ground before the Germans could fully unload them. The 99th airmen left fire and destruction in their wake as they droned back to Navarin, Algeria.

On the same 20 April, however, Lt. Col. Bruno Dinort took off from Gerbini, Sicily, with 27 DO 17 bombers from his KG 26 bomber geschwader. "We will extract a measure of vengeance for these losses."

"Yes, Herr Colonel," Maj. August Lambert answered.

In the late afternoon, the US and RAF airmen never expected the air raid by German bombers all the way from Sicily. At 1700 hours, sirens suddenly wailed across the Allied Theleple airbase. The NATAF air units had not had time to scramble pilots for interceptions but only to scatter for cover before Lieutenant Dinort arrived with his waves of light bombers. The DO 17s blasted both the airfield and campsite with 500 pound bombs. The attack destroyed nine P-40s and three Spitfires, while damaging eleven other planes. The German KG 26 bombers had also destroyed six buildings, killed 14 American airmen, killed seven RAF airmen, and wounded 23 more Allied airmen.

"We have done well, Herr Colonel," Maj. Gunther Unger radioed Dinort.

"Fleigerkampft Sud-Ost will attack them again tonight," Dinort said.

"Tonight?"

"Who would expect it?" the KG 26 kommodore said.

True enough. At 0200 hours, 21 April, 17 Heinkel bombers came over Theleple to once more catch the Americans and Britishers off guard. Again, Allied fighter pilots had no time to man their P-40s or Spitfires before whistling bombs once more laced the airfield and campsites. This second attack within 12 hours knocked out four P-40s and seven parked Spitfires and destroyed an operations room, while killing six Allied airmen.

The two German air raids on the 211 Group's Theleple base did not cause the damage the Americans had caused on Palm Sunday and the next day, but Fleigerkampf Sud-Ost had reminded the airmen of the 211 Group that Allied pilots could not carry out devastating attacks with total immunity. When Col. Arthur Salisbury and Lt. Col. Dan Loftus surveyed the damage, Salisbury shook his head.

"The bastards," he cursed.

"Who can blame them?" Dan Loftus grinned.

On 22 April, Lt. Col. Dan Loftus surely avenged the two bombing raids on Theleple. This time the Germans were sending 21 of the huge ME 323 transport planes into Tunisia. The formation of Gigantens, with 23 ME 109 escorts, had come within 40 miles of Cape Bon when they ran into the NATAF combat air patrol. Dan Loftus had just turned north at Ras el Fortass off Cape Bon when he ran into the aerial convoy coming southward. 7 Wing had left Theleple at 0700 hours to begin the second 211 Group CAP, once more with 36 Kittyhawks from the 5, 4, and 2 Squadrons, with 2 Squadron as top cover.

The Junker escorts included some of the best Fleigerkorps 2 and Fleigerkorps Tunisien pilots and the air battle off Cape Bon on this 22 April morning became the most vicious yet in the April confrontations. Like all the other dogfights, the Germans lost, despite their many excellent Luftwaffe pilots among the escort complement. Lt. Harti Schmeidel of II/JG 53 was shot down by Kittyhawks but he bailed out wounded and was picked up by an American destroyer. Lt. Wolfgang Fisher of III/JG 27 died when he tried to land his damaged fighter at Tunis and the FW 190 blew up. Lt. Heinrich Perzina of III/JG 51 was shot down and wounded when he tried to get his ME 109 back to base.

Some of the German pilots excelled. Lt. Herman Schneider of II/JG 51 got two Kittyhawks, while Lt. Heinz Benne of I/JG 77 got three P-40s with his FW 190 to raise his kill score to 147.

But these German victories were academic because 7 SAAF Wing shot down all 21 of the big ME 323s, most of them around Zembra Island on the approach to Tunis. Both Major Parsonson of 5 Squadron and Lieutenant Colonel Loftus, the wing commander, got two of the huge Gigantens. When the battle ended, only 11 of the 23 German escort planes reached Dejedeida airfield, while the

South Africans lost 11 of their Kittyhawks in the vicious air battle.

Only an hour later, 23 B-25s from the 321st Bomb Group attacked Sidi Ahmed Airfield. Lt. Col. Ed Olmstead and his Ruinator bomber crews did not find many planes on the ground, but they destroyed several buildings and some 14 motor vehicles. Several ME 109s intercepted, but American gunners drove them off with Sgt. Larry Rider of Perry, N.Y. downing one of the Messerschmidts, while Sgt. Ray Lankford of Waco, Texas, also downed an ME 109, his second during the Operation Flax campaign.

On the evening of 22 April, at 2100 hours, Field Marshal Albert Kesselring called his Luftflotte 2 kommandants into conference at his Naples headquarters. "Gentleman, we must acknowledge that Operation Bulls Head has failed. We cannot send large transport formations into Tunisia from Italy and Sicily. The enemy has overcome the loss of his spy system by instituting a round the clock fighter patrol in the Strait of Sicily. They have invariably found and destroyed our aerial formations. From now on, only small flights of transport planes will attempt to fly into North Africa and these will only be flown at night."

None of the officers answered. They realized that Kesselring was right. They could not make further attempts to continue Operation Bulls Head.

The disastrous culmination of the German attempts to resupply Tunisia by air quickly accelerated the defeat of the Afrika Korps in Tunisia. Allied ground forces were already pressing hard against the Germans and the cessation of Operation Bulls Head had only worsened matters.

Gen. Jurgeon von Arnim had tried to encourage the men of his hard pressed Afrika Korps as the Allies flexed their muscles for a decisive blow. "If every German soldier justifies the Fuhrer's reliance on him," von Arnim told his troops, "and if he fights with unshakable resolve in this historic hour, we shall destroy the enemy's hopes and victory will be ours."

But no amount of bravery by the Afrika Korps could stem the Allied tide, whose GIs, Tommies, and French troops were receiving increased reinforcements while provisions for the Wehrmacht soldiers dwindled to near nothing. By 23 April, according to Allied intelligence, the shortage of fuel in Tunisia had paralyzed all Afrika Korps activities except for localized fighting. Between 23 April and 1 May, not a single Axis supply ship reached Tunisia and less than a 100 transport planes had successfully run the gauntlet of patrolling Allied fighter planes.

German defenses rapidly collapsed on all fronts. By 2 May, the British had cleared the Germans from the Kairouan area and began the drive on Tunis. On 4 May, French units stormed and broke the Enfidaville Line in the center, wrested the peaks of the Djebel and Takrouna hills, and pasted retreating Germans with heavy artillery. In the northern sector, the U.S. II Corps mauled the Germans at Mateur and drove the Wehrmacht remnants north. The Americans then swept across the open plains with tanks and motorized infantry toward Bizerte.

Meanwhile, Allied air forces were again concentrating on support missions, hitting Longstop, Ksartyr, Crichel, Oved, Ain el Ashker, and anywhere else where the battered German forces tried to regroup in Tunisia for a counterattack or to reform a new defense line. By 6 May, the Americans had taken Djebel Zaghovan on the outskirts of Bizerte and the British had reached the outskirts of Tunis.

On 7 May, the last German resistance in the east crumbled and the British entered Tunis. At about the same hour, American GIs rolled into Bizerte. Two days later, the American and British ground troops met at Protville to isolate the Germans at Tourbaba on the Cape Bon Peninsula. On 10 May, the local German commander asked for surrender terms. For all practical purposes resistance in the American II Corps sector had come to an end. On the same day, Allied armored units had broken the weak resistance on the neck of Cape Bon to entrap enemy troops along the seacoast area at Hammanlif.

The British and French converged on the totally spent Afrika Korps that no longer had ammunition, supplies, or air support. Allied air units pounded the Germans at will while British and French artillery pummelled the trapped Germans unmercifully. On 12 May, Gen. Jurgeon von Arnim surrendered.

At 0830 hours, 13 May, General Freyburg of

the German III Korps and General Mancinelli of the Italian Supremo Corps met with British 8th Army staff members to end all hostilities. The two Axis officers agreed to unconditional surrender and von Arnim sent a final message out of North Africa.

"I have accepted the terms of surrender and have ordered all troops of the Afrika Korps to cease fire as of 1230 hours today, 13 May 1943."

At 1315 hours, the German radio in Rome wired OKW headquarters in Berlin: "The last German radio in Africa has closed down at 1312 hours. Control Rome is no longer in contact with Africa."

General von Arnim had surrendered 101,784 German troops, 89,447 Italian troops, and 37,000 non-specified troops of the Afrika Korps, a bitter blow indeed for Germany. The Wehrmacht could have surely used these experienced combat forces for the inevitable Allied assault on Sicily, Italy, the Balkans, or somewhere else in Fortress Europe.

Allied casualties had not been light in the Tunisian campaign. The British had suffered 4,000 killed, 13,000 wounded, and 10,000 missing. The Americans had lost 2,700 men killed, 9,000 wounded, and 6,500 missing. The French had lost 2,000 killed, 10,200 wounded, and 7,000 missing.

No doubt Operation Flax had played the major role in the collapse of the Afrika Korps in Tunisia. During the month of April, fighter and bomber pilots of NASAF and NATAF had destroyed 263 German transport planes, including 74 of the big ME 323s. They had downed 241 ME 109s, FW

190s, and MC 202s, and 34 DO 17 and HE 11 bombers. The Allied airmen had also probably destroyed 138 more Axis planes and damaged 54 other Luftflotte 2 aircraft.

Gen. Carl Spaatz told Washington at the end of the Tunisian campaign: "Air power can no longer be considered an adjunct to ground power. In North Africa, air power and land power were co-equal, with neither one acting as an auxiliary. Air superiority assured success in the Tunisian campaign."

Gen. Jurgeon von Arnim told interrogators after his surrender: "Allied air superiority made the difference. If we had controlled the skies over the battlefield and over the Mediterranean, we would still be in North Africa. But how could we fight without air support and reinforcements in men and supplies? The enemy air forces deprived us of both and defeat thus became inevitable."

The April massacres by U.S. and RAF airmen in Operation Flax had hastened the final German defeat in North Africa.

PARTICIPANTS

Allies

NAAF (North African Air Forces) — Gen. Carl Spaatz

NASAF (North African Strategic Air Force) — Gen. James Doolittle

1st Fighter Group — Col. Ralph Garman
14th Fighter Group — Lt. Col. Troy Keith
82nd Fighter Group — Col. William Covington
325th Fighter Group — Lt. Col. Gordon Austin
2nd Bomb Group — Col. Ford Lauer
99th Bomb Group — Col. Fay Upthegrove
310th Bomb Group — Col. Anthony Hunter

321st Bomb Group—Lt. Col. Edward Olmstead

Also: 350th Fighter Group, 3rd Recon Group, 17th Bomb Group, 97th Bomb Group, 301st Bomb Group, and 320th Bomb Group

NATAF (North Africa Tactical Air Force)—Air Marshal Arthur Conningham

211 Group—Col. Kenneth Cross

12th Bomb Group—Col. Earl Bates
57th Fighter Group—Col. Arthur Salisbury
314th Squadron—Lt. Col. William McKnown
92 Squadron—Maj. Neville Duke
7 SAAF Wing—Lt. Col. Dan Loftus
Also: 31st Fighter Group, 52nd Fighter Group, 79th Fighter Group, 239 Wing, 244 Wing, and 285 Wing

OSS Intelligence, Algiers—Gen. William Donovan

Codes: Sicily—Pilgrim; Italy—Franklin; Algiers—Roman

Axis

Luftflotte 2, OB Sud-Ost—Field Marshal Albert Kesselring
Lufttransport Mittelmeer (transports)—Gen.

Ulrich Buchholtz

Fleigerkorps II (fighters) — Gen. Hannes
Trautloft

Fleigerkorps Sud Ost (bombers) — Gen.
Erich Hammhuber

JG 27 (FW 190s) — Col. Edu Neumann
JG 77 (FW 190s) — Lt. Col. Johannes
Steinhoff
JG 53/II — Capt. Wolfgang Tonne
JG 51/II — Maj. Hartman Grasser
JG 51/III — Maj. Erich Rudorffer
12 Gruppo (Italian fighters) — Capt.
Franco Bisleri
KG 26 (DO 17 bombers) — Lt. Col. Bruno
Dinort
KVT 16 (transports) — Col. Walter Hagen
KVT 5 (transports) — Col. Lenz Krumwey
SS Gestapo — Col. Heinz Jost

Afrika Korps — Tunisia — Field Marshal Irwin
Rommel

Deputy commander — Gen. Jurgeon von
Arnim

Fleigerkorps Tunisien — Gen. Hoffman von
Waldau

BIBLIOGRAPHY

BOOKS

Bavousett, Glen, *More World War II Aircraft in Combat,* Arco Publishers, New York City, 1981

Bekker, Cajus, *The Luftwaffe War Diaries,* Ballantine Books, New York City, 1964

Craven, W.F. and Cate, J.L., *The Army Air Force in World War II, Vol. II: Europe: Torch to Pointblank,* Univ. of Chicago Press, Chicago, 1949

Cruickshank, Charles, *Deception in World War II,* Oxford Univ. Press, New York City, 1979

Fitzsimmons, Bernard, *Warplanes and Air Battles of World War II,* Chapter 7, "Desert Bomb Runs," BDC Publishers, London

Ford, Carey, *Donovan of OSS,* Brown, Little & Co., Boston, 1970

Johnson, Brian, *Mediterranean Sweep,* Chapter 6, "Palm Sunday Massacre," British Broadcasting Co., London 1976

Johnson, Brian, *The Secret War,* British Broadcasting Company, London, 1978

Killen, John, *A History of the Luftwaffe,* Doubleday & Co., Garden City, NY, 1967

Maurer, Maurer, *Air Force Combat Units of WW II,* U.S. Air Force Historical Division, Washington, DC 1951

Playfair, S.O., *The Mediterranean and the Middle East: Vol. IV, The Destruction of the Axis Air Force in North Africa,* His Majesty's Stationery, London, 1966

Rogers, Edward, *German Airborne Troops,* Doubleday & Co., Garden City, NY, 1974

Rust, Kenn, *Checkerboard Clan, History of the 325th Fighter Group,* Aero Publishers, Fallbrook, Cal., 1978

Rust, Kenn, *The 9th Air Force in World War II,* Aero Publishers, Fallbrook, Cal., 1975

Rust, Kenn, *12th Air Force Story,* Historical Aviation Album, Temple City, Cal., 1975

Tantum, T.H. and Hoffschmidt, E.J., *The Rise and Fall of the German Air Force,* WE Publishers, Greenwich, Conn, 1969

Van Ishoven, Armand, *Messerschmidt BF 109 at War,* Charles Scribner & Son, New York City, 1977

Woerpel, Dan, *Hostile Skies,* Andom Press, Marshall, Wis., 1975

Wood, Tony and Gundrum, William, *Hitler's Luftwaffe,* Crescent Books, New York City, 1977

NEWSPAPERS

"U.S. Air Units in Africa Destroy Junkers," *New York Times,* April 7, 1943

"Destroy 29 Axis Planes and Ships in the Mediterranean," *New York Times,* April 11, 1943

ARCHIVE RECORDS: Albert E. Simpson Historical Research Center, Maxwell Field, Ala.

Action Reports and Narrative Reports:
Document #743, "The Battle Story of Flax," NAAF Review #1
Document #744, "Analysis of Flax Operation for Period 5 April 1943 to 22 April 1943," NAAF Review #2
NAAF Operations Bulletin, 1 April to 30 April 1943
RAFME Review #3, pp 18–30
NASAF Summary of Tunisian Campaign, pp 47–116
NATAF Summary of Tunisian Campaign, pp 30–131
Monthly Combat Summary, 47th Wing, April 1943

Combat Unit Action Reports:
14th Fighter Group
Mission #16, 10 April 1943
Mission #19, 18 April 1943
Summary of Combat Activities — March–April 1943

82nd Fighter Group
    Mission #106, 5 April 1943
    Mission #135, 10 April 1943
    Mission #140, 11 April 1943
    Summary of Activities in Tunisian Campaign, 12/23/42–4/21/43
321st Bomb Group
    Mission #14, 4 April 1943
    Mission #17, 10 April 1943
    Summary of Activities, March–April 1943
57th Fighter Group (including 314th Squadron)
    Narrative Report, Operations for 18 April 1943
    Summary of Activities, March–April 1943
    Biography of Maj. Archibald Knight
325th Fighter Group, Narrative History, March–April 1943
1st Fighter Group, Narrative History, March–April 1943
310th Bomb Group, Narrative History, March–April 1943
2nd Bomb Group, Narrative History, March–April 1943
99th Bomb Group, Narrative History, March–April 1943
97th Bomb Group, Narrative History, March–April 1943
History of the 7 RAAF Wing, RAFME Review #3

GERMAN SOURCES

Air History — Luftwaffe, "Battle for Tunisia"

Bucholtz, Gen. Ulrich, "Supply by Air of the En-
larged Bridgehead in Tunisia"

German Document #,QU, Operation Bullshead,
March–April 1943

Italian Document #2829, May 1943, "Merchant
Shipping Sunk in the Mediterranean"

Luftflotte 2 Weekly Reports, from 6 April
through 27 April 1943, including German and
Italian Air Forces operations

OB Sud Ost Summary, "Operation Oschenkopf"
(Bullshead)

MAPS: Albert Simpson Historical Center

PHOTOS: Albert Simpson Historical Center
         DAVA (including Bund Archives &
         USAAF), Washington, DC
         99th Bomb Group Association mem-
         bers

ACKNOWLEDGEMENT

I would like to thank retired Maj. Gen. Fay
Upthegrove and Mr. Carl Mitchell of the 99th
Bomb Group Association for information on the
99th Group during Operation Flax. I would also
like to thank Mr. George Coen for extensive information on NASAF operations and Mr. Don
Woerpel for his excellent information on NATAF
operations. Finally, I would like to extend my ap-
preciation to Mr. Cargill Hall and his staff at the
Albert E. Simpson Historical Research Center.

ZEBRA WINS THE WEST
WITH THESE EXCITING BESTSELLERS!

PISTOLERO   (1331, $2.25)
by Walt Denver

Death stalks the dusty streets of Belleville when a vicious power struggle tears the town in half. But it isn't until a beautiful rancher's daughter gets trapped in a bloody crossfire that someone with cold nerve and hot lead goes into action. Only who would've guessed that a stranger would be the one to put his life on the line to save her?

RED TOMAHAWK   (1362, $2.25)
by Jory Sherman

Soon, deep in the Dakotas—at a place called Little Big Horn—Red Tomahawk will discover the meaning of his tribe's fateful vision. And the Sioux will find a greatness in his enduring legend that will last through all time!

BLOOD TRAIL SOUTH   (1349, $2.25)
by Walt Denver

Five years have passed since six hardcases raped and murdered John Rustin's wife, butchered his son, and burned down his ranch. Now, someone with cold eyes and hot lead is after those six coyotes. Some say he's a lawman. Others say—in a low whisper—that it's John Rustin himself!

Available wherever paperbacks are sold, or order direct from the Publisher. Send cover price plus 50¢ per copy for mailing and handling to Zebra Books, 475 Park Avenue South, New York, N.Y. 10016. DO NOT SEND CASH.

THE BLACK EAGLES
by Jon Lansing

THE CONTINUING SHELTER SERIES
by Paul Ledd